D1623987

WHAT WE SAW AT NIGHT

JAQUELYN MITCHARD

Published in the United States in 2012 by Soho Teen
an imprint of Soho Press, Inc.
853 Broadway
New York, NY 10003

Library of Congress Cataloging-in-Publication Data
Mitchard, Jacquelyn.
What we saw at night / Jacquelyn Mitchard.
p. cm.
ISBN 978-1-61695-141-2
eISBN 978-1-61695-142-9
1. Xeroderma pigmentosum—Fiction. 2. Serial murderers—Fiction.
3. Survival—Fiction. 4. Racially mixed people—Fiction] I. Title.
PZ7.M6848Wh 2013
[Fic]—dc23
2012033360

Interior design by Janine Agro, Soho Press, Inc.
Interior art by Michael Fusco

Printed in the United States of America

10 9 8 7 6 5 4 3 2 1

For Danny and Pamela
Hearts and minds

Être et durer
"To be and to last"
(the unofficial motto of Parkour)

I

DARK STARS

"Don't move and don't scream too loud, no matter what you see," Juliet told Rob and me. "Promise? On pain of death?"

"I promise," I said readily.

Rob shot me a furious glance. I forced myself to shrug with a chilly deadpan.

What else was I supposed to do?

Juliet was a force of nature. I could ask her why we might scream. I might as well chew on air. She wouldn't tell us. She was my best friend—in fact, aside from Rob, my only real friend—and the sum total of what I truly knew about her would have filled a teaspoon. She'd probably spent two hundred days at my house, and I'd spent another hundred at hers. None of that mattered. Still, I was always guessing at how headstrong she was and how unattainably different . . . and we were about to see that proven all over again.

Rob shivered in the Washington Wizards team jacket his father had given him. It was meant to be comforting, to include

Rob in the real world. Rob was a natural athlete, especially when it came to basketball, but couldn't play because of what he had, what we *were*. He could never be exposed even to the lights in a gym during a real game. The jacket was one of thirty or so. His dad stockpiled them, being a sporting-goods buyer. They were actually a kind of mockery. But Rob's dad was such a sweetie that he would never have realized that. So Rob dutifully rotated among the Bucks, the Bulls, the Pacers, the Pistons, and yes . . . even the Wizards.

I was wearing my leather coat and two layers of scarves. It was April 8, but Iron Harbor didn't know it was technically spring. At two in the morning, in the brick passageway between the Smile Doctors dentistry and Gitchee Gumee Pizza, we could see our breath every time we spoke. The temperature couldn't have been much above freezing.

"I'm going to die," I said. "And be cryogenized. Standing here."

"Such a weenie," Juliet said.

She didn't seem to feel the cold. Ever. In a black bodysuit that made Rob stare and a black turtleneck sweater that gathered at her knees, Juliet braided up her waist-length dark blond hair and looped it into an elastic band. Along the left side of her face, from her cheekbone to her lip, she'd stenciled in iridescent face paint a line of blue stars that glowed in the faint light from the street corner.

Face paint! For a Tuesday night among the Nothings of Nowheresville, Minnesota. For the excellent true adventures of three people who had absolutely no lives.

"I've been called a lot of things," I said. "But never—"

"A weenie? Consider yourself called," Juliet interrupted with a wicked laugh. "In fact, I have called you a weenie myself."

She had, in fact: the previous summer, when I balked at breaking into Valerie Meyercheck's house again. After all, it was the *third* time. Valerie spent about ten days a year in Iron Harbor and the rest of the time whirling among her houses in Switzerland, Paris and Lake Forest. I'd finally followed Juliet inside, but I did *not* try on any clothes. Juliet took two sweaters, two of countless heather cashmere cardigans. Juliet insisted (and I believed her): no one who had a hundred color-coded sweaters could be sure if the moths had eaten some, or if the dear old family servant Valerie, probably called "Mammy," had given them away to the poor.

Maybe I was a weenie.

Of course, none of us could trump what Henry LeBecque had called Juliet last fall, though we should have seen it coming for years: a "wannabe vampire." As if she'd chosen to live the way we did. First off, how could any guy with a pulse dump Juliet, no matter what her limitations? Henry said he couldn't stand being with a girl who basically had to go home every morning and sleep in her coffin.

He paid for it, though, a month later. Just before Halloween, the former librarian, Mrs. Taylor, died at ninety. Torch Mountain Home Cemetery happens to be a place where a lot of kids like to drink. Nobody was thinking about the fact that they would dig old Mrs. Taylor's grave before they actually buried her, and cover it with a piece of canvas and a blanket of sod. Henry never knew what hit him. His "friends" (loyal allies that they were) took off when they heard Henry scream and tumble into a black hole. He was lucky he had his cell phone to call his parents and explain and them how he ended up alone in the deep bottom of a new grave in the snow on Halloween night. *He* was a weenie.

"Don't look yet!" Juliet called back. "I have to go through this mentally before it happens."

Biting my tongue, I watched Juliet stretch, an old habit from her days as a competitive skier. She patted her hands over her clothing, to make sure nothing was sticking out or unbuttoned. She checked her shoes to make sure the laces were tied. Then she ran off into the darkness.

Rob nudged me as we heard Juliet's light step on the fire escape, far down the cobbled passageway. The metal was old and rusty and probably a decade out of code. Most public things ran about forty years behind schedule in Iron Harbor. Who would know better than we? People were careless enough not to lock their doors. Many didn't even bother, much to the convenience of the only three teenagers who would be out all night, whose parents either were fine with what we did, or never bothered to stop us. Who dared to try to keep us out?

There was no fire escape, roof terrace, restaurant back entrance, abandoned cabin, deck door on a lakeside mansion, no unused boat, construction site, or gated park that Rob, Juliet and I didn't know about—even *before* we all got our driver's licenses last winter. The three of us had been born within four weeks of each other. What were the odds? January was obviously a very good month for freaks. Now the streets of Iron Harbor—all twenty of them, plus the resorts in the hills around the tiny town—belonged to us.

"What do you think she's doing?" Rob said.

He noticed me shivering and pulled me close to him.

My heart skittered. I resisted the urge to say: *Hold me tighter.* My fingers flickered at the level of my chest in the ASL sign for "I want": the one we taught my little sister to use to ask for food when she was three and spoke only baby

Chinese. But Rob didn't see. He never saw. My sign language was from me to myself, a sort of prayer, like the way people cross their fingers behind their backs when they tell a lie.

It wasn't a lie, though. It was the central truth of my so-called emotional life. For the past three years, Rob's touch could brand itself in a way I would be able to feel the next morning when I lay in bed, as though I'd been bruised and there was a sort of pleasurable agony in probing the injury. Rob could pull the pin on my emotions just like that, and then leave me on fire as he walked away. He had no idea, of course. Worse: it was the effect he wanted to have on Juliet, and never would.

He hunched down on his heels and started poking at the mortar between the cobblestones. We waited.

One, one thousand. Two, one thousand. Three, one thousand. . . .

You can think a lot in three seconds, I'd learned from being in an MRI machine.

My mother knew how I felt about Rob. I'd never told her. I didn't have to. My mother should have been a clairvoyant on TV and made us all rich. ("I see an older man, very handsome, a thick head of hair. He's with a baby. He wants you to know they're both happy.") People would have believed her. She could see through walls and straight into my skull. And phones? She could name the person at the other end of the call by the tone of my voice or who I was texting by the number of keystrokes.

A telling example of how my mom operates: about six months ago, I got dressed for the night and came down for dinner. There, at my place at our butcher block table, was this little pink bag. In the bag was a year's supply of birth control pills.

"Well," I said. "Uh, thanks. I was hoping for a digital camera for my next birthday. Which isn't for quite some time. What's the occasion?"

"Just in case," my mother said.

My little sister, Angela, who'd just turned nine, started laughing so hard that milk came out her nose. I'd bet that Mom had sat her down beforehand with a matter-of-fact "Allie's a young woman now," and "sexual feelings are a part of every young woman's process of maturity." Having been adopted at the age of the three by a single mom (who happened to have an older biological daughter with a life-threatening disease), Angie was disturbingly wise beyond her years. Either that or just disturbed.

"I hope these have a really long, uh, shelf life or whatever, because I don't have acne and Mr. Right isn't anywhere around," I said. "Or even Mr. Wrong, for that matter."

"I was thinking about Rob Dorn," Mom said.

"So have I, but he thinks about Juliet."

"Are they. . . ?" Angela put her fork down. Spaghetti sauce was way too volatile a condiment for this conversation.

"Most certainly negatory," I said. "Rob has as much of a chance with Juliet as Howard." (This in reference to a custodian of indeterminate age, who had worked at the hospital and clinic since shortly before time began. All of us knew Howard because he never really seemed to leave. Any time any of us had ever been there, he was either pushing the big rubber dumpster through the halls or lying down inside it, singing some of his favorite religious hits.)

"I just thought you should have them," Mom said.

"Isn't this the kind of thing you're supposed to find hidden away somewhere? Then start crying and saying your little girl is all grown up?"

My mother sighed. "That would be conventional," she said.

Even now, I couldn't tell if she would be happy if I actually took the birth control pills or if I didn't. So I kept them in my underwear drawer. *I* was the one who almost cried whenever I saw them, because I knew I was the last person on earth who would ever need them. . . .

Juliet's voice came down from above like a mortar shell.

"Live once!" she shouted. "Ready?"

"For a year now," Rob muttered. "What stupid thing is she doing?"

"She's okay," I said, and I called softly, "Ready, Juliet!"

"She doesn't have a light," he pointed out.

"You don't know that. She could have had it in a fanny pack under her sweater."

Until recently, my little sister actually assumed that people with XP could see better in the dark, like cats. Which is absurd: on average, we probably see worse. A lot of people with XP damage their eyes with light when they're little before they even know they have it. Rob and Juliet and I kept miners' headlamps and little Maglites in our backpacks if we had to pick a lock or peer down a ravine or around a dark corner.

"Are you right where I left you?" Juliet called, very far away. "You have to watch every second of this. You're my witnesses!"

I called back, "We're right here!"

One of the things you learn pretty quickly if you live your life at night is that—unless you're literally standing on someone's front porch—you can pretty much be as loud as you want. No one will hear you or see you. Definitely, no one will care. We had Juliet's dad to thank in part for our freedom, of course. Tommy Sirocco was one of the Iron County sheriff's deputies, and he worked the midnight shift solely because his family's life was set up around his daughter. Whenever he spotted Rob's Jeep, Officer Sirocco would quietly turn his squad car away to give us privacy.

I heard a shuffling and loud scraping above. Rob tensed. Juliet was making her way across the flat graveled roof of Gitchee Gumee Pizza. The Indian name for Lake Superior is Gitchee Gumee; that wasn't just something Longfellow made up for a poem. (Hiawatha was real, too, by the way.) The second floor of Gitchee Pizza housed the apartment of its owner and founder, Gideon Brave Bear—also a genuine Indian, a Bois Forte Chippewa; he got pissed if you used the term "Native American." Every kid in town ate at least one meal a week at Gitchee. Fortunately, in addition to being a very good purveyor of pizza, Gideon was also a very stereotypical drunk. He wouldn't have heard Juliet if she had been up there setting off fireworks.

We heard the scraping again, and then a few short taps.

"Juliet!" Rob cried out. "What the hell?"

Then Juliet jumped.

FOR A SHATTERING instant, I thought I was a witness to my best friend's death: a spectacular original suicide, for an audience. It was just the kind of stunt Juliet would pull. My mind slowed to syrup as I waited for her body to hit the ground between Rob and me. Juliet had always sworn she would die her own way. Not in some bed in the darkened living room of her house or hooked up to an IV in a sterile hospital . . . or after an overdose with a note pinned to her pillow, which is how many lives end for people like us.

But this wasn't death. This was *life*. The moment Juliet

launched herself from the roof, she became a whirling constellation. I couldn't see her face. A long line of glow-in-the-dark blue stars, outlined in silver, soared out above our heads between the buildings, wheeling in space, completing a full circle. Then the stars were gone. She'd already landed on the opposite roof—hooting in her victory dance—when my brain caught up to my eyeballs.

Juliet Sirocco had just traversed a twelve-foot gap, twenty feet off the ground . . . while performing a front flip in mid-air. She must have shed her sweater on the roof. That explained the feverish swirl of glowing stars. She'd stenciled them on her bodysuit, all up one leg and one arm, as well as her face. Rob fumbled for the switch on his Maglite. The faint beam flickered over the roof. Juliet was punching the air and grinning down at us. I broke my promise, because I screamed. I couldn't help it. The word exploded from deep inside: "Amazing!"

"Shut up, Allie!" Rob hissed.

"What? That was pretty amazing."

"She could have been killed!"

I had to laugh. "What else is new?"

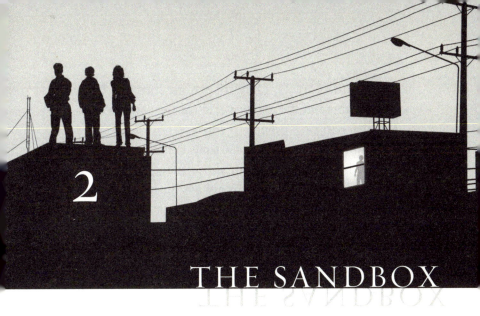

2

THE SANDBOX

The three of us met in the sandbox. In the sandbox, at night.

You think of a happy child. That child is playing in the sun. She's picking flowers in a field with the sun's rays painting threads of platinum in her hair. She's running with a kite, her chubby legs just a little tanned with the balmy blessings of midsummer. Think about it: even the *Sesame Street* theme song begins with the words, "Sunny day, sweeping the clouds away."

That sunny day would kill us.

We were happy children, I suppose, but we ran to the swings to play when kids our age were listening to bedtime stories. In the hospital, I'd once overheard a toddler telling his parents he'd seen ghosts in the Iron Harbor playgrounds, the ghosts of children. I remember I was afraid to speak to the nurse after that because I thought I might cry. We hadn't come back from the dead, but we did live in a parallel universe. It was our own country, the night country. We lived

there with our parents, many of whom chose to be Perse-
phone and abide in the netherworld for the sake of love.

We also had each other.

I couldn't even remember a time before the three of us
were friends. So I knew from those playground days that
Juliet would never stop. She was always the first to dive naked
into Ghost Lake, black water so cold that it would freeze the
blood in your veins. She was the first one to get a set of lock
picks so that we could steal a joint from the back room of the
guy who hand-loomed ugly ponchos for tourists. We got the
weed but we only had one toke apiece. If you have XP, you
really can't smoke. Heat damage risk is huge. You can, however, drink. Juliet helped us celebrate the New Year last year
by sneaking into the hot tub of a famous New York talk show
host's ski chalet, drinking the champagne we'd lifted from
one of the twelve cases of Veuve Clicquot in his wine cellar.

But there was a flipside to Juliet's adventurousness, the
side that haunted Rob and me. She was the only one who
took off, for weeks at a time, alone, away from us. First she
had a legitimate reason: for four years, from ages eleven to fifteen, she managed to ski competitively. Sunlight be damned,
she hurtled down the slopes swathed like a mummy in oversized goggles. But then, a year and a half ago, she'd suddenly
stopped. Yet the disappearances continued. Like every month
or so, for a few days or a week, we wouldn't hear from her
beyond a text saying *C U Soon*.

She always came back though. That was the silent mantra
I repeated to myself whenever the absences seemed to reach a
breaking point. *Juliet always comes back.*

JULIET CAME CLATTERING down the fire escape.

"Did you see me? Did you see me?" She was jumping

around like one of the Cat Dancers on the pom squad at Iron County High where we were students but never actually went.

"I saw you!" I said. "What made you do that?"

"What in the world would inspire even you to do something that idiotic?" Rob snapped. "That was screwed up, even for you."

"What do you mean, even for me? Somebody who's not a wuss?"

Rob rolled his eyes. "My point is: you don't even know what you're doing. People work out for years before they try anything like that."

"I've been practicing it for months!" Juliet's hair had come loose from its braid and cascaded around her shoulders. Her face blooming in the cold, she looked like a movie star, the only imperfection a little shadow of a cleft in her chin.

When she got mad, her eyes changed color, like somebody had retouched them with gold flecks. Juliet had no scars. Most people with XP who don't find out until they are two or three years old have a lot of dark freckles: scary dark scars from sunburn. Rob had some on his back and neck. They found out he had it when he was one, and they were pushing him in his stroller at Disney World. Some lady looked at him. His mom thought she was going to say how cute he was, but instead she screamed, "What did you do to your baby?" Rob's neck and back had morphed into an angry field of huge, dripping blisters.

I didn't have any scars, either. But they found out I had it before I was born. Ironically, my dad is a genetics researcher. He had a cousin with XP, the fatal allergy to sunlight. (Clinically, *Xeroderma Pigmentosum*.) So they tested the unborn baby for it. And they found out—yay!—she didn't have it.

Then she was born. Surprise! I did have it. Tests aren't always right.

Then Dad took off.

Lots of dads do. I hadn't seen him since I was four. He existed for me as some very nice handwriting in a few letters and a bunch of fat guilt checks that allowed us to own our house and have some nice things. Mom adopted Angela instead of latching on to some guy, which I completely admired her for, because most XP kids are only children.

What makes XP even stranger is that there are seven kinds of variations involving eight genes. Some kinds only affect your eyes and skin. But others involve cell changes from exposure to sunlight, too. Juliet and I have Type A, and Rob has Type C, but none of us have the kind that makes a child start out smart and beautiful but lose more and more every year . . . reading and drawing and words and steps just disappearing, like water into dry earth. If you can be grateful for something that's impossible to be grateful for, I was grateful for this small blessing. And for my mom, especially. I couldn't even imagine trying to raise a kid who was not only doomed to a life without sunshine, but also to lose her mind.

Juliet continued to pirouette before us.

"You've been practicing this alone? What if you hit the ground?" Rob demanded.

"What if I did?" Juliet said. "I'd die. Gideon would find me the next morning. Somebody's going to find me dead sooner or later anyhow."

As the douchebag Henry LeBecque pointed out, one of the truly extra-terrific things about XP is that you're forced to live like a vampire, except you're not immortal. Most people with XP die before they're forty, although in every other way, you're totally normal. Juliet lived like she was dying. Some XP people do. Others just hide in the dark and wait.

Nobody said a word.

Juliet finally glared at both of us and growled, "I'm getting my sweater." In a flash, she hurtled back up the rickety fire escape to the pizza parlor roof and came stomping back down, clearly outraged at Rob—and me, too, although I hadn't done anything. "Go on and leave. I'll walk home. I'm taking it you're not interested."

Her home was a long, lonely uphill hike from Gitchee.

"Interested in what?" I asked, glaring at Rob, too. "We're not leaving you."

"She can do what she wants," Rob said in a toneless voice. He was shaking out the keys to his Jeep, mumbling about going home early. It wasn't even three. We hardly ever went home before five. Then he relented. "Get in the car, Juliet."

Her eyes sparkled in the darkness. "Don't you even want to try it? Don't you want to learn? I have two DVDs and some books. It's the most incredible feeling. Like flying. Like an orgasm while you're flying."

"Sounds good already," I said under my breath. I'd never flown in an airplane or had sex, at least with anybody else.

"I can show you how to be safe," Juliet encouraged.

"Yes, I could absolutely see how safe you were up there," Rob replied.

Juliet stopped in the middle of the street, her hands on her hips. "It's a discipline, Allie. It's called Parkour, Rob. It was invented, like, fifty years ago in France, and it's based on strength, speed, skill, self-confidence and safety." She opened her blue eyes wide. "*Safety?* Get it? It's a way of getting so strong you can move as fast as you want past obstacles, or over or under them, without ever being hurt."

"I've seen the videos on YouTube," Rob said. He was already in the driver's seat.

"One of the founders said it's a way of touching the earth and everything on it, being part of it instead of just having it shelter you." Juliet ran over to Rob's side of the car. "We've had enough shelter, don't you think?"

"I've seen the memorials too." Rob made air-quotes. "'He died doing what he loved.' That's as stupid as one of those stories about how some fourteen-year-old kid's uncle shoots him while they're deer hunting and everybody's okay with it."

Juliet kept smiling. "Everybody dies," she said, turning her face so it was out of the light. "But not everybody really lives."

3

REAL LIFE

Within a month, Juliet had converted half of Rob's barn into our Parkour Skill Gym, with mats and parallel bars Rob's father had scraped together from work. I wasn't surprised by how easily Rob caved, and frankly I didn't care. I'd become alive, like Juliet. I would wake up at sunset sick with pain in my belly and shoulders from the endless crunches and handstands. *This is how she must have felt during ski training,* I thought. And when that ended . . . what was she going do with all that excess energy? Within a few weeks, I could leg-press two hundred pounds and do a handstand on the bars.

The three of us were all over the playground at the elementary school, and then all over the bleachers at the high school. At first, we ran the bleachers sideways, skipping up one row at a time to the top, for agility. After we could do that without tripping, we would swing our way down the supports. Rob even stopped saying the word "safety" every five minutes. He was in the thick of it, too. I could hear it in his laugh.

We used the playground equipment to practice vaults until we could hurtle the little merry-go-round touching it with only one hand. (In Parkour terms: a *passement*.) But while Juliet and Rob mastered the backflip right away, I needed a hundred tries to run up a wall and hurtle backward to a standing position. I never landed like they did. Although I will say in my defense: everything I've ever read says that the backflip is not really a Parkour move as much as a show-off move, since the point of Parkour is to get you quickly from one place to another, defying obstacles.

After a series of my progressively more embarrassing wipeouts, Juliet said to Rob, "She's un-teachable. Allie, how did you ever learn to do a backflip off a pier?"

"I *can't* backflip off a pier," I snapped, with what little breath hadn't been slammed out of my body.

When I finally mastered it, though, I couldn't stop. I must have done thirty in one night.

Once in a while, we saw the beam from one of the police cars: Juliet's dad or one of his friends. They must have thought: *Nice.* What good, clean fun we were having, just playing like the kids we were. . . .

At the beginning, my mom, who—did I mention?—has always had a problem with boundaries, would walk into my room and say, "You're burning through the Ibuprofen. What are you guys doing out there? This doesn't seem prudent, Allie."

But I rarely had a cut or scrape because I soon learned to drop and roll. I would land on the balls of my feet and then tumble to a standing position. To a bystander, it would look like I'd whammed myself, but it was a way of harnessing momentum to land lightly. The feeling of being able to run to the end of a wall twelve feet up and make this controlled dive into mid-air . . . and knowing you weren't going to twist an ankle or break your collarbone. . . . Juliet was right about the sensation. It was a part of something magical. It was like being *on* the earth instead of hiding inside it. And she was right about that part, too: we'd hidden all our lives.

IN JUNE, JULIET decided we were ready to try a gap leap to a cat grab and then swing down five stories to a ten-foot turn vault to the ground. She was going to set up a camera with a filter to film us. It would be the first "Dark Stars" video feat. Dark Stars would be our "Tribe," which is what the Parkour "*traceurs*" call one another. (To perform Parkour was to "trace." Juliet had memorized all the Parkour terms in French. I had no interest in the words, so I rarely used either the French *or* English. I was only interested in the action.)

Our launch pad was a six-story building under construction, perched on the bluffs above Lake Superior. Juliet had chosen the spot. From there we would land on the roof of an older neighboring five-story building: Tabor Oaks, an upscale apartment complex. Then we would *"lache"* (pronounced la-chay): swing by one arm to the other from one balcony to the one below it. The bottom-most balconies were differently built, ten feet down and about five feet to the left or right of the balconies above—with nothing directly below them except open space.

If you missed that final move, you would plummet to the grass, thirty feet down. You'd be lucky if you only broke your neck. If you had a lot of momentum, and you kept flying, you'd eventually tumble down to the boulders washed by the waves below. I'd assumed that this was the motive behind Juliet's choice for the Dark Stars on-camera debut: the thrill, so close to the certain death on the rocks of Lake Superior, and also so close to a bunch of rich strangers who had no taste for adventure.

Of course, Juliet must have known we might glimpse something. Only later did I realize that she'd always known.

OUR TRANSITION FROM the playground to the pit—to the end of an innocence we only saw in retrospect—was abrupt. If you had asked us, Rob and I would have said that we were very mature for our age. People think that, and say that, and we were among those who would have *meant* that, what with our life-threatening illness. But in fact we were, if anything, slow to "grow up." I thought of drinking booze and smoking weed and (eventually) having sex as big markers of adulthood. I had no idea how sheltered we really were.

It began on a Thursday, right before I fell asleep in the morning.

Juliet zinged me a text: *B ready*.

I shot back: *?*

Something new and big We R READY! READY 4 MORE! The CHALLENGE!

When?

2 morrow! Juliet replied.

And that was all.

Why so soon? I wondered tiredly. Why tonight?

THAT FRIDAY MORNING, before our epic night of "bouldering"—a Parkour word that supposedly combines the word "building" with "boulder," from mountain climbing—I had a clinic appointment.

If I had to go to the doctor, it was usually after midnight. Many XP doctors and nurses (my mother among them) worked the red-eye shift for obvious reasons. All the patients in the XP Family Study got free care, so we tried to make it easier for those who did the caring. There were people who'd moved all the way from Wyoming and California. The Siroccos had moved from the Twin Cities, just to bring their kids to the XP Family Study at the Tabor Clinic—the most extensive treatment facility for XP anywhere in the world. They knew it was worth the headache and expense of travel to a lackluster ski resort town, all thanks to the Tabor family.

Dr. Andrew Tabor, who was around sixty, took care of us. His younger brother, Dr. Stephen Tabor, took care of the dead. (At least that's how I thought of him.) He did research for the XP Family Study, too, but as the county medical examiner. He dissected bodies to figure out how to prevent what kills us, which is usually skin cancer—the worst kind. Every year after New Year's Eve, the Tabors had a big party for the XP families, and Dr. Andrew would always give the same cheery toast.

"We're THIS close. Forty years ago, my father, Simon, could never have believed how far we would come."

Dr. Simon Tabor, who was easily a hundred and still kicking, founded the Tabor Clinic. Why he'd decided to make XP his life's work, none of us knew—nobody in his family had been afflicted. But half of the year-round citizens of Iron Harbor worked at the Clinic. The Tabors also owned a lot of other places in town, including the canoe and SCUBA rental places, some buildings, and the three restaurants that aren't Gitchee Pizza. Gideon wouldn't give in, although they tried to buy him out. He said he wanted to leave Gitchee Pizza to his son, even though he doesn't have a son and he's been married four times.

Sometimes, I had to ask myself why, though . . . why this whole community has grown up around the Tabor Clinic.

These families are trying to buy time, basically. Time for what? Time to be with their kids, which used to strike me as selfish if the kid was suffering. Time for the kids to have a life, which is fine, I guess, until they get old enough to know what XP really means.

People talk about "genetic engineering" and "stem cell research" and "DNA repair" like it'll be available next week at Walmart. But even if God or the government doesn't forbid it, that stuff takes more time than we have. It takes longer than one short lifetime. Like, ordinarily, people would say to a girl my age: *You have your whole life ahead of you.* Sure, you have to grow up in Nowheresville, but someday, you'll remember the huge storms and the loon's lonesome moans and you'll be happy you had that girlhood. And that would all be fine except the odds are, this fairy tale doesn't apply to me. This is my girlhood and my everything-hood. You can't blame us for wanting to *carpe* that *diem* if our diems are numbered.

I went back and forth on this subject. Sometimes, I thought I would be better off if I'd never been born. Sometimes, I thought I would hang on long enough for somebody to find a biological switch that could turn this thing off. There were some adults with XP in Iron Harbor, sure. But not too many. And we didn't see them much. Juliet and Rob and I were among the older patients.

When my mood was especially black, I'd think of Dennis Ackerman. He was one of my tutors—super cute and the nicest guy. He taught me math and science three nights a week. He tutored other kids who couldn't go to regular school, too, the ones on chemotherapy or recovering from mono or what have you. But having XP himself, he had a soft spot for us.

Four years ago, at the age of twenty-five, he'd decided he'd had enough.

That morning, my mom came into my room and woke me out of a sound sleep. The look on her face was so awful, in the truest sense, as though she'd seen a vision. I was sure my little sister had been diagnosed with some awful disease, too, or that Juliet, who was still skiing competitively as a freestyle jumper, was paralyzed. In a flat voice, Mom told me that Mr. Ackerman's mother had found him dead in his car that morning. He had shut the garage and stuffed rags in all the cracks and just let the car run until he fell asleep. I asked if he'd left a note. My mom said he had, and it said that he knew this was a lousy thing to do to his mother and his "kids," but he couldn't stand the wait anymore.

I more or less understood that, too. But thanks to Juliet, I had long ago vowed never to go that route.

MY FRIDAY APPOINTMENT got off to a lousier start than usual because I forgot my umbrella. Mom and I fought the whole way to the clinic. She wanted me to be more serious about my illness. I figured I was as serious as I could get about something beyond my control. With my mom being a nurse, though, she was pretty vigilant. She was over-protective. Let's be frank: she was crazy. She would have had me bubble-wrapped if she could have.

I was so absorbed in thought about our upcoming expedition that nigh,t I just spaced on the umbrella. It wasn't raining, of course: I needed an umbrella the size of a palm tree even when the sky was clouded over, which was pretty often in Iron Harbor.

My mom had gone out early for a run with her best friend, Gina Ricci. In addition to being my godmother, Gina was also a nurse who specialized in XP.

When they burst through the door, sweating, Mom rushed upstairs to shower. (Mom held the North American indoor record for speed-showering: five minutes from foot on the bottom step to fully clothed.) Gina gave me a kiss and slipped me a ten dollar bill. One of the benefits of having a chronic illness is frequent monetary giftage. I thanked Gina with a hug—but before my mother could slip into the shower stall, she stopped at the second floor landing and eyed my outfit.

"You're half-dressed, Allie Kim!" she yelled.

I ignored her. That always lit her fuse.

You wouldn't refer to *not carrying an umbrella* as "half-dressed," unless you were my mother. So much crap to wear just to run from my back porch to my mother's car and then the ten feet into the clinic! You can't have one inch of skin exposed. Not for a minute. When I go out during the day, I have gloves and veils and goggles on, so that I look like I'm studying killer bees. She dashed back down and pulled the umbrella out of the closet, shaking it at me like a sword.

My mom is good. A good mom. She so believes that I will outrun XP that I sometimes let her believe it, too. If I live to a ripe old age, her reasoning goes, I won't want to end up looking like I was deep-fried early in life, will I?

"Allie!" she said again. My mom's natural voice is a less-than-soothing bellow that makes neighborhood dogs howl. "Did you hear me?"

"I'm sorry, Jack-Jack," I told her. My mom's name is Jacqueline.

"Don't call me that," she said.

"Okay, Jack-Jack," I said.

"Someone has to take this seriously, Allie Kim!"

"Jackie, calm down," Gina chimed in. "Allie is a very serious girl."

"And I'm an adolescent. I'm supposed to feel immortal."
Mom shook her head. "You have bruises all over you. If
Rob Dorn is—"

"He has bruises all over him, too, Mom. We're doing
this . . . mountain thing."

"In the dark?"

"How do you think they climb Mount Everest?" I replied.
"Fog and storms. No oxygen. You can't see. It gives you character."

Gina laughed.

"I'll give you character," Mom finally muttered. "And *I*
see everything."

"That you do," I agreed.

She hit the shower. Gina bit her lip to keep from smiling
back at me.

I JUMPED OUT of the car while Mom was in mid-resumed
eruption. She would have to circle around for twenty minutes and (maybe?) park illegally and get a ticket that someone
would fix for her because she worked there. By then, she'd
have calmed down.

The Tabor Clinic is part of Divine Savior Hospital,
which is huge, *completely* huge, with, like, three hundred
doctors. But there were only three Tabors. At the Clinic,
they call me Chinese Ginger. Gina is to blame, because
she knows I am half-Chinese. But Dad must have been
crossed with some hot European way back to leave me
with straight auburn hair and weird amber-colored eyes.
My mother is fair and Irish, although she kept the name
"Kim" after they got divorced, for no reason that I could
ever discern—given that I don't look Asian and she surely
doesn't, either. Maybe it was to pave the way for Angela,

my adopted sister from China. I hoped she would last after I was gone so my mother wouldn't be childless.

Whenever I hinted at something like that, at the inevitability of Angie's outliving me, it drove my mother savage. It either made her think I hated Angela or that I was "giving up." Maybe sometimes I was, but only for the moment.

Anyhow: red hair is recessive and so is XP. Both parents have to be carriers—not of the disease, but of the gene. The kind that seems to occur mostly with Asian people, especially the Japanese, was not the kind I had. This was a mercy, again, if you can say a thing like that about a thing like XP, because other strains leave you with an IQ of 50 by the time you're ten years old. The weirdest part is that the doctors can't explain why this happens. Sun damage should have no effect on neurology. That's why the Tabor family is convinced that there is a partner gene involved.

Gina was already waiting for me in the lobby. I wasn't surprised she'd beat us there. She hadn't bothered to shower. "Ready to give up a ton of blood and skin?"

"I live for it," I said.

"Good. Don't spend that ten bucks all in one place."

I GAVE UP all my samples and then went to the neurology lab. They did a bunch of peering into my nose and eyes and making tones I had to raise my finger if I heard. Then I went in to wait for Dr. Andrew.

I liked him. For an older graying guy, grandpa-aged, he always smells good and he's super-fit, like all guy doctors (although not most nurses, I've observed). I would sometimes see him jogging when I got up at night before dinner.

He gave me a hug, per usual. "You lost weight," he said.

"Nah, just buffing up," I told him. I had lost a few pounds from Parkour, and although I was five-six with big shoulders and strong legs, it showed.

"Nothing else? No problems?"

"Well, I have this chronic problem with sunlight. I can't get a base tan."

Dr. Andrew snickered. "And how's that career in stand-up comedy coming along?" He flashed a big fake smile that would have looked dumb on anyone else his age, but on him it was just sweet and goofy.

The drill took an eternity of two hours, like it always does. But I was grateful, as I always am, not to have to endure a full checkup every month.

Nothing about me had changed. That was good news.

Once I was home, I only had four or five hours to sleep—not enough. I was also freaking out, because hang-dropping your way down a ladder or the monkey bars is one thing, but trespassing on private property is another. Juliet kept insisting they were the same.

I texted her: *2 Tired.*

She texted me: *2 Chicken.*

I texted her: *Bring it.*

She wrote back: *Live once!*

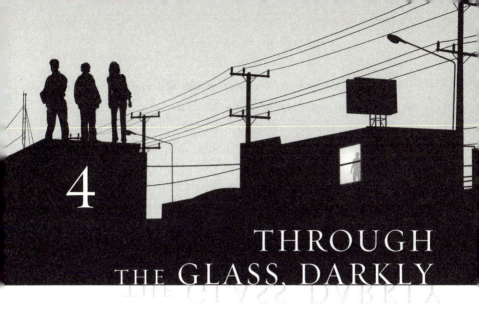

4

THROUGH
THE GLASS, DARKLY

Rob picked me up around nine, after I was finished with what little school work I was going to do. It was June and junior year was a week away from becoming a memory. The gloves I'd bought for traction were already getting worn, but the light, grip-soled shoes were still good.

"Are we both insane?" I asked him, when I got into the front seat of the Jeep.

He smirked.

Without XP, Rob would have been able to run Iron County High. There would have been minions and maids hanging off him. Instead, he was a shadow presence, like the rumor of a spectacular guy. He supposedly had "friends." We all supposedly had "friends." I was on the yearbook committee. Once a month they met at my house. Nobody knew what to say to me. *Melanoma yet, Allie?* Or—*did you hear that Kayla and Jeremy broke up? She was out for two weeks . . . she's on antidepressants.* Random gossip about strangers unknown to me.

They tried, at least the nice ones. When Juliet was still skiing, I'd mostly hung with Nicola Burns. I really liked Nicola, and we still did things sometimes—rarely, but enough that we could say we were "friends," with quotes. The key: she never pitied me.

Regrettably, in eighth grade, I'd also briefly hung out with Caitlin Murray, who went through this brief period of trying to be a saint. I don't know what inspired it. She'd been a horrible, spoiled child, a cosmetic surgeon's daughter, and had matured into a horrible, spoiled teenager. But then her parents got divorced; her mom was briefly single before marrying a guy who had been a singer in some ancient band. Maybe for a while, Caitlin felt the cold wind blowing through the cracks of the universe and briefly identified with the doomed and the lost.

Then she did something to Juliet, and I never spoke to her again.

It was Homecoming Dance of freshman year, although technically we were never really "freshmen" or "sophomores." Because we had tutors and because we did everything fast to get it over with, we were a year ahead of everyone else. There's so much happy bullshit and plain old babysitting in school that it would otherwise take us two and a half years to get through all four. At least that's my understanding.

Anyhow, our parents wanted us to try to have normal friends to the degree we could. We didn't blame them. *They* had normal friends in high school.

We tried to do what normal friends do. Go to the dance. Stand by the wall. Watch the Daytimers *e-lab-or-ate-ly* pretend to not notice you, until one of them bursts into tears because, Oh! She just feels so bad for you, and all her girlfriends have to run to the bathroom to comfort her! Meanwhile, most guys stand there and do boob-feeling pantomimes like some kind of idiot puppets. I have to admit, these guys don't bother me, because they don't pity us, either. Then there are the guys who unwittingly pretend to be robots whose batteries have died; they stare into space with no emotion in an effort to convey a mysterious, hidden, deep soul that doesn't exist. I'm not a violent person, but it would have been bad for me to have an automatic weapon just then.

This particular night also happened to occur during Juliet's first year away from skiing.

She was miserable and restless, and was packing more attitude than usual. She said that the people on her ski team used to call her "The Great and Terrible." I believed it. After that last winter, she'd returned home with a tiny tattoo just above her navel ring: the initials G.T. I don't think that even Rob ever noticed it, although we'd all gone skinny-dipping many times. It was dark blue and hard to see in the dark, especially if you were distracted by the wink of the little piercing ring in the moonlight, which he would have been. But I saw why she'd earned the nickname that night.

The band started to play an old song from the distant past, with a chorus that repeated "more and more of you." It must have struck a chord in Juliet, because she just got out there. We'd scoured our parents' discarded jewelry (in lieu of being able to shop during business hours) and Juliet had picked out eight impossibly slender silver rings her mom, Ginny, used to wear as a kid. Juliet called them her "ringlethingles." That night, she wore one ring on every finger.

Having balance like no one else, insanely agile in five-inch heels, she danced.

Danced.

The whole gym froze. It was as if someone had pressed a giant pause button. But the music played, even though the guys in the band stumbled over a few notes. No one came out to try to dance with her or even beside her. It was *art*: her hips in a perfect grind of a figure eight, her hands down at her thighs tickling an invisible piano, gradually working their way up to all that hair, her eyes closed in invisible ecstasy.

When the song ended, Juliet walked out of the spotlight and jerked her head at me. I had to snap out of my own trance. Passing Caitlin Murray and some of her coven, I heard a purr: "You know, there are ways you can make your living at night. On a pole."

Juliet just kept walking. "Daytimers," she said under her breath.

Rob was outside already. He hadn't even witnessed the Juliet-Caitlin exchange. But he said something right, something I never could, even though I saw the same sea of parked cars. "Do you notice the irony in our society?" he joked. "Wannabe size-zeros in a crowd of beached whales. America is this obscenely fat society of self-deniers. It's fried mayonnaise balls or death, and everyone buys into the hypocrisy. It's *sad*. These moms need to get out of their cars and dance. Look how unhappy they are!"

Juliet beamed.

That night I knew Juliet had somehow united us in an unspoken belief: we had it over the Daytimers. We were smarter and funnier. And when Juliet whirled in a dizzying constellation over Gitchee Pizza, I knew this to be truer than ever. We could do things they could never do, *but at night*. Even most of the jocks with heads the size of fire hydrants couldn't do Parkour. It was hard. Harder than hard. Demanding of body, in flexibility and strength. Demanding of spirit, in creativity and fearlessness.

Most of all, it demanded constant improvisation.

AS WE DROVE to Juliet's house, I asked Rob, "Do you think she's already tried this?"

"I wouldn't be surprised at all, Allie-stair," he said.

For Rob, it was "Allie-stair;" for Juliet, "Allie-Bear." I could never figure out why neither of *them* had nicknames. It made me feel like a stuffed animal they tossed back and forth, like the little penguin on skis Juliet still slept with.

"Well, if she did, I'm glad," I said.

"Why?"

"Because she's still alive and that means it's doable," I said.

Before we even reached her house, Juliet was dashing out the front door with a sack that could have been Santa's. Inside was a tripod plus a lot of power food, like bars and dried chili, as if we couldn't have set everything up and then driven to the Gitchee for a meatball sandwich. We set up a camp in the little private beach park area about a quarter of a mile down the road from Tabor Oaks . . . and ended up eating a whole lot more than we needed.

"Stupid," Juliet muttered after we'd finished, standing up and burping. She could make a burp both graceful and adorable. "Now what do we do? My stomach's about to explode. It's going to take hours to digest."

"We have to wait hours anyway," said Rob. "Why are we out here at ten o'clock? What the hell are we going to do except offer ourselves as a sacrifice to mosquitoes until everybody is nighty-night?"

With the mention of the word nighty-night, the

combination of two power bars and bowl of mush hit me like a cloud of pixie dust. "I'm . . . just so . . . tired. . . ."

Juliet laughed. "Go ahead, Allie-Bear. We'll wake you at the stroke of midnight."

I WAS CURLED up in the back of the Jeep when Rob roughly shook my shoulder.

Apparently I'd been asleep for two hours. The first thing I noticed when I stumbled out of the door was that the wind had kicked up.

"That weather crap has nothing to do with us," Juliet said. "Unless it's pouring."

I scowled at the waves. Mist tickled my cheeks. "Why didn't you guys wake me up and tell me this was off?" I asked. "There's no way we can trace now."

"Of course we can." Juliet laughed. "It's fine. And we just got back. We went to Gitchee for pizza and hung around talking to Gideon. He's getting married again, by the way. This makes five times, a Northern Minnesota record."

I ignored her. You would never try anything on a wet surface or if you were sick or out of whack, even a little. David Belle—the son of Parkour's creator and really the person who pioneered the sport—is no show-off. He says bare feet are the best shoes. And everything he did, he did with grace and safety. But I also knew I could calm those waves easier than I could stop Juliet going up that building.

A tall rock wall already had been built around the construction site, probably meant to shelter any cars there if the lake was feeling frisky. We *could* have walked around to the front entrance. Instead, Juliet sprinted to the wall, grasped the top, pulling up to a standing position, and dropped onto a vast concrete slab that would eventually become the parking garage. I glanced at Rob. He took off after her. I had no choice but to follow.

Juliet and I wore La Sportive Fireblades because they fit narrower feet. Rob had K-Swiss. That kind of shoe costs over a hundred, easy. Rob's dad got the shoes for us for practically nothing, because of his job. He'd also bought us rock-climber gloves, with "sticky" pads on the fingertips and palms.

In less than a minute, we were up the side of the skeleton of that new building, though we'd agreed we wouldn't make this a speed course. We adjusted our headlamps. Faces in the dark are always silvery, but Rob's was lighter, almost glowing. The waves were slapping down now. I could see whitecaps in the black abyss. When I was really little, and we moved to the north shore, the waves used to keep me awake—until my mother told me that they were saying, "*Shush. Shush.*"

Years later, long after the time they had put me to sleep, I thought of them as saying, "*Now? Now?*"

My pulse pounded as we stood silently on one of the construction workers' platforms and studied the roof next door. It looked further than twelve feet away, the distance Juliet had assured us. (Later, I would find out it was twenty feet.) To me the roof appeared tiny, distant—as though we were going to try to jump from a mountaintop onto a dinner plate. Rob said, randomly, that the building was much nicer than the taller one upon which we were perched. Juliet sniffed. Of course the building was nicer: It was old, with thick walls, and the apartments were huge. Each took up half of one of the floors. Except the top floor. That was all one even huger apartment. . . .

"So we're going to land on top of some rich person's roof like a bunch of giant raccoons," I said.

"Yeah, but one at a time," Juliet said. "Remember, you drop and roll. No one will care. It's two in the morning. And anyhow, the bedrooms are in the front bit, not back here."

Only later did I wonder: *How did she know?*

"I'll go first," Rob said.

Before either of us could speak, he backed up and hurtled himself over the gap and down. We heard him land, but for a second, both of us were afraid to look. Then we heard a yell: "It's good! The wind's behind you and the drop helps."

The waves were thrashing the shore now. His voice was almost lost.

Juliet turned to me. "I don't want to leave you alone," she whispered.

I could barely hear her over my thumping heart. What the hell were we doing?

"I know you think that I don't give a damn if I live or die," she added. "And maybe I don't. But I would never, not ever, willingly hurt you." She hugged me briefly. "So you go ahead, Bear."

The moon burst from behind a mound of cloud and I didn't give myself time to think. *It's just a jump*, I said to myself. Then I was in the air, my back arched, my body poised to drop and barrel-roll. As I did, I expelled the air from my lungs.

My eyes bulged as Juliet landed, softly as a gull, several feet past me.

Parkour is not competitive. I would have been jealous otherwise. On the other hand, Juliet had saved me and bested me. I *was* jealous.

"Down," she said.

We lined up at the edge. I could feel my heart pounding again. We would need to drop and hang from the edge of the roof and then swing, building up enough momentum to let go with one arm and grab the rail of the balcony below, about five feet to the right. After that, we'd grab the railing with our other hand and "muscle up" onto the balcony before the next drop—to another balcony, about five feet to the left.

The balcony of the penthouse apartment was long, with room to spare for the three of us.

Rob swung down first. But he shook his head in the shadows.

"It's harder than it looks," he hissed. "I can give you a hand." Obviously, Juliet wouldn't allow that. Her biceps were like little apples under her jersey. She copied his exact moves and scrambled up the railing onto the balcony beside him. When my turn came, I gave myself a boost by taking a few steps and swinging myself two-handed. I'd planned to grab the railing of the balcony with my free hand and pull up, but I ended up hurtling myself over the rail and into my friends' arms.

At that moment, the sky above the lake split open.

Two crippled fingers of lightning reached down for the black water. Only a few seconds passed before a deafening thunderclap. The air sizzled with the smell of sulfur. I winced. That stink is probably why the ancients believed lightning and thunder were harbingers of all things demonic. Why not? My idea of Hell could easily include being exposed on a balcony as a Lake Superior tsunami kicks in.

We crouched together.

"Let's see if there's a fire escape," Rob said. "And get the hell out of here."

We looked back toward the town. Another blast of lightning blotted out what few lights there were above Oxford

Street. To my shock, I realized I was high enough up to spot my house on Trinity. If the thunder woke my mother, she would be up roaming and accelerating into hysterics after realizing I wasn't there.

I leaned over the balcony, looking for a way down that didn't involve becoming a human lightning rod, when the lights in the penthouse came on.

Rob pulled me back. Juliet scrambled into the shadows beside us.

All I could see was white. One massive room: white walls, white carpeting, white woodwork. Except . . . right in the middle of the floor, next to the sliding doors, a young woman with dark hair—probably not much older than we were—was on her back. She wore only a bra. A man with his back turned to us was leaning over her. He seemed to be kissing her, then slapping her, then trying to pull her up.

Rob swore, softly, under his breath.

We stared for an instance in horrified silence as the man lowered his face to hers. He had short-cropped dark hair, darker than Rob's, with a wide white streak of platinum blond down the back in what appeared to be a dyed slash of a lightning bolt.

Rob pointed to the fire escape: a sleek ladder that descended straight from the far side of the balcony. The glass doors were floor to ceiling but he pointed and guided me toward it. We dropped to the balcony floor and crawled past a potted pine to get to the edge of it. I was already ten steps down when I heard Rob say, "Juliet! Juliet! Come on."

The rain began to fall, hard, cold drops on my hot face.

Rob said again, "Juliet! He'll see you!"

Juliet didn't seem to care who saw her. She descended

languidly, almost like a ballet dancer, and leaped the last few feet to the ground. The rain began pounding. The inside of my eyeballs were wet.

After a fevered sprint, Rob and I threw ourselves into the car. Juliet ran around in the dark, picking up her tripod. When she jumped into the back, I turned to her. She was messing with the camera, dripping wet though not breathing as hard as either Rob or me.

"I think this stuff is okay," she gasped. "I was scared it blew into the lake!"

I couldn't seem to catch my breath. "Was that girl . . . what was wrong with her?"

Juliet lifted her shoulders. "She looked like she was passed out. And he was trying to wake her up."

Rob didn't even seem to be listening to our conversation. "We triggered some alarm when we landed on the balcony—which is why the lights came on . . . right?"

I said, "That girl looked dead."

"Dead drunk maybe," Juliet dismissed, drying her camera with her shirt.

"He was doing, like CPR, right?" I asked, mostly to myself.

"Good date gone bad," Juliet replied. Her voice was flat. "It scared the hell out of me, though, when that light went on."

The lightning crashed again. We heard a hollow boom—a tree or a light pole down. It happened all the time.

Then Rob said, "Who has a date in a room with no furniture?"

We all turned to the apartment. It was dark.

5

WANT AD

I woke up screaming, my sheets drenched with sweat.

At least Angie and Mom weren't there.

You try to breathe through things like that. Out with the bad air. In with the good air. Out with the bad mind pictures, in with the good mind pictures. That girl's face was slack and rubbery. She was a young person with an old person's skin. A dead person's skin. I felt my throat constricting.

My little sister has allergies. So we probably occupied the only house in Iron Harbor except the hospital and the assisted-living facility that had air conditioning. I rolled out of bed in my T-shirt and underpants and tugged at the window—panicking when it would not open, forgetting I had to slide the latch—then finally laid my face against the blackout screen and sucked in as much piney air as my lungs could hold. In the distance, I heard birds chirping. Back in bed, I began to text Rob.

Then I realized it was noon on a Saturday. Rob and Juliet were asleep.

As I should be. My mind raced, wondering why I didn't have alternative, non-lethal pursuits and alternative non-criminal friends. Maybe I could stay away from Juliet for a little while. There was still Nicola. True, school was out for the summer, but she'd be on yearbook committee with me next fall, right? We could plan ahead. We could even do some non-yearbook stuff. We'd gone to the movies precisely six times in my life. Once I'd stayed over at her house, too. Plus her dad collected all these old pinball machines, all with horror themes, that were definitely fun. He also had the first edition of every single Stephen King book, signed. That was sort of cool.

Come to think of it, I would probably have been better friends with Nicola if Juliet hadn't taken up so much real estate in my friendship pasture. But how could I call Nicola out of the blue? I hadn't seen her for months. (*Hi, Nicola! I just saw a girl who was possibly dying and I'm totally creeped out, so I don't want to hang with my best friend. . . .*) My thoughts wandered back to the penthouse.

The dead-looking girl probably *was* dead drunk.

Why wasn't there any furniture in the apartment?

The guy was probably a construction worker. Maybe he'd snuck in there with his girlfriend and they'd gotten wasted.

Why was he trying to revive her?

They were just two innocent people looking for some privacy.

Why was her face bone gray like that?

Not for the first, fifteenth, or fortieth time, my friendship with Juliet disturbed my sleep—though I was sure, not hers.

I had knockout pills I could take. I only needed them once a month, when I had cramps. Some XP kids had to take them routinely because they could never get used to the reversed biorhythmic schedule.

I rummaged in the drawer and took two of them. Then I prepared to do my whole sleep ritual, which I had neglected the night before. I made my Goodnight tea with honey. I put fresh sheets on the bed. I jumped in and out of a dangerously hot shower, smeared myself with my one vanity—expensive cream that smelled of the Caribbean Islands I would never see—and pulled and pegged my blackout shades so the room was utterly lightless. Then I got out my big sleep mask, the one that was ten inches long and lay across my face like a soft log filled with flaxseed and lavender . . . and after all that, I still could not banish the lurid image: the guy with the platinum streak down the back of his head, jerking that girl's limp body up off the white carpet.

But that's what you did to revive someone. It wasn't gentle. Right?

And if he really was a guy who was working on that new apartment and in there with his wasted girlfriend, the last thing he'd want is for her to barf all over a pristine sea of total whiteness. Of course she wasn't dead. If she was dead, there'd be blood. And gunk. Bodily fluids. I'd spent half my life in a hospital; I *knew*. That place was spotless. Still . . . living-but-passed-out people shouldn't be that pale.

On the other hand, what was I basing this on? The number of passed-out-drunk people I'd seen in my life numbered zero.

I lay back on the bed. The best way to put yourself to sleep is to listen for a sound that's almost outside your ability to hear. I closed my eyes and searched for the loon and finally found it, a sound as familiar to me as my own music after all these years, yet still, even during the day, lonesome and eerie.

My legs began to tingle. *Please, let the pills kick in*, I thought. *Please.*

I woke up at eleven that night and quickly grabbed my phone.

Rob had texted: *Sleeping in.*

Juliet had texted nothing.

THREE DAYS PASSED. Then three more. I didn't hear from Juliet once. She didn't answer any texts or calls. *Here we go again,* I thought. *Another vanishing act.* Rob became oddly withdrawn too, claiming he wasn't feeling well. I couldn't argue with sickness. The nights seemed to grow longer, even though summer shortened them. This was supposed to be our time together.

I devoted myself to not thinking about Rob or Juliet. Not thinking about best friends is almost a discipline in itself. I tried to start a journal. Unfortunately, I'm no writer, and the entries kept coming back to Rob in ways that were at best embarrassing and at worst excruciating. I wondered if he was as shaken by what we'd seen as I was.

Of course he was. That's why he was ignoring me.

On day seven, I decided to capitalize on our shaken-ness.

Spending as much time in a hospital as we do, you learn a few things—namely that certain ER admittances must be recorded by the police, and while names are never given, you can deduce an identity from certain details: age, ethnicity, and reason for showing up in the first place. Juliet taught me how to access the police records the night we pushed Henry LeBecque into that open grave. (*Male Caucasian, 17 yrs old, intoxicated, admitted to Tabor Clinic ER for panic attack, 12:17 A.M., November 1. Released 3:45 A.M. after exam.*) I scoured the records for any sign of the woman with the gray skin. But there were no matches. In fact, not a single woman had been admitted to the ER the night or morning of our little stunt. So if that guy with the blond lightning bolt had been trying to revive her, he must have succeeded.

On day eight, I found myself crying.

Why wouldn't Juliet and Rob return my calls or texts? What had I done? Was I going to spend the entire summer— or worse, the rest of my life—without the two people who knew and understood me better than anyone in the world? That night, I even tried to sleep, which was a very weird feeling, trying to fall asleep without all the daytime sounds of Iron Harbor to provide my bedtime lullaby. I clung to the belief that Juliet and Rob were going through some variation of what I was going through, that both of them had to be missing me, but both of them were scared to talk about what we'd seen.

By that morning, crying felt like a job.

The word clicked in my brain.

It was summer. School was out. I should do what normal kids my age did. I decided to get a *real* job.

THE FUNNY THING: my own mother didn't even need a job. We could have paid off our house and bought new clothes every season and gone to Italy in August on what my father sent. But for the very first time, I understood why my mother needed to work. She needed a goal, a distraction, a purpose.

Still, what could I do?

Literally, I had no talents. I could type people's papers. I couldn't work at Gitchee; Gideon lit the place like a hockey rink. I could be a server in a dark restaurant, like that one in California where the waiters were blind. None were dark enough here. I could clean houses at night. I was good at harassing my little sister. . . . *A-ha.*

I decided I was a babysitter. I made advertisements.

REST EASY!
EXPERIENCED BIG SISTER
CAN BABYSIT AND CLEAN 4 U NIGHTS.
AMAZING REFERENCES

Okay. "Amazing" was pushing it. Not counting my mom, I had two: Gina and Dr. Andrew. I could add Juliet's dad. He was a cop, although he'd never seen me do anything that required talent except paint my nails while eating popcorn.

I pressed send. Then I waited.

I GOT TWO calls that day: two more than I expected. There isn't a lot of demand for sitters who only work the graveyard shift. One came from a single dad who was clearly drunk when he left the message. I didn't call back and neither did he. The other came from a young woman, Tessa—a nurse at Divine Savior, no less, who worked midnights—with an infant named Tavish. (I had to ask twice if I was pronouncing it right. TA-vish.) She'd just moved to Iron Harbor into a building on Lakeshore Road. Although it couldn't be the *same* building, as in *that* building (could it?) I decided to go and talk to her anyhow. We made a date for the following Tuesday.

And almost as soon as I hung up—at least that's how it felt—Juliet called.

She sounded as chirpy as though we'd just spent the previous night on an online body-butter-buying binge.

"Rob and I went to Duluth to scout," she said all in one breath. "We found some good stuff for us."

I blinked. My throat caught. "May you be happy always," I replied.

"It's a long drive though," I heard Rob chime in from the background. "You take an hour or more to get there, you don't have much time."

"But once you find spaces for traces, you have places to go to," Juliet added. "You don't have to search. You just sing."

"And you have the soul of the poet!" I managed. "What about me?"

"We didn't think you'd be into it," Juliet said.

Right, but you were into each other.

"So do you want to be into it?" Juliet said.

"Well, let's see," I said. "I'm busy. Cheer practice is Monday and Wednesday. . . ." Then I exploded: "It's been ten days since we did that building but who's counting and neither one of you bothered to do so much as text me more than five times, and that was only Rob! Why should I want to do anything with you?"

"We love you," Juliet said.

I hung up.

THAT NIGHT, I found myself in the Jeep with Rob and Juliet. We weren't going to do Parkour. We were going swimming.

Normally we'd borrow a boat from the snazzy side of Ghost Lake. But no one owned a boat that fit our needs: conveniently located and not very well tied up. We ended up in the bass boat owned by the gym teacher, Mr. Callahan—one of the few boats we used with the owner's permission.

Once we were out in deep water, Rob and I jumped in. We gasped as we splashed. It's never warm. It's so cold in fall that you could die, like the people on the Titanic. In summer, it's cold enough to be a shock. The water always smells of pocket change, like old nickels and dimes, because of all the minerals in it. Minerals are why there are beaches on Lake Superior that have inches of black sand on them, and agates and garnets and gold that old people are always finding because this was all once a volcano. There was also a lot of glacier action and earthquakes and such that, for me, it was God's way of saying, *This is not land meant for habitation, people! Move to the Twin Cities* . . . but what do I know?

"I want to try Tabor Oaks again," said Juliet, rocking back in forth on the boat's little bench. Rob and I treaded water, teeth chattering, avoiding each other's eyes. "They've put floors down now on the other building, to climb up. . . ."

"Forget to call me that night," I said. "Like you have the last two weeks."

"Fine," Juliet said. "We'll do it. It's a good course."

"Who's we?" I spat, enraged. "Am I not part of 'we'?"

"It's good in a semi-sick way," Rob said, ignoring me. "The course."

"Somebody lives in that place now," Juliet said. "It was probably just, like, the mover, or the new owner's brother or something and his girlfriend."

"How do you know?" I demanded.

She shrugged.

Again, later, long after, I would close my eyes in the dark, and see Juliet's legs, the spokes of a starry-silvery-blue wheel, glowing in the dark that first night above Gitchee Pizza, and wonder, *how-did-she-know-how-did-she-know?*

"Maybe it was some crazy drifter who dragged some random girl into an empty apartment on a stormy night," Rob said.

"How would he get in there?" Juliet answered, seriously.

"I was kidding," Rob muttered.

Juliet shook her head. "Rape is a crime of opportunity."

"It isn't usually, in fact," Rob said. "You should know better, Juliet. Your dad being a cop and all. Some rapists plan very carefully. The smart ones do. They stalk people for weeks and months. If they're really crazy, they work up this whole thing where the girl is coming out of her house—"

"You read too many books, boy detective," Juliet interrupted.

"It's a fact," Rob said. Their eyes met. They both smiled. "I deal just in facts, ma'am."

He ducked under the surface. Part of me hoped he would stay there.

THE NEXT NIGHT, I had my job interview. I needed my mom's car. It was eight o'clock, and there was still plenty of light left in the sky, so I wore a ball cap with my ponytail poking through the gap, and a long-sleeved shirt.

The speed limit in Iron Harbor is 30. My mother's car is a six-seat Toyota mini-van. Very used. But very sturdy.

"Be careful," Mom warned. "No speeding."

"Not even any drag racing," I said.

"Be back by—"

"Morning. Yes, Mother. Do you know how many other mothers are saying, now, 'Miss, I don't want you out one minute after sunrise!'?"

"Don't change the subject Do you think you should put gloves on? I can still see everything. It's *light* out."

"I already look like some old lady in an English mystery novel, Mom."

She started laughing. "You do. You look like that woman on an old TV show who was always solving mysteries by

herself. I used to think, it was this little town in Maine and
people were dying there like flies. How could there be a murder every week in a town that small?"

How, indeed?

I dumped my dinner plate in the sink, hugged Angie until
her feet were off the floor and she was literally unable to
breathe, and left my mother ranting at the beef stroganoff.

Out on Island Road, I turned off at Red Beach, just to
look at the water, since I was too early for my appointment
at 9 P.M. The young mom had a certifying class, and it
ended late. I'd learned I was going to meet Tessa's mother,
too, also a nurse—and of course, Tavish, the baby boy. I
stopped for a while and just breathed. I rarely do this, but
Island Road is a little strip that leads to the natural turn
onto Lakeshore Road. That night, the lake was too breath-
takingly beautiful to miss. Any scrap of daylight counts if
you're protected.

Some of the beaches are black sand. Others, besides being
black, have particles of red in them. The other half of the
people who work in Iron Harbor—those who don't work at
the clinic—are on the boats, the ones that carry iron ore all
over the world. The town tries to cover up the pit mines with
fast-growing trees now, birch and maple. My mother says
this once was a paradise with everything a person could want
(especially if the person wanted mosquitoes). In any other
country, Lake Superior would not be considered a lake, but
an inland sea.

When I tried to pull away from Red Beach, some asshole
practically sideswiped me. So much for the peaceful feeling.
I figured he had to be from Chicago, in the kind of Italian
convertible guys use as metaphors for certain parts of their
anatomy (or to overcompensate for the lack thereof). I took

a moment to breathe, to collect myself. The moon was on the horizon, laying down a strip of gold.

Finally I drove to the address.

Looking back, I have no idea why I chose not to acknowledge the connection until I pulled into the parking lot. (Actually, I do. I was overwhelmingly obsessed with what was going on between my two best friends.) Just to make sure that there weren't two vintage condo buildings on the bluff right next to a modern condo building under construction, I pulled into what would be the lot of the building next door.

It was Tabor Oaks, of course.

Just staring across the pavement at the small lighted address panel next to the foyer door—not even up at that balcony—my heart thumped again. I thought of the platinum streak on the back of that otherwise dark head of hair. Why would he dye his hair in such a weird way? Maybe he wanted to be a blond. *Blondie*, I thought.

Maybe Blondie was Tessa's husband. Maybe he was having an affair.

Talking to myself, aloud, like a crazy person, I said, "Allie, chill. Calm down."

At that moment, I had a disquieting thought. I didn't want to be here, but I was here. What were the odds of ending up in the same place? (The odds were actually not that bad, given that Two Harbors has a permanent population of six hundred people.) But what were the odds I'd get a call from a person who lived at the place where I had seen something so creepy? I stared up at the penthouse. There was someone living there. That whole floor must have cost a big dime, given the private beach and astonishing view. I almost didn't hear the voice calling.

"Hello!"

I didn't move.

"Are you Allie Kim?" The voice floated down from above. "Ring at 4B." I looked up. It was an older woman, with short silvery hair, waving from behind a screen on the third floor, holding a little boy, who was madly waving, too. She said, "Crier!"

Was she talking about the baby? Who was a crier? I should have trusted my instincts and bolted.

I glanced around the parking area. There were about six cars in the ten slots. I even recognized a few of them, although I couldn't have named the owners. Finally I forced my wobbly legs to march up to the door. There were ten address slots; except for two handwritten names, all but two were printed in uniform type. One of the handwritten names, the one for 4B, read CRYER.

I almost giggled. Tessa had never bothered to tell me her last name, or if she had, I hadn't remembered. I needed to focus a little harder if I was going to pull off this babysitting gig for real.

The name for the penthouse, scribbled on a piece of envelope, read RENALDI. The thought that I might come face to face with "Blondie," if he lived there, filled my throat with hot and undigested Stroganoff. But I shoved the thought aside and pushed the glowing 4B. The front doors buzzed open in return. I forced myself to relax as the elevator ascended and I got off on the fourth floor. The door at the far end of the hall opened, and the woman with short silvery hair popped out, holding the boy—who was by then yelling his head off.

She smiled as she closed the door behind her. "Are you from New York?"

"What?"

"You're wearing a hat and sunglasses at night."

I pulled them off. "No, I . . ." *Try the truth,* my mother once said. *It catches people off guard.* "I have XP. It's a genetic thing. . . ."

Her eyes widened.

"You're Jackie Kim's girl."

I couldn't help but laugh. "Yes."

"I know her from work."

"Oh, wow! Well, maybe you know then XP isn't contagious. Parents of kids with XP insist that they wear the seven veils if they go out—"

"I apologize," said the woman. "I acted like *I* was from New York. That was very rude! My name is Teresa Kaminski. I'm Tessa's mother. And this is his majesty, Tavish." The little baby abruptly reached for me and started to giggle. Without thinking, I let him come into my arms and pull my ball cap off my head.

A moment later, a younger woman burst into the apartment. She was practically a clone of the older woman, minus the gray hair. When she saw me, she slumped against the door. "Are you from Heaven, then? That's the first time he's stopped crying all day."

"I'm from not from Heaven or New York," I said. "I'm just a local, like you."

The baby smiled up at me, all gums and soft cheeks.

After that it was a whirlwind of re-introductions and explanations. Grandma was Teresa Kaminski; the young woman was Tessa Kaminski-Cryer. Tessa met her husband when they were little kids; both their families spent summers in Two Harbors. Tessa's husband sold insurance to hospitals. He was on the road a lot, and she was freaking out because she was going to start doing two midnight shifts on top of a class and needed someone to babysit from eleven to six, when her mother (who had just started doing private duty) got off work and came to stay with the baby. Tessa finished with an exhausted "I'm desperate. I only have a week to find somebody."

"I'm a good babysitter," I lied.

The truth was, I was already smitten with Tavish. I had taken care of Angie before. But taking care of your own siblings requires no skill, only the willingness to follow through on your threat to punch a cute little Chinese girl with an arm the circumference of a broomstick. I had never changed a diaper. I assumed there were package directions for the diaper and a quick manual of sorts you could get for the baby, with the parts labeled.

"You can ask anyone at the hospital about me," I added.

We had a cup of tea. The baby never stopped smiling and cooing at me as I told Tessa about the hot spots in Iron Harbor. She knew about most of them, including Gitchee Pizza. She showed me around the apartment: the décor was exquisite, very sparse and Pottery Barn. "This is a great place," I said, in a voice that clearly signaled, how can you own a place like this if you're thirty at most and working the midnight shift?

"It belongs to my husband's family friend, Steve. The whole building does. Dr. Tabor? Steve Tabor?" Tessa said.

I nodded. Of course I *knew* Dr. Steve, although not as well as Dr. Andrew, obviously. I didn't hang around accidents and crime scenes and examined deaths of any kind. But I felt a warm rush of relief. Mentally, I slapped myself. I was a paranoid idiot. Juliet was right. It would take someone even dumber than me to use this property as a private crime den: the *medical examiner's* property.

"So, Allie, can you start next week?" Tessa asked. "Or for

a practice, paid of course, on, like, Sunday? How about . . . ten, no eleven dollars an hour—if you do a little cleaning?"

I had been thinking she'd offer me six or seven. Life brightened. I began to see visions of my own car. Lime green. A Beetle. I said goodbye to young Tavish, who immediately burst into tears again. "One-year molars," Tessa said wearily. "They start six months after six-month molars."

WHEN I REACHED the parking lot, it was full dark, no moon—but I saw him right away.

Blondie hopped out of a little red sports car and slammed the door.

I froze in the dull light of the foyer. It was the same car that had nearly sideswiped me. I stared, petrified, as he yanked a large sack from his trunk and hobbled over to the edge of the parking lot, disappearing over the bluff to the lawn at the water's edge. In the shadows, it looked like a sailboat's canvass, rolled up like a rug. So I did the only thing I could think of. I ran to mom's car and grabbed my Maglite.

When I returned to the parking lot's edge—and aimed the spotlight at the spongy grass below—I saw nothing.

Since that night, many times, I've tried to imagine this moment from an outside perspective. You've seen a guy (whom you've suspected of doing something horrible). You've seen him carry a suspicious looking package over a bluff. And when you've decided to chase him down, he's gone. No rolled-up sail. Nothing except the lake demanding softly, *"Now? Now?"*

So what do you do?

You drive seventy in a thirty, all the way home.

6

SECOND GLANCE
SECOND GLANCE

We did go to Duluth.

Both Rob and Juliet apologized again for blowing me off. The excuse? They were just concerned given how skittish I'd been at Tabor Oaks. As if they hadn't been skittish! (Well, Juliet hadn't, but still. . . .) And yet, I let it go. I figured that if I accepted their apology and thought of us as "we," maybe they would again, too. Besides, I'd been doing my own thing. I had a job. I was maturing, even if they weren't.

I focused on the positives. School was out. Summer was here. We were ready to trace.

The first night, we didn't expect to be able to do anything. But we didn't count on the very excellent Duluth Orchestra Hall. Nor did we count on the way some hah-hah public sculptor had set up what essentially was a Parkour garden. Rob laughed when he saw it: a piano keyboard set in a series of pillars, each about ten feet long and ten feet wide and ten feet apart, pillars in a row that grew taller and taller—from a height of four feet to about twenty feet. Some were dark rough granite and others were a pale gray, almost white. Apparently, at least according to what Rob Googled on his phone, it represented piano keys. It had cost the city of Duluth more than a million dollars.

"These guys must have a convention every year where they laugh their heads off at city government," Rob said.

Juliet said, "You think?"

"Maybe they believe it's really art," I said.

"I think *they* think it's all a big gag," Rob said, typing away at his phone. He summoned up a bunch of pictures, including the Detroit giant bathtub (The Heart of the Lake) and the Pittsburgh Horseshoe (called—God help me—Irony), as well as the one we dubbed the Seattle Rattle, which was supposed to represent an ancient anchor. As far as we could tell, it was a baby toy that would not have passed a safety inspection.

"Well, I'm not complaining," I said. I made a point of looking into both of their eyes. "This is a perfect setup for a Tribe like us, right?"

BEFORE WE STARTED, we treated ourselves to a fairly lavish dinner at La Prairie Rouge. I'd found myself flush with more money than I'd ever had in my life, as Tessa insisted on paying me $12 an hour because Tavish liked me so much. Still, we shared two entrees among three: oysters and salmon with dill. Then we hurried back to Orchestra Hall. In the car, Juliet and I changed out of our long black skirts into our long black Spandex pants. We did a few long vaults over the lowest "key," to warm up.

After that, we tried a standing jump to balance on its top, whereupon Juliet did a back flip off the second-highest key . . . whereupon we began to notice that a man in a dark blue uniform was more than casually interested in our abilities . . . whereupon we noticed him walking, then jogging toward us . . . whereupon we got arrested.

"Good evening, ladies and gentlemen," said the police officer. "May I please see your driver's licenses?"

Reluctantly, we extracted them from our backpacks. Slowly, and very respectfully, Rob said, "Please excuse me. But we are not driving."

The cop looked at us in that measuring way certain scary people have: as though trying to decide whether it's worth messing up their hair to bloody your face.

"I did not ask you if you were driving. I asked for your driver's licenses," he said.

"What we were doing is a kind of discipline, a sport called Parkour," Rob said.

"I don't care if it's Parcheesi. My kid brother got caught doing it, at the parking garage, outside the Macy's. It's like skateboarding without the skates, and surfboarding without the surfboard, or like suicide without the—"

"Sewer?" I said helpfully.

He acted as if he didn't hear me. Normally I would never have said a thing like that in a situation like that. I still have no idea why I did. Juliet gave me a look of such alarm and disgust that I would have turned myself into a giant granite piano key at that moment. But it prompted her to draw her trump card.

"My father would not do this," she said with a sad sigh.

"And who is your father? The mayor?"

"No, he is your brother officer. Thomas Sirocco, deputy chief of the Iron County Sheriff's Department but former detective in the Minneapolis Police Department."

"He get in trouble?" the cop asked plainly.

"No, he moved to Iron County because he wanted to. Fifteen years ago." She blinked several times and swallowed. "So that I could be treated at the Tabor Clinic." Juliet could really turn it on when she wanted to. She was so pitiful a drama-dolly that I wanted to cry, myself. "I have a fatal illness. *Xeroderma Pigmentosum.*" With that, she withdrew a medical dog tag from her wallet. We were all supposed to wear the tags on chains around our necks. We preferred to pin them to our backpacks, or failing that, pretend we had lost them. I've often wondered what you are supposed to do if you found a person with XP in a dangerous situation . . . which, to any other person, would be a normal situation, like, walking down the street at noon. Throw a blanket over him? Call the vet? However, I retrieved my own poignant ID badge from my back pocket. Rob did, too. It was squirm warfare at its finest.

Now it was the police officer's turn to blink several times. "Go on then," he said to her after a moment. "Get home safe. You guys too."

He turned and walked stiffly back to his car.

We turned and ran for Rob's Jeep.

"World famous brainimus minimus!" Juliet hissed at me as I cowered in the back seat. "How could you do that? If my dad found out, I could have gotten grounded for this. I have never been grounded. That would be the equivalent of death for me."

In truth, I wasn't sure that she would get grounded, even if we *had* been locked up in a Duluth jail for a night. Many counties had been littered with warnings in lieu of speeding tickets issued to Juliet Sirocco.

"So let's go home," Juliet said. "We can do Tabor Oaks again."

"No," I said automatically. I thought of Blondie. *There.*

Then not there. He knew his way around the property. Which meant that he probably *lived* there, right alongside Tavish and Tessa. People can vanish in the time it takes to start a car and drive it ten feet, yes. But people have to be very fast to vanish completely.

"I saw him again," I said.

"The guy in the apartment? The penthouse?" Juliet asked, as casually as if I had mentioned my own mother. She sounded almost bored.

"I'm not going back there," I said.

"You go there all the time," Juliet replied with a patient sigh. "You spent the entire car ride telling us about how you are babysitting there."

I glared at her. "Well I'm not going near that penthouse," I insisted.

"What did he say?" Rob asked. "The guy? When you saw him?"

I scowled. "We didn't have a chat. Whatever. I'm not going back there. You go for it, you little tribe of two."

"Okay," Juliet said. "Are you fine with that, Rob?"

Rob chewed on the inside of his cheek.

"Because I can do it myself," Juliet added.

"I'll do it," I said. "But just this once."

Rob shrugged. "Obviously, I was going to do it anyhow."

No one else said a word for the duration of the trip.

NINETY MINUTES LATER, we were up on the nearly completed building, preparing to leap onto the roof of Tabor Oaks—home both to a scary disappearing man and to my new employer.

Rob gaped at Juliet as she launched herself down and out and over. I was so pissed at his idol worship that I ran right after her. I realized midair that I had not turned on my headlamp. If I had pinwheeled my legs or done any-thing to break form, I would have fallen to my death. But I landed hard, right beside Juliet. I was breathless, and my cheeks were damp. I blamed the tears on the wind. Rob leaped and rolled to a stop at our feet, then hopped up. Before either he or Juliet could say a word about my stupid headlamp oversight, I growled, "It was a mistake. I won't do it again."

"I was just afraid for you, honey," Rob whispered.

Honey? He'd never called me that before. The word kicked at my heart but also my brain. I wondered how it would feel if he'd called me "honey" in a way that didn't sound like what I called my nine-year-old sister. But over any other shred of emotion, the movie reel of what I'd just done played over and over again in my mind. I fought to slow my breathing. I had one of those moments of clarity—not for the first time—realizing that what was risky in daylight was sheer imbecile business by night.

We prepared for our descent. The plan: down to the pent-house balcony, and then *lache* swings to the next diagonal balcony (including Tessa's) . . . and all the way down with a leap to the soft ground from the second floor.

"I'll go first," I insisted. "I need to. I'm fine. I really am fine."

Screw Rob, I thought, using my anger to focus. *Honey? Really? Screw Juliet, too, for making me do this.* Lightly, using one arm to hang and swing and the other to grasp the balcony, I lifted myself over: a perfect traverse. I stood straight. The curtains were drawn, and only one small light burned in the living room, next to the long curved sofa. Too late, I noticed . . . the door was open. Of course it was. This was summer. There was a nice quiet lake breeze. Cool, beautiful night. Just a screen.

Somehow I whispered, "Stop."

Rob leaned over the side of the roof and waited for my cue.

I froze. *There.*

Blondie's form hovered over a girl on a blanket. Was it the same girl? Short, dark hair? I spotted the lightning streak. The girl looked straight at me, her all-pupil eyes as motionless as a doll's, her blue lips parted in a gasp. Her head was bent far to the left and forward. An unnatural position. You couldn't have held your head that way, even lying down. And her neck. . . .

I whirled and pushed against Rob's legs, just above me.

"Go back up!" I whispered. "Pull me!"

"What?"

"Go. Back. Up."

It took Rob a moment to get his bearings. *Breathe,* I thought, *breathe.* Rob grasped my wrists. They slipped out of his hands. I pulled the long sleeves of my jersey down over my hands and got up, crouched, on the railing of the balcony.

Rob reached down for me again. "You have to face the door, so I can grab both of your arms," he whispered.

"It's okay. I can pull myself up," I whispered back.

"Just give me your wrists, Allie."

I looked down.

Blondie's hands were pressed against the screen, his fingers splayed. And even though our eyes never met, he smiled.

He'd seen me, too.

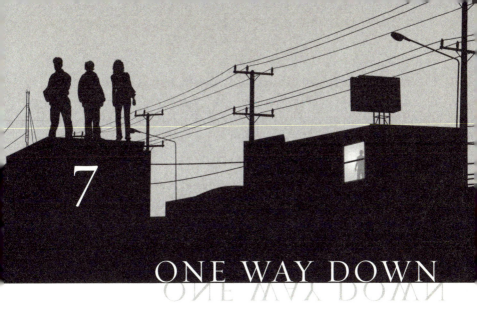

ONE WAY DOWN

ONE WAY DOWN

I would have loved Rob, anyway. Even if he hadn't thrown himself over the edge of the roof and then pulled himself and me, with my body almost dead weight, back up beside him and Juliet. (I still have little scars on my ribcage where he dragged me over the gutter.) I pushed myself to my feet, and there we all were: on the roof, the calm lake before us and the starry sky above us. But I was the only one hyperventilating. The things I'd seen tumbled from my cracked lips in a harsh whisper, until Juliet cut me off.

"How do you know the girl was dead?" she demanded.

"Juliet, her eyes were open!" I nearly shrieked. "Her neck was all covered with bruises and her face was all dirty or bruised. There was—"

"We believe you," Rob interrupted. "Wait. Wait a minute. We can't go back the way we came."

"How do you know it was the same guy?" Juliet asked in the same monotone.

I turned to Rob. "Will you hit her in the face? Are you

kidding? We find the freaky guy with a naked dead girl once and we come back and you think there's a different guy in a different apartment with a different dead girl? He saw my face, Juliet! He smiled at me!"

Rob said, "Let's just get down."

"Tavish!" I gasped. "Tessa and the baby. What if he gets them?" I fumbled for my cell phone in my fanny pack, sitting down hard. Mace *(thank you, Mom!)*, a scream whistle (*THANK you, paranoid Mom!*) and finally my cell phone. I punched Tessa's number. Before she picked up, I realized it was three in the morning and snapped the phone shut.

Instantly, it rang.

For a delusional moment, I thought it was Blondie. I couldn't bear to look at the Caller ID.

"Pick it up," Juliet ordered.

I opened the phone. "Hello?"

It was Tessa. Of course it was. She was alive and well. She was twelve hours south with her husband and the baby, and not at all perturbed that I'd accidentally dialed her number. I wanted to sob for her to call 911, but instead I apologized for the "accidental dial" and told her I'd see her soon.

Rob saw me start to shudder. He gently rested his arm around my shoulder. To Juliet, he said, "Call your dad."

She shrugged. "I'm thinking about it."

I pushed Rob's arm away. "You're *thinking* about it? Call him now!"

"Chill, Allie," she groaned. "Of course I want to call him. But I want us to get out of here first, because, if we don't, I'll never get out of my house again."

Juliet started to pace back and forth, and then spotted the fire escape and raised a finger over her lips.

One by one, quiet as kittens, we descended the metal

stairwell and alighted soundlessly on the gravel. Rob's car was nearly hidden on Lakeshore Drive in a little grove of pine trees, off the road, in case anyone chanced to come by.

I don't know why I kept silent. Did Juliet have that much power over me?

There is a moment in everyone's life—and I guess I'd never had one—when everything stops. Time stops. Motion stops. That was the first time it happened to me. The journey of a thousand miles may begin with a single step, but the sprint to Rob's Jeep might as well have been a million single steps through quicksand. I thought I'd fall. I thought I was being punished. For what? A life that wasn't long enough to have piled up any serious sins, unless you counted the champagne and Mike's Hard Ice Tea and the weed (only six times and once, respectively)? Then again, stuff happens to innocent people all the time. Just look at anyone with XP.

Rob later said I'd sprinted like an Olympian.

NONE OF US wanted to go home, Juliet included. Rob decided to take us up the old fire road to Ghost Lake—to our old hangout spot, down the shore from where we'd borrowed Mr. Callahan's boat. I hadn't been there in years. There was our phony metal sign, posted when we still had to bike everywhere; it claimed the property was protected by Sirocco Security. It cost us thirty bucks to make. But people stayed away, even kids drinking or screwing, figuring the alarm was connected directly to the police.

If somebody peeked through one of the boarded windows, they would think slobs lived there instead of nobody. Not all the windows were even broken. Stacks of bottled water blocked most of the view, anyway. We could always stay overnight, not that I had. I'd like to think Rob and Juliet hadn't, either. Nicola Burns once told me that some kids at Iron Harbor High still believed that this part of Ghost Lake really was haunted.

We sat in the car, Juliet up front, me in the back.

"Where did he go?" Rob asked over his shoulder. "That night you saw him?"

"If I knew, I'd know," I told him, exasperated. "He just disappeared."

"Maybe he ran to where we hid the car," he said.

"He ran in the other direction, toward the beach," I stated.

"He must have had a car hidden," Juliet chimed in. "It would be easy to hide a sports car."

Had I told Juliet about the little red car that nearly creamed my mom's mini-van? I couldn't even remember, I was so freaked out.

Rob suddenly burst out, "What are we doing? We're sitting here chatting and that girl could still be alive!"

"She's not alive," I said.

"Lots of people who are in trauma recover," Rob said. "People shot through the head recover. It's been twenty five minutes now."

"How about we make something up," Juliet suggested. "But I have to figure out how my call to 911 won't be from me."

Rob glared at her in a way that made me think he knew she was lying. "That's easy. You dial 5-5 before and it blocks your number."

I poked my head through the front seats. Of course Juliet would have known that, but she hadn't shared it with us. "I didn't know that," I said purposefully.

"I read it somewhere, and not on the Internet," he said, his eyes still on Juliet. "You know, reading? Books? It can be useful. You didn't know that, either?"

Juliet didn't respond. We sat silently as Rob, cussing under his breath, dialed 5-5 and then 911 on Juliet's phone. In a phony voice, he reported a woman who was injured in the penthouse of Tabor Oaks Condominiums on Lakeshore Road. *No*, he said, he wasn't interested in leaving his name. *No*, he said, he wasn't interested in any reward money. *No*, he couldn't leave a number.

He shut the phone and we waited. My skin writhed, as if my body were coated with stinging ants. We sat in the silence of his Jeep. We sat and sat. . . .

Then we heard the sirens. Had it only been a couple of minutes since Rob had made the call? First a police car, and after that, an ambulance. . . .

More than one car had been dispatched. The sirens blended in the kind of alternating shrieks and whoops that woke my mother up at night, making her cross herself in panicked prayer: *Lord, I beg that medics aren't scraping my daughter and her dumb friends off the highway* (although Juliet's dad would have called her or shown up if that had been the case). The sirens stopped.

Would there be shots?

For an agonizing three minutes, we sat still together, barely breathing.

Finally, Juliet broke the silence. "You think they have him by now?"

Rob said, "Of course."

"So we can go down there and find out what happened," she said.

Rob glanced back at me. Neither of us had thought of

that. "Wait just a minute. I don't want it to look funny for us," he said. "We can't just come driving by."

"Of course we can!" Juliet exclaimed. "You're an XP kid! I'm Tommy Sirocco's daughter!"

Rob turned back to the wheel. "True."

Just to be safe, we waited another interminable two minutes. *One-one-thousand* 120 times in a row. An MRI would have been preferable. Then Rob rattled down the hill. Leisurely, observing the speed limit, he proceeded back along Lakeshore Road. We almost overshot Tabor Oaks. There were lights, two on the third floor—but not on the top floor. There were no police cars, either, no sirens, no ambulance . . . no sign of life except for the cars we'd seen in the parking lot when we'd bolted.

"What the hell is going on?" Rob said, as much to himself as us.

Juliet one-dialed her dad. "What was all the excitement? It was like *Law and Order* down by Tabor Oaks. I didn't see a fire truck." She paused, listening to him speak. I held my breath, avoiding Rob's eyes in the darkness. "Where were we? Up by Ghost Lake, fishing. . . . No. Nothing . . . shiners. I guess." Juliet made big circles with her free hand, implying an ever-rolling spool of words. "No, Dad . . . no. We heard the sirens and came over to the new building." Silence. "We thought someone lit a fire in it or something. Well, so, what *did* happen?"

Juliet touched her finger to her lips and put the phone on speaker. Her father's tinny voice filled the charged air of the Jeep: ". . . what they were talking about. Maybe somebody heard something. Sorry, darling. Just another big night in Mayberry!"

Talking about Mayberry was a favorite joke of his, and

we'd only recently figured out it referred to an old TV show. At times like these, it was clear that Tommy Sirocco missed his life as a detective down in the big city. (Listen to me. *The big city! Minneapolis!* Nicola once said she couldn't die without seeing Paris. I would be lucky to see Chicago.) Officer Sirocco always maintained that he was happy, though, because there was happiness and safety for Juliet, and for his wife, Ginny, in Iron Harbor. But Juliet still managed to wander. With the state's ski team, she traveled all over the region.

"Dad, you didn't see anybody?" she demanded. "Why did they send like, the Marine Corps?"

"We have to send the whole crew if there's a chance there was a victim. Fire truck. Ambulance. You know the drill, sweetie."

"So who was it?"

"It was a prank call. We sort of knew it from the get-go. If I could get my hands on whatever punk's ass it was." He stopped. "Am I on speaker?"

"No, Dad."

"You sound like you're underwater."

"I am underwater." She shot us a panicked smile, then clicked off the speaker and held it against her ear. "I'm glad it wasn't real. Thanks, Dad. Bye. See you soon."

I held my breath. Then I shouted, "No!"

One, loud shriek from the bottom of my feet. Now, looking back, I guess it seemed like high drama. But then, it felt as though if I didn't let loose with something ear-splitting, my guts would boil through my flesh. "I saw him! You saw him, too, Rob. Didn't you?"

He stared at the steering wheel. He wanted to say he had. But he hadn't. I had pushed Rob back up onto the roof too fast for him to see anything below except me.

"I'm going back there now," I said. "I'm going to search—"

"Allie," Rob gently murmured. "Allie-stair. The sun is going to be up in an hour."

"But I saw him. I saw that girl. Juliet, won't your dad's team search the carpet for hair and fiber evidence?"

"That's TV, Allie," Juliet said. "There was nobody there."

"I want to talk to your dad. We could call in a sketch artist. Someone could draw her, from what I saw."

"But my dad was actually in there, Allie. He didn't see anything."

I stared at her, pleading with my eyes, my belly filled with rage, my heart breaking. "You don't believe me. You really don't."

She shook her head. At the time, I was certain she truly doubted me. But she didn't doubt me at all.

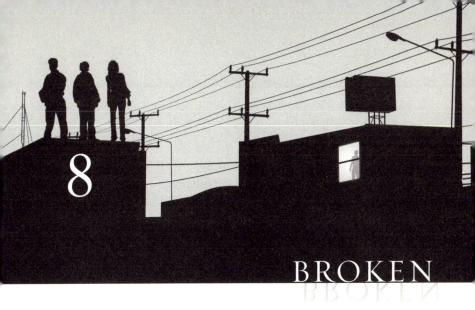

BROKEN

BROKEN

"If you had a long life for sure, what would you do?"

"Nobody has a long life for sure," I told Rob. "Especially people who jump off buildings."

We'd had the what-if-you-weren't-doomed-to-die conversation before, many times. But not recently, not since we'd started Parkour.

We were sitting in the Jeep, on the top story of the parking garage in Duluth: the one that widened in big concentric loops until it filled an entire city block at the bottom. It was the same one that the cop's son had been caught scaling. In fact, the cop had inadvertently given us the idea. The sky was a deep blue, the kind of blue it turns just before kids like us can begin unwrapping our scarves and hats and sunglasses. And the best part? The part I want to kill myself for admitting?

Juliet wasn't with us.

Three days had passed since *the incident*. The whole ride home that night, she'd been on this weird campaign that was probably based on diluting her own fear: She'd tried to talk to me about *the incident* as though it hadn't happened quite in the way I thought it had. She'd dropped dismissive hints. ("Maybe you were thinking of that other night, before, and you thought you saw something . . .") I'd dismissed her dismissal: I knew she was shaken. Juliet was cool. And not in the slang sense. She never got agitated. She was cool like a pool hustler.

The key to Parkour isn't just strength, and it definitely isn't daring. It's absolute focus. From her ski jump days, Juliet was able to focus far better than Rob or I could. She'd applied that gift to Parkour, the gift for drilling straight down to the moment in front of her. Still, she was more challenged than we were, because even with contact lenses, her vision wasn't 20-20 in either eye. Her poor vision was partly responsible for the bad fall that ended her fledgling ski career. Although she covered it up, she was losing a little more vision every couple of years. Dr. Andrew said that eventually laser surgery would correct the kind of loss she had, which was a complicated form of astigmatism. But no one would even try it until Juliet was eighteen.

"If I could live a long time and be sure of it, I'd travel," Rob said. "I'd . . . you know. Take a sabbatical. The way professors do."

Or Juliet, I answered silently. She'd gone on another "sabbatical" these past few days. Just up and disappeared. And I did hate myself for being relieved that I could spend time alone with Rob. The problem was that she could be so persuasive that there were moments I did doubt myself. *The incident* had been an adrenaline-drenched blur. Juliet's excuse for her break from us was that she needed to "rest a little." This would be like a promiscuous athlete who made

$20 million a year announcing that he would spend the next few seasons as a Buddhist monk.

But like I said: it gave Rob and me time to talk. And I was not hallucinating this much: we did talk differently when Juliet wasn't around.

We'd gone for sushi. We'd even tried out gruesome sounding combos, like Marching Dragon Tail. (It was awful.) Then we ran for the car—a sun below the horizon can still be dangerous—and Rob grabbed my hand without thinking to pull me along.

Feelings change fast when you're a teenager. Mom told me that it still amazed her that she would start a school year thinking about one boy constantly, relating every song and every bite of food and every glance in the mirror to complete absorption in him . . . and then, a few months later, be able to look at him with cold detachment, noticing his blackheads and his girl butt. But my feelings for Rob hadn't changed, ever, except to grow stronger. I fantasized about explaining to him why we should get married when we were eighteen, because it corrected for our presumed lifespan.

How could he not know? Or care? Being with Rob meant more to me than having a real grown-up life—whatever that even meant—in part because I didn't think of my condition as really suited to having a big life, unless I could telecommute for everything. But I could have a home and a love. I could be happy. Eventually he would cave in and admit he was attracted to me.

Two nights earlier, I had cut my hair in face-framing tendrils. Tonight, I'd even tried alluring cologne. (An oldie called Shalimar; my mother said that her mother had used it; but magazines said that it turned guys on because it smelled like vanilla—in other words, like something they could eat like a cookie.) Predictably, Rob didn't try to eat me like a cookie. As always, he treated me like a kid sister. Worse: a kid brother.

In the silence he said suddenly, "There are lots of places, like Paris, that are better at night. I'd keep a little room in some big city like LA, with just a Nerf basketball hoop and computers and my music and books. I wouldn't even have a stove because I'd get takeout from a different place every night."

"Refrigerator?"

"I'm not a barbarian."

"What else?"

"A Murphy bed."

"What's that?"

"It's a bed you pull down out of the wall. If you have one, you only need one big room. You know, with a table and a couch. A very big TV. Stands for the guitars. A Strat like Jimi Hendrix."

"You don't play guitar. A what like Jimmy who?"

"Never mind. I'm dreaming here."

Rob was the only guy I knew who shared the exact same musical tastes as his father. (True, I didn't know many guys. But every guy in Iron Harbor our age listens to rap.) Both Dorn males insisted that "all great music was created between the years 1966 and 1974."

"Anyway, just one room to live in and one room to clean," he added.

"Is this a guy thing? Like, it's okay to do everything in one room?"

Rob sniffed. "Juliet told me she would live on a motorcycle and carry everything she would ever need in two saddlebags."

My shoulders sagged. Even when Juliet wasn't here, she

was here. I couldn't think of a response. She had one-upped me in absentia.

"It's not appealing to me, to tell the truth," Rob continued. "If I didn't have to take care of it all by myself, I'd actually have a real bed and more than one room."

"Why would you have to take care of it by yourself? Why wouldn't you have a roommate?" *Like me?*

"You have to be on your own sometime. I'm just not really necessarily the kind who wants to. I'm not a solitary guy."

I smiled in the gathering dark. That was a lie. But I was smiling because I had to strain to hear him. That was really the crucial difference: he spoke so much more quietly when Juliet wasn't around. She made the air around her hum just by being in it. Every time we did Parkour, we clamped our gloved hands together and shouted, "Live once!" And that was okay. It ritualized Parkour, which *should* be a ritual. But tonight . . . sitting alone with him was a fantasy glimpse into the lives of two regular people, who had regular habits and did regular things.

"If I had a life for sure, a long life, I would be a judge," I said.

"A judge? Now that would be difficult."

"Not for me. I would be firm but fair."

"I meant, practically, it would be difficult," he said.

I laughed. "Night court. Someone has to be there. I think, being used to what you see at night, I would be more tolerant than a Daytimer. We aren't very easily shocked."

"Tolerance. So you wouldn't be a hanging judge?" Rob said.

"Ha! So what would you do?"

"In my room? My studio would be downstairs. There

would be an inside staircase, maybe a fireman's pole. And since I don't play guitar, I'd record. I'd mix. The old rock stars, you know, like The Beatles or the Rolling Stones? They would start their day at five or six at night. They would be in the studio until dawn. Like that old song, 'Beth' by Kiss. '*Me and the boys will be playing . . . all night.*' So that's what I'd be."

"Why don't we ever say: what we *will* be?" I asked without thinking.

"I guess we're trained out of it."

"I'm sick of being trained out of it. I'm opposed to thinking my early death is a foregone conclusion."

Rob smiled. "Allie, you don't face the facts. Never did."

"Never will," I said. "Facts are overrated. All geniuses ignore facts."

He kissed me then.

We both pulled back, instantly. For a frozen moment, his eyes met mine as though we'd spit on each other or something.

Then, he leaned over and undid my seatbelt and his. He kissed me again, pulling me under him. The times I had been kissed before amounted to once, in eighth grade, by our then-neighbor, Eric. I had worried about how it would be when it happened for real, doing silly little kid stuff like kissing the mirror and my pillow. And of course, I'd only ever imagined it being with Rob. But now that it was happening . . . everything fit like finely chiseled wood, smooth and soft and funny, tasting like the wasabi we'd had with dinner. Then he stopped.

I said, "What? What?"

"Is this going to be our time?" he said.

"It is if you say it is."

He blinked. "Here?"

"Not, well, not in the Jeep. I'm not a contortionist. But I want it to be with you, if that's what you mean."

"You don't feel like you're cheating on Juliet?" he asked.

My eyes narrowed. "What are you—?"

"I didn't mean that . . . I, listen. If you were bi-curious, I think I would have brought that up a few years ago, Allie. But I feel like I'm cheating on the three of us. As you know, like a unit. The *tres compadres*."

"Stop," I said. My heart thumped so hard I thought it would burst out of my ribcage. "Let's just go back to talking about the future we aren't going to get instead of talking about the girl any guy would have the hots for, or feelings for, or give anything to get over. . . ."

"Any guy but me."

"You don't?"

"I used to, but now I don't. Please let me finish. If we do this, now, we can't be the *tres compadres* anymore. We can't be the three friends together. We'll be two and one. Is that okay with you?"

Was that okay with me? Why did he have to bring up long-term consequences of instant gratification?

Rob added, "Maybe us being here, right now, this way, it's a sign. Although I don't believe in signs."

"Since when?"

"I never did," he said.

"I mean, since when do you not want Juliet?"

"Since I kissed you just then."

"But you did before."

"Allie, there you go. This is a fact. You can't be jealous of before."

"Oh," I said.

I drew in a deep breath, and then settled back into the cold Jeep cushions. The moment had not just been broken; it had been broken and then stepped on. Gradually my pulse slowed.

"Let's see how you feel after we make short work of this building. We came here to trace, right?" I had to say something. Both of us were strung wire tight and needed to do . . . anything. I honestly didn't know if it was our moment to do *everything*.

Rob grinned, as if nothing had happened at all. "You're on," he said.

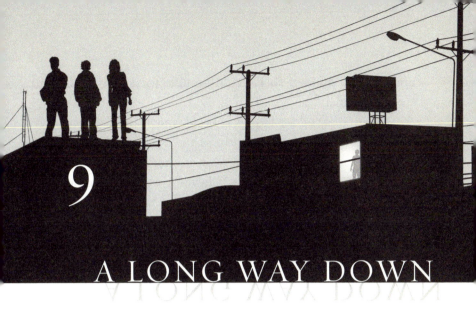

9

A LONG WAY DOWN

A LONG WAY DOWN

What we planned wasn't so dangerous, unless you missed your footing or your grip. But we weren't going to miss.

I pulled on my gloves.

Rob went first, roped to me, while I filmed him with his camera. Something had changed tonight. It was as though we'd done Parkour all our lives, instead of for three months. From the roof of the parking garage, down floor-by-floor, he perfectly "derived" (as Parkour speakers say) his relationship to the space—walking that little beam, then hanging from it, as though it were as wide as a boardwalk on the beach. He finished with a standing jump and a flip off onto the grass.

I applauded and stowed the camera in my flat front pack.

As I prepared to take my turn, while Rob raced back through the parking garage, something came over me. I decided what the hell, to be a girly girl for once. I yanked off my skullcap and my headlamp and let my newly-shortened hair fall free. For the first run, I'd be roped to Rob anyhow and he'd be filming, so I would be able to see by the light from his camera.

The all of a sudden Rob was beside me, roping our waists together. Before I began, he kissed me again. It was a long kiss, hard and involved, as if we were both preparing for a battle I'd win. As if we both believed the future would be wide open: some sappy happily-ever-after fairy tale. It was a beautiful lie, and I grasped it tight. We both did. I began my first passage down the wall and turned fast to leap and grab the edge of the next level. Focusing, my breath even, I made my way one more level down.

Vaguely, somewhere above, I heard a car start. I tried to ignore it. Focus was all. But the car kept revving, like some kid horsing around. Had Rob and I missed someone? Rob couldn't have been messing with me. Besides, I knew the sound of his Jeep. Anyway, the rope was still taut; he was on the other end.

Then I heard the squeal of tires.

Rob yelled, "Christ, no!"

There was a clatter and his headlamp went out. Camera light: gone. Rope: slack. Darkness. Nothing.

Steady. Steady, Allie.

The car corkscrewed down the shadowy interior of the parking garage, plunging toward the street. I couldn't stop the car; I was tethered to Rob. Not unless . . . I unhooked the rope. Who knows what had happened to him up there? My fingers trembled. I stopped breathing. Parkour is all about using momentum in your favor, turning jumps into rolls where you can't get hurt—

So I jumped.

Without preparing, I hurtled into the air and became a part of it, twenty feet straight down. Tried to roll but only hit. *Snap.* A thunderbolt in my right forearm, a lightning flash behind my eyes. My arm felt heavy and numb. *It's broken,* I realized with curious detachment. The kind of break that would tear skin. Not my head. Not my neck. But it was hard, sickeningly hard. . . . I reached out with my left hand. No grass. This is how mistakes happen. And deaths. You can't derive what you can't see. I must have landed on concrete, not the lawn where Rob had beamed up at me only minutes ago.

Rob. . . . Was he hurt?

I tried to sit up. No, no, no.

The car. I heard it. It was coming. I could see it. Lights down around the back of the garage . . . then appearing again—bearing straight towards me down the exit ramp. I squinted in the glare of the headlights. The driver aimed that car like a gun.

Roll, I commanded myself. Roll over that useless, limp, pain-shriek arm. *Hide.* Where? The fountain nearby? The one we'd passed on the way back from sushi? Jerking up to my knees, I crept behind the lip of the giant stone bowl. The light grew brighter, the engine louder. This was the end. Not by the sun. By the night. By some maniac.

The car revved and roared. I begged my brain to go black. And then—

Another screech. And a shout: "Allie!"

I peered over the lip of the fountain. Rob seemed to be sprinting toward me in slow motion, like some cheesy old film of runners on a beach. "Allie! Allie!" The car was speeding away now. I could see the silhouette of the driver: a shadow puppet. Shouting to himself? Or talking to someone beside him. . . . My brain began to slip pieces of information back in, like cards into a deck.

The car was small and sleek, a dark metallic convertible

with the top up. Too dark to see color. But it was the same: *Blondie's*. His car. Here. But how? Why? Trying to scare me into silence? No. Trying to *silence* me into silence. For good.

Another card: a vague mental picture as the convertible vanished into the night. There was someone else, hunched over in the passenger seat—someone small, who sat up as they cleared the turn onto Canal Street.

The final card: Rob, cradling me against him.

"My arm is broken," I gasped. My voice sounded funny. I realized I was whistling through gritted teeth. "Don't move me."

Rob laid his windbreaker over my shoulders, more a gesture of gallantry than utility, since I was drenched in sweat and his jacket was filthy. Then he used his shirt to tie my arm to my rib cage.

"I don't know why I'm doing this," he said. "I saw it in a movie."

As I lay there, he forgot there was an elevator and sprinted up five flights to get the Jeep. "Hold on, Allie," he shouted over his shoulder, and despite the agony that was now rolling through me with the immensity and intensity of a cement drill, there was a spurt of satisfaction. My boyfriend was taking care of me.

IN THE ER at Duluth Summit Hospital, a woman doctor and the trauma nurses took a quick look at my arm, then shuttled Rob and me into an X-ray room. There we waited with a guy who was so drunk that he clearly felt no pain at all despite a head wound the size and shape of golf ball, and a little kid who either had a 104-degree fever or was under sedation. I wouldn't have minded some sedation.

"Do you have any nausea? Did you hit your head?" the

doctor asked. She wasn't that old—mid-thirties, maybe—very slender with thick blond hair like Juliet's in one of those pretty, no-nonsense bobs like mine was attempting. She wore big red-framed glasses that should have looked absurd but didn't. She could have stepped right out of an ad for the young professional woman. She peered into my pupils with a little penlight.

"My arm," I said. "I didn't hit my head at all. The only nausea I have is from the pain. And somebody tried to kill me, incidentally. The tire tracks are right there."

"Dilaudid," the doctor replied. "Two milligrams."

"If this is a police matter," the nurse said. "Then—"

"We have time," the doctor interrupted.

The room was dark, which was a comfort, and the staff moved fast, which also was a comfort. They led me into a little curtained cubicle.

Rob sat down next to me on the bed and turned the lights off. The doctor left. Then she came back in and turned on every light there was.

"Please leave the lights low," Rob pleaded.

"I need to examine Miss. . . ." She glanced at her clipboard. "Kim. Allison Kim, is that right?"

"Yes," I said. "More or less. Alexis."

The doctor flipped on a huge new control panel of lights, the size and intensity of a space station. She shot Rob a cold glare. "You need to leave."

The syrup of the Dilaudid was beginning to distance me from the throbbing bawl in my forearm.

"I'm her friend." Given what had happened earlier in the car, the description stung. I'd already moved to the boyfriend-girlfriend stage. Though technically, Rob still was only my friend, nothing else.

"Young man, just step outside for a moment. I don't want to have to ask for security." Rob—dirty, scraped, and practically hyperventilating— must have looked to her like a Yeti.

When Rob stepped outside the curtain, the doctor said, "Sweetheart, tell me how this really happened. Nobody has a right to hurt you."

"Wait," I said, as she turned the lights on again. "Please turn the lights off first."

"You have other, older bruises—"

"I have Xeroderma Pigmentosum. The bruises are the least of my worries."

At the mention of XP, the doctor blinked, then stood up and snapped off the lights. "I'm sorry," she said.

"Rob is my best friend. We were doing Parkour stunts on a building and this crazy person came along in a car and Rob dropped the rope. I fell off a wall. That's all."

"He didn't hit you?"

"He'd rather break his *own* arm. We've been friends since we were babies."

The doctor hooked a piece of her blond hair behind one ear. "It must have been a big wall."

"It was. I fell from the third level of that circular garage, you know, about a block from Orchestra Hall. Near Shimata, the Japanese restaurant."

"That's quite a fall. Why did you say someone tried to kill you?"

"Did I say that?"

"You did say that."

"Because after I fell, a car drove up over the sidewalk and drove straight at me, and then turned away. But not until the last minute." I licked my dry lips. The air around me seemed fuzzy. A police officer had arrived. He leaned against the wall of the cubicle. Even though he was wearing a light linen jacket, a black T-shirt, and cowboy boots, you could tell he was a cop. Maybe I could tell because I was so used to seeing Tommy Sirocco try to act like a regular person and look just silly at it.

"Did you see a license plate, Miss Kim?" he asked, without bothering to introduce himself.

"No. But I've seen the car before. I think I have. Up in Iron Harbor, where I live." I told him about Red Beach and the sports car.

The cop smirked. "Guy probably lives here in the cities. Gets his thrills playing games with his car." He tapped his notebook. "Can't be too many Italian sports cars around here. I'll run it."

"You go to the Tabor Clinic, for XP," The doctor said to me. It wasn't a question; it sounded like an accusation. "Why are you down here then?"

"The bigger the building, the better the trace. Don't you do anything for fun?"

I could see the doctor's smile in the faint glow from her penlight. "I knit," she said.

"Oh."

"Joking. I surf."

"On Lake Superior? Dude!" The drugs were sillyficating my already loopy brain.

"Yes, but I come from San Diego. We aren't talking about me." She tried to stop smiling, but she was having a hard time. So was I. "So you've been doing this a while. Hence the other bruises. I'll apologize to your boyfriend."

"We wiped out a lot last spring. And yes, it is harder at night."

"It's borderline," she said. "No, it's clinically insane to do it at night."

"We use headlamps." I tried to point to my head with my right hand but the pain made me breathless. "Now, I wish you would call my mother, Jacqueline Kim, who is a nurse. Although *she's* going to need the ER when she hears this."

"Do you have a permission to treat?" the doctor asked.

"In the outside pocket of my front pack," I said.

You don't leave home without it, in case you fall down in the street and wake up lying on Miami Beach at high noon.

"Both bones are broken, the radius and the ulna, Allie. You need a screw in there. I am a reconstructive and hand surgeon, which is good luck. Everything else is bad luck. We need to act before there's more swelling, and that's part of the bad luck. And I have to do it in a situation that won't hurt you, and quickly, and with your whole body draped in . . . I'm thinking out loud now . . . Helen!" A nurse appeared, as though she had been waiting to read her lines. She was chewing gum, and her red hair, unlike my own, came directly out of a box. I liked her immediately. "Let's get Brent and Martina to find out which OR is open stat. We need to repair this girl's arm and get her and her boyfriend home before daylight."

"Is she a vampire?" the nurse said.

"Yes," the doctor said. "So don't piss her off. I need the OR with low light and a microsurgical headlamp. . . . Allie, would you like us to call your mother right now? Or afterward? You aren't seventeen yet."

"Please, afterward. My sister is asleep. Might as well let her sleep. Because she won't be . . . won't be. . . ."

"Be sleeping for a while. I get it. This will hurt worse later than now. We'll med-flight you to Divine Savior, so I need to warn the doctors there."

"They have rooms for us. Darkrooms. As though we're developing. . . ."

The doctor patted my thigh. "I'll see you upstairs. But you'll be out of it by then. You'll have a tiny scar. And no jumping off any more buildings." She stopped and peered back through the curtain. "For a while."

I heard her stop and say, "I'm very sorry, Rob. Most times, when you hear hoof beats, it's horses. But sometimes, it's zebras. You can stay right there and we'll bring some pillows and blankets to make you comfortable. You did good work getting her here and immobilizing her arm. She should be ready to leave by four, four-thirty. I'll go with you in the helicopter."

I BECAME PROBABLY the only patient in the history of Duluth Summit Hospital to be medevac'd in order to beat the dawn. I had never seen the sunrise from high in the sky, and of course, I'd never been in a helicopter. From the way they appear to move, so fleet and graceful, you imagine they'd feel swift and weightless as a dragonfly. But the experience was like being shaken in a soup can, hot and noisy and bumpy, each voice echoing and the chuffing of the blades deafening, infernal.

Except for the patient, everyone's issued big rubber ear muffs. They all end up shouting, straining to be heard over the sound of the rotors. The ride was also weirdly unstable, scary, not the flying carpet of efficient medical reassurance you expect for those in the worst case. In the worst case, though, most of the injured are probably zonked.

After an eternity, we landed. The rosy pink glow of morning filled the air as the door opened. The doctor said, "Give her . . . *blur of numbers* . . . Dilaudid . . . *blur of words* . . . push. No, right now. Before you move her again."

I went flying again, but without leaving the bed. My mother's stern, sweet face loomed over me, then Dr. Andrew's . . . and then nothingness. My last thought was that this was the closest I'd been to sunlight in a long, long time.

I SLEPT AND woke. There was Rob: cleaned up and child-like, with little-boy comb marks in his wet hair. He sat in the chair beside my bed, in a dark room where a small lamp was softly shaded. Only after smiling at him did I notice the dark circles under his eyes.

"What time is it?" I sounded like a frog. My throat had never been so parched.

"Seven."

"All this time, just two hours?"

"It's seven at night, Allie."

"Oh, wow."

"Juliet just left," he said. "She said to give you a kiss from her." He kissed me, on the forehead.

I wanted to say, what about us? What about last night? I'm sure that about a billion girls everywhere on earth were saying just that, in those precise terms, at that exact moment. Rob added, "Now, I want to give you a kiss from me. But I don't know if I should."

"Well, I think you should at least give me some ice chips." At that moment, I realized that I had already been chewing ice chips. The drugs created a very weird set of feelings, as though I were remembering my present, instead of my past.

He chewed his dry lips.

"Maybe it was a sign. Your getting hurt," he said.

"A sign of what?"

"That we weren't supposed to be together. Like that."

"You don't believe in signs," I croaked. "Maybe that was

a sign that you should believe in signs." Abruptly I felt weary and nauseated and dizzy, as though the doctor had somehow misconnected some of my strings so that I had a pulse on the front of my elbow instead of my wrist. "I don't feel like kissing or debating kissing, Rob. I feel like sleeping."

"Go ahead."

"Okay." I shut my eyes. Then I opened them. "Did you see your film?"

Rob smiled, and I had to reconsider the kissing.

"It was awesome. That was sweet of you, Allie." His smile flickered. "I had my phone on to film you, too, and when you fell, I was running to you but I tried to get the license plate. I didn't. But it's an Alfa Romeo. There are only three Alfa Romeos in Iron County. One belongs to Warwick Quinn, you know, the anchor. . . ."

I thought I had said something wrong, something that I wouldn't remember I'd said until he left the room. "I know who he is."

"And the other two belong to Stephen Tabor."

"So that was *Dr. Steve* who tried to wipe me out?" I tried to sit up, and moaned so loudly that a nurse hurried into the room and pushed my pain medicine button. I collapsed back against the pillows and winced. "That would be funny if it wasn't so nuts. The country coroner is trying to kill me? For what, body parts? And that girl in the apartment, too? The only problem being, of course, that the guy wasn't Dr. Stephen?"

"That's the weird part."

"*That's* the weird part?" I was the one on drugs, yet the previous eight hours of our lives had contained more sheer weirdness than the previous eight years. "What's the weird part?"

"He's not here," said Rob. "Dr. Stephen's not here. Dr. Andrew and Dr. Stephen are in London for the week, for some graduation or something."

"But he owns the apartment building." Just as fast as I'd been worked up, I was slipping back down into the welcome haze of the drugs. "Where Tessa and Tavish live—you know, the lady I work for and her baby. Where the body was."

"The car's in his garage on this kind of lift thing he has to stack his sports cars up when he's not using them."

I squinted at him. Since when had he become an expert on cars? "How . . . you . . . know?"

"I told Gina, your mom's friend, that I saw a car like he has. And she said he must be from Chicago. That's Dr. Stephen's baby. He would never let anyone else drive it. There's no way it's the same guy you saw that night. There's no way it was the same guy who tried to sideswipe you. Are you sure, Allie?"

"Sure . . . and not so sure."

"I mean, are you sure that you saw anyone in there, I mean the second time?"

"Rob, I'm tired. My head hurts and my arm kills. I'm sleepy."

"I'll let you sleep for a little while," Rob said. "The cop is out there. I'll tell him to come back."

WHEN I AWOKE, only Juliet was in the room with me. She stood over my bed. For a moment, alone with my best friend, I was afraid. Then, I took a deep clean breath. Juliet kissed me on both cheeks. Funny: it was something we'd decided to do on a whim about a year ago: kiss each other on both cheeks Euro-style. It was an inside joke that never really took. We hadn't done it in months. The last time we had, our lives were a lot less complicated. Or at least mine was.

"I can't leave you alone for one day," she said. "Much less a couple of weeks."

Was this her way of saying she was sorry she hadn't been with us? Was it her way of saying she was sorry she hadn't protected me from Blondie? What the hell was it her deliberately obscure way of saying?

"You're supposed to have a close relationship to the earth, but not that close!" she joked. Leaning near to my cheek, she added, "Bear, quit scaring the hell out of me. I never thought I'd say I was glad anybody had a broken arm, but when you consider the alternative. . . ." She clucked her tongue.

What's wrong? I wondered. Her voice was off. Her posture was too posey-phony. She stood like an actor in a play, as though she wanted everyone in the cheap seats to see how very sincere she was. It wasn't the drugs playing games with my brain. Everything about her was false.

She turned toward the door. "Rob, how much of this do you think is Allie-Bear seeing things? Or did a phantom really try to knock you off the parking lot?"

"Somebody did," Rob said. He came in without knocking, not that anyone expected him to. "Somebody really did. It's absolutely *not* funny, Juliet."

"It sounds like a foreign movie," she replied.

"Juliet, it happened just like I said, before she woke up." Rob's voice flattened. "I got the ripped up elbow to prove it."

"You're hurt?" I said, trying to sit up, to look in his eyes.

He hesitated at the foot of the bed. "I jumped away from that car and cut my elbow up. It's nothing."

"I thought the rope was around your waist."

"It was. I was just adjusting it when I heard the car behind me. Basically, I wanted to tie it, so I could adjust the camera

. . . I had it in my hands for a couple of seconds, right at the wrong time."

There was something wrong in his voice too, something wrong with what he said. It sounded rehearsed.

"It couldn't have been the guy from that night," Juliet explained, as though I was a trauma victim, as though Rob had not just admitted to breaking focus with me before Blondie ever came along. I'd never considered the mechanism by which the rope went slack. That would have happened only if Rob had been hurt. That's when it hit me: *He's ashamed*. Rob hadn't been messing around with the camera. He'd dropped the rope. Which meant he'd dropped *me*. Out of fear. He'd had my back, literally, and he'd let go.

"Maybe it's some effect from her medication," Juliet said. "That makes her keep thinking she sees him."

I glared at her. "Why is this about my mental problems instead of some freaky stranger? I don't take medication. Just sleeping pills and not very often. And hallucinating cars and dead people isn't a side effect." On the other hand, I wished I had imagined it. A little crazy in exchange for a lifetime of fear? It would have been a good deal. Before I could raise my voice even louder, my little sister burst in with my mom. Angela took one look at me and started to cry.

"Angie, I'm okay," I said. "I'm really, really okay."

"I don't want to go to school," Angie sobbed, leaning against Juliet. "I should stay here and read to you." Despite my pain and confusion, I almost laughed. I saw my mom's lips twitch.

"You can come back right after school, Angela," Mom said.

Juliet kneeled down and hugged Angela. "Pick which pocket," she whispered.

Through her tears, Angela mustered a grin. She *was* nine and greedy as a crow. She pointed to the right side of Juliet's suede jacket.

"I can't fool you!" Juliet cried. She pulled out a tiny bottle of nail polish, the kind of garish pink-orange only a girl who'd just recently stopped using her hands as shovels could have loved. I felt vaguely sick. I could have scripted this scene myself. Angela had always worshipped Juliet in a starstruck sort of way. Juliet was everything glamorous and carefree that I wasn't, like someone on the red carpet, at least by the standards of Iron Harbor. In turn, Juliet had always treated Angela like a midget princess: first bearing gifts of sequined hair bands and matching plastic clogs with light-up Disney princesses on them, then nail polish to compliment the skinny jeans, butterfly tops, and chocolate bars as big as her head. "If Allie was really going to stay sick, wouldn't I be crying too?"

Angie nodded.

"So, I'm not crying. After she takes you to school, your mom is coming right back here. And Rob is here. And I'm here. And we'll take care of her."

My sister's gaze focused on Juliet. "Okay," she said. "Okay."

Mom cleared her throat. "Let's give Allie some time alone with her friends. We'll be back soon."

When my sister was gone and the door closed, I asked Juliet, "Are you psychic or a sociopath? Nail polish?"

She looked at me as if I were the one who'd been body-snatched. "I'm logical, Allie. I figured that she would be here, and I figured she would be upset the first time she saw you."

"You're good."

She didn't respond. No, having performed a magic trick,

Juliet then decided to disappear down a rabbit hole. *Poof!* How convenient! Yes, it seemed that she'd forgotten she had to be somewhere right at that moment, somewhere else. She started busily fussing with her hair and her jeans. If body language could be translated into speech, Juliet's would have announced: *Well, my work here is done. Attempting to muddy the brain of a drugged, post-surgical girl was my mission, and now I'm history.*

She kissed me. Her "love you" was light, the drop of a leaf. The door closed.

I waited for Rob to say something. Finally he did. Of course, they were the words every girl fantasizes when she wants to stab herself through her own heart. "Allie. I hate to do this."

"Don't then."

"I have to."

"Just don't."

"I don't think I'm good enough for you, Allie. Not after what happened last night."

"What really did happen?"

"I heard the car. And he was coming right at me. And I . . ."

"And you let me go. You dropped the rope to get away."

He stared down at the floor and squeezed his eyes shut. "Yeah. Which is why I can't be with you. I don't even have the right to be your friend."

I forced myself to take a deep breath. "Everybody gets scared Rob. You acted out of instinct. You knew I could take care of myself." The words sounded as if someone else were speaking them. I couldn't tell if it was the drugs or the pain.

He shook his head, still avoiding my gaze. "I should have held on to you. No matter what. But I let go."

"Well, I shouldn't do Parkour if I can't take care of

myself," I said quietly. Maybe it *was* the drugs, but I added the thing you should never say, even if you're being tortured. "Don't you want to be with me?"

Rob straightened and shrugged. Finally he looked me in the eye. "The question is, how could you want to be with me? Shh. Don't answer." He leaned over and kissed my hair. "I'll come by tomorrow."

"You don't have to," I said. "I have a lot of thinking to do."

Rob bit the inside of his cheek. "Okay. That makes sense," he said. I watched him leave. The door closed behind him. We were no longer the tres compadres or even a Tribe of Two. I was alone: a Tribe of One, a single Dark Star.

10

SABBATICAL

Maybe it's not possible to experience a broken heart when you've had a mutually exclusive relationship for less than thirty minutes. But that's how it felt.

Still, I had pride. I used it like a fossil fuel. I ran on it. Every time I seemed certain to scream or wail or sob if Rob hadn't called (not to mention Juliet, for whom I'd wrestled with the kind of feelings you have for freshwater sharks and Ebola virus), I topped off my pride tank and kept going. Like Juliet, I went on sabbatical. I vanished for the rest of the summer.

I'd left the proverbial balls in their courts. They had to make the first moves. I'd done what I could. Besides, *I* was the one with the freaking broken arm.

Another dull night.

Another sleepless day.

More pain in my arm. More painkillers to numb it.

If being in my room for basically eight weeks didn't do much for my mood or sanity, it did do a great deal for my mind in other ways—good, bad, and pathetically useful. I became the living authority on *Ellen* and the newest incarnation of *Oprah*. I learned all the things even smart people will do to fawn on celebrities. I learned how dysfunctional families will rip each other to shreds for a piece of the limelight. On one show, a woman who'd married her daughter's boyfriend revealed her pregnancy. How would Christmas morning look at that house, a year down the road?

In addition to these lofty pursuits, I discovered that a semester's course work in AP English takes just about exactly four weeks of seven-hour days. When school actually started, I'd read Virginia Woolf and who was afraid of her; I'd read James Joyce (Dublin), Joyce Carol Oates (not Dublin), and the Millers, Henry and Arthur (way more exotic than Dublin). I'd written papers about all of them.

On top of all that, I started something new.

I began to research serial killers.

Of course, this only began after I'd once again scoured the police records for any sign of any injured or dead young women with dark hair. There were none. But the total number of missing young women in a two hundred mile radius of Iron Harbor over the last decade was truly horrifying: there were over two dozen.

What I learned confirmed the few things I'd probably gleaned from snippets of A&E shows. These types of murderers looked and acted like everyone else so much of the time, nobody could believe what they did the *rest* of the time. They worked in restaurants. They drove buses and went to law school. They wrote poems for Comp II, one about "reaper's eyes" that didn't refer to harvesting the corn. Their histories, their kills, their habits of mind, their stealth, boldness and uncanny good luck (if you can call it that) opened a new world: the world of the abyss. There was no bottom. Ted Bundy abducted and killed two girls in one night, not once but twice. Alex Rendell brought his Big Ten soccer team a national title; but his real gift was as a marathon death merchant: he cut the throats of groupies in twenty states.

Oddly, the more I read, the less I feared. These guys weren't animals; that would be insulting to animals. And they weren't Quantum Physics, either; they were Algebra I. They did the same things over and over, for two reasons. The first? They were compelled to do it. At first they loved it, too. It was their addiction, their crack. They'd gotten a taste and just couldn't say no again, no matter how disgusted they were with their own actions. They'd created a wall of denial that would make any drug addict or alcoholic seem like a saint. The other reason? They were good at it—probably better at it than they'd ever been at anything in their lives. And that private victory, that "another-one-down-and-nobody-knows" feeling was tied up with the thrill of secrecy and denial, too.

Sometimes after reading a particularly gruesome passage, I thought of Rob and me. I pictured that first moment we hopped into his Jeep to sneak to Duluth to do Parkour without Juliet. I remembered that first kick of excitement, what it felt like to let Juliet go. To kiss Rob and know that I was the one. I also remembered a lot of weird and terrible stuff, though, too—mostly about the absence of life in the ghoulish faces of those poor women I'd glimpsed in Blondie's apartment. I remembered Blondie's car disappearing into the night after trying to kill Rob and me. I remembered all those moments a thousand times, and I still felt just as icky and unsettled.

A "sabbatical" does that to you.

EVERY WEEK, I had to get my arm checked.

My cast was a flexi-mold. I felt like barfing whenever they changed it, despite the efforts of the medical appliance makers to amuse me with a choice of subtle blue or wild paisley. My arm transformed into an old-lady's arm: pale and shriveled. I couldn't exercise, so I lost strength. The pain lessened but the itching drove me mad. Babysitting Tavish became my only real connection to the outside world, beyond my immediate family and doctors. I had to admit, showing up at Tabor Oaks three times a week *was* a thrill, like I was getting one over on Blondie.

Besides, Tavish and I were in love. Together, with the help of YouTube, we tried to learn to tap dance. He wasn't even a year old. But to Tessa's delight, Tavish danced on top of my feet.

The summer nights grew shorter. School was coming soon.

One night Tessa said, "Did you know that somebody made a prank call to the police about this place? And they said there was a murderer in here?"

I was changing Tavish, so I had a good excuse to look away. I had mastered the left-handed diaper change and was pretty proud of myself—especially since Tavish, now strong and solid, was a pretty squirmy challenge. I took a deep breath. "My best friend's father is a police officer," I said. "So yes, I heard about it. Small town. I didn't know it was this very building though. Does that creep you out?"

She nodded. "Kind of. You know what, Allie? I don't want to creep *you* out, but I came out in the morning, and there was dirt, like, soil, all over my balcony. There was a plant knocked over up there. And I thought I saw a shoe print in the dirt. But the rain washed it away." Tessa looked at Tavish and me and laughed. "It's so out of the way and quiet here. You start seeing things. . . ."

The shoe print? My jaw flickered. It couldn't have been one of ours. We never got down that far.

"Crazy stunts like that happen every summer, Tessa," I replied. "Kids around here get bored. Believe me, I know."

"That's exactly what my husband said. It's the reason we ended up here, besides the fact that his company has a hub in Duluth. He says it's an innocent place. But he's never around!"

I forced a laugh. "Maybe it was your own shoe. I do stuff like that all the time."

Tessa sighed. "You're probably right. The only time I'm not spaced out is at work, now that I'm pregnant. . . ."

Having finally managed to suit Tavish up in a new diaper, I lifted him and squeezed his little body against me. "You're pregnant? Congratulations!"

She rubbed her tired eyes and laughed. "Well, it wasn't the plan, but thanks. I wanted to wait three or four years and get my Master's to be a nurse practitioner. Babies happen, though." She took Tavish from me and snuggled with him.

Cautiously, I said, "You never see anyone around here who doesn't belong here, do you?" I glanced out the floor-to-ceiling windows at the blackness of the lake.

"How could I? I sleep half the time during the day, when my mom or James is here. I hope I get past the exhaustion stage of pregnancy pretty soon. The only person I ever saw was somebody that was James's friend, the old doctor. . . ."

"Stephen Tabor."

"He sent somebody to try to fix that old hole in the ground."

"What hole?"

"Down there by the bluff. You know, where the parking lot drops off, the lawn by the lake? There used to be stairs that led down to this old boathouse that you can't see from

here. It was like a garage underground, in the wall of the
bluff. It scared me because Tav's walking now. But there's
this little door thing in the ground covered by the grass. You
know how little kids are. Steve's putting up a fence back here,
next week, a big sturdy chain link fence. But if we're staying here, particularly with two babies, we're going to need a
place that's not crawling with traps."

My throat constricted. I forced myself to murmur something about being right, and something about being sensible,
and that Tabor Oaks would end up being fine for a toddler
with the right precautions.

Tessa handed Tavish back to me. "You're such a sweetie,
Allie," she said. "I don't know what I'd do without you."

TWO MINUTES AFTER Tessa was gone, I'd wedged one
of my shoes in the door to the apartment and one in the lobby
door, just to keep both open and to be safe. (It would be like
me to drop the keys and I didn't want to take the chance that
I might not be able to get back in). After that, I rocked Tavish
to sleep. Once he was gently snoozing, I strapped him into his
back carrier and headed down to the grassy area in back of
Tabor Oaks, at the water's edge.

First, I just kicked around with my bare feet. Then, I
sunk to my knees to get a closer look. All of a sudden Tavish
awoke again and began to laugh. He pulled out strings of my
hair while I scrabbled through the grass, hunting—

There.

Jesus. The door was hardly hidden. You couldn't miss it,
unless you were looking towards the lake from the parking
lot, where Blondie had disappeared on me. But where the
lawn sloped down near the bluff, it was plain to see: a clever
mat of dry grass and weeds pegged to the ground by a tent

stake and sealed with a thick lock. Tavish began to fuss, and though I hated to give him a pacifier, I found the one attached by a shoestring to his carrier and stuck it in his mouth.

His lips bobbed angrily, but soon he surrendered and his eyes fluttered closed.

What was down there? Boating equipment? A bundle of sailcloth? Something else? Suddenly, it seemed urgent to get the hell back into the apartment. Maybe I was paranoid. I didn't really care. If someone wasn't actually watching me, it felt as though someone should be. I thought of that old line from sophomore AP English, *"By the pricking of my thumbs, something wicked this way comes."* Standing up, I hurried back toward the apartment building. My phone vibrated in my pocket.

Rob? I wondered, or hoped. I grabbed my sandal from the lobby door and took the elevator up. The phone stopped buzzing. I froze in the hallway on the fourth floor.

The apartment door was closed.

My sandal hung from the doorknob.

Maybe Tessa's mom was here. Or maybe her husband had come back early. It would be nice, as I'd finally get to meet him. . . .

This was all fine. I was tired. If Rob had called, I wanted to use this as an excuse to reconnect. I wanted to tell him about what I'd discovered out there on the grass. Reaching back to pat Tavish's sleeping head, I knocked him with my cast. No one answered. I rang the buzzer. Still no response. I fished in my pocket for the keys, but when I put the key in the lock, the knob turned easily.

The door was open.

Someone had closed the door but not locked it.

"Tessa?" I shouted, my pulse racing again. "Teresa? James?"

I'd left the living room lights on; now they were off.

I stopped breathing. With both hands, I reached back to Tavish. He squeaked in his sleep. No one, not even a monster, would hurt a baby.

My legs turned to jelly as I hurried back into the elevator and pushed the button to make sure the door stayed closed. The elevator alarm blared. Everyone in the county would wake up. Good. Fingers trembling, I dialed 911.

A COUPLE OF minutes later, I heard the lonely sound of a single cop car's siren. I could finally breathe when it screeched into the parking lot. Juliet's dad was on a fishing trip; the next in charge, Mike Beaufort, was a man I barely knew. He was young and slim and built, kind of like a younger version of Will Smith, Northwoods style. He completely understood my panic after all that business a few weeks before. Better to take no chances, especially with the sleeping baby still on my back.

There was no one in the apartment.

I followed Officer Mike from room to room as he searched everything, even dresser drawers. He asked me some casual questions; they blended into yes, yes, yes. I agreed that there had been vestiges of light in the sky when I'd gone out with Tavish. I agreed that I might easily have turned the lights off. I agreed, lying through my teeth, that discussing all that freaky stuff about the murderer must have scared me—and I agreed that it made me curious about the hole in the ground. I agreed that it was stupid to investigate in the first place, but thought it was a boathouse. Yes, yes, yes.

Officer Mike called Tessa at the hospital and asked her to come home. I wasn't sure if I was ashamed or relieved. Probably both.

After that, Officer Mike escorted Tavish and me back

down to the door in the lawn. He said he had no idea what the door was—an old boathouse seemed about right, as far as he could tell—and he called his boss on his cell. I could hear Juliet's dad laugh on the other end. Yes, yes, yes: the door opened to a boathouse no longer in use. Just like we'd all suspected. A derelict stairwell down to the lakeshore was all that remained of the structure, and Dr. Stephen would get rid of it when he built the fence next week.

That was that.

I had to hand it to Officer Mike: the whole time, he didn't once treat me as if I'd done the wrong thing or overreacted. Back in the safety of the Cryer apartment, I finally summoned the courage to ask: "So, who hung my sandal on the door? I left it wedged in the door in case I dropped my keys."

"That wasn't very wise, to leave a door open," he replied.

"I know. But still, when I got back, my sandal was hanging from the door knob."

"If I had to venture a guess, I'd say someone came along, saw the open door, and closed the door for you. I'd say it was a kind neighbor who's trying to avoid this misunderstanding, and I wouldn't blame him or her." He sighed, but his tone was not unkind. "It had to be one of the other building residents. Let's go knock on some doors and we'll find out which one."

Let's not, I thought. *Let's not increase the percentage of people in Iron Harbor who think I'm nuts.*

"I'm fine now," I said. "I guess you're right. You don't have to knock on any doors. Seriously."

Officer Mike sat with me, waiting for Tessa to return home. I laid Tavish in his crib and suddenly remembered that I hadn't even looked at the text I'd received. I dug my phone from my jeans pocket.

It wasn't from Rob.

It was from BLOCKED.

Have fun but don't get hurt.

Instinct usually doesn't lie. Human beings are the only animals who ignore instinct, but, like Rob once said, we're trained out of it. Parkour was a way to rediscover instinct and tap into that buried ability to survive, no matter what the cost. That crawling sensation I'd felt by the lake, the same sensation I felt right now, amounted to a pure reflexive reaction: a warning that someone knew what I was looking for.

Who would have known that?

Only someone who was watching me.

II

FREESTYLE SOLO

The next day, out of the blue, Juliet left a big bouquet of daisies on my porch, along with a handwritten note.

> *Is the cold war over? Can I come and see you tomorrow night? Even for a movie? I'll bring enchiladas.*

I texted her back: *There's never been any war.*

A moment later my phone rang. Juliet was a gush of "How are you?" and "I'm so sorry I haven't stopped by!" and other crap that sounded as if it were coming from some random XP staffer at the hospital, not the best friend I thought I'd known my whole life. But I played along. I told Juliet that I was okay. Just recovering and babysitting. She was probably right that I had been hallucinating dead girls and demon drivers. For now, I was just laying low and getting better. Was that cool with her?

"I guess it's cool?" she said. If it sounded like a question, it probably was, for the both of us.

How could I say what I felt? That she should have been with me the whole summer? Bringing me magazines and lip gloss, staying over, driving me around, taking me to the movies, French-braiding my hair, filling a bucket with soapy water and giving Angela pedicures, regaling me with her last triumph of running into Caitlin buying size 9 pants at the used boutique, then verbally slaying her?

Nothing is more pitiful than asking for what you know you can never have.

Along those lines, Rob wasn't there, either.

Sure, there had been the kiss. And the accident. Was he really that tortured over it? I'd forgiven him! *I'd* have dropped the rope if Blondie had been gunning toward me. I'd hid behind the fountain like a coward, hadn't I? By now, Rob should have still been able to be one of my best friends if he couldn't be my boyfriend. But the longer we went without communicating, the harder it became for me to make the first move. We should have been able to overcome any awkwardness. Rob should have been sending me crazy YouTube videos of Parkour, or just random stuff to make me laugh, or texting me dumb jokes with excruciating puns. (*Don't speak, my love. Just be mime.*) He should have been buying me gross desserts too greasy and fattening for any girl to eat and ordering pizza from Gitchee with four kinds of meat—one that Gideon insisted was venison, but which made us want to count the dogs in town.

Yes, with Juliet, there had always been that little crackle of caution, that inner voice: *Be slow, take care, nothing is what it seems.* Instinct. I knew to trust that now better than ever. But I'd never felt it with Rob. Something had changed though, as sure as you wake up after a night so hot you sweated through your sheets, and suddenly, it's the fall. We couldn't have stayed the same forever, even if none of this had ever happened. The *tres compadres* could only last so long. Somewhere deep inside, we all knew it.

On the other hand, this was such a one-eighty that it seemed almost otherworldly. I was guilty; I hadn't reached out. But that poisonous jealous notion kept snaking its way back into my brain, too. *Maybe Juliet and Rob have finally hooked up.* If that were true, they'd be ashamed, given what had happened between Rob and me before the accident. Still, they owed me, if not their loyalty, then an explanation. Right? They couldn't be *that* selfish and spineless.

Maybe we weren't *ever* the *tres compadres.*

In fact, although we'd always been friends, the true "forever" for Juliet and Rob and me—when we were inseparable—had been only the last three years, since Juliet stopped skiing.

What had I done all the years before that?

Not much. In fact, pretty much what I was doing now. Reading. Hanging with my mom. Watching the tube. I'd always been a little too omnivorous with TV, able to recite whole episodes from shows other kids never heard of, from *The Twilight Zone* to *The X Files* . . . although there was one difference now. I spent more time with Angie when we both were younger. I guess I really did have some babysitting experience.

By the time she was about six, Angie could recite whole episodes from *The Twilight Zone* and *The X Files,* too. Sometimes, after a marathon of old reruns (and when Mom's heroic efforts to keep her eyelids aloft were finally met with defeat) Angie and I would even sneak out into the backyard late at night. We would lie on our backs and I would show her things other kids don't see during the day. If you could lie still, a black porcupine would walk right past you, or a spectral opossum, carrying her grotesquely beautiful babies on her ridged back. During those days, I thought often of deaf people, how some make a choice to depart from the world of the hearing. It just doesn't have much to do with them, as the Daytimers' world increasingly had less to do with me.

A hard truth: even those days were lost to me now. Angie was worried about me, yes. But she no longer relied on me to explain why certain creatures only came out at night.

Three nights after Juliet and I spoke on the phone, I could have sworn Rob passed my house after dark and slowed down. The night after that, I was sure of it. The sound of his Jeep was unmistakable; I didn't even have to part my blinds. The next night, he stopped. I lay still in my bed, listening. A door slammed, but the Jeep sped off into the night. He couldn't bring himself to see me. Why? One part of me longed for him. The other part seemed to be closing up, like moonflowers do at night, and hiding the most private self away.

I'd been too naked, too honest with him that night in Duluth. Maybe he felt the same, as though he'd ripped some part of his soul and left it behind in my hands. Neither of us could pretend it was just a moment that happened because he was a boy and I was a girl. If it had been like that, if we hadn't been best friends beforehand, there would have been two possible answers. Both started with "no." That's what girls did when guys wanted to have sex with them, wasn't it? *No, I don't think I'm ready.* Or: *No, not now, it's a big step.* I'd done the opposite. I'd said, right here, right now. Or, if not, then whenever you say, with you.

How could we go back to before?

❖ ❖ ❖ ❖ ❖

AS SOON AS the doctor gave me an okay to be active again, I was able to channel my anger and confusion. I poured it straight back into Parkour. I tested my weight on my little sister's old swing set, which she never used anymore, and found that it was stable. Slowly, I began to swing, forcing myself to rely on and work my bad arm.

They say a broken bone heals stronger than before, and I had no reason to believe otherwise. But at first, using it hurt so much it made me want to give up, or at least to throw up. I asked for Vicodin. If you're presumed to be a short-timer in the world of the living, doctors usually give you almost anything you want. (Although I learned from the absurd amount of TV I'd watched recently that this is not true for those on Death Row.) I doped up but kept going. When the pain consumed my whole being and not just my arm, I wrapped it in cold packs and took my knockout pills.

I used weights and my own weight. I grunted and sweated through progressively greater numbers of pushups and finally pushups only on my right arm. Sometimes I exercised for two or three hours, despite the torment of the mosquitoes. When I started to do jumps, I first had to re-master my balance. I worked until standing on the top crossbar of my sister's old swing set became as natural as standing on the ground, and I never missed landing my back flip.

The nights grew longer and colder; the mosquitoes began to fade. The air emboldened me. Too much time had passed. If I really was a lone Dark Star, what could be braver than making the first move? Finally, one night, I picked up and put the phone down ten times—and then managed to call Rob's landline. Worst case scenario: I wasn't calling him, I was calling his dad.

"Hey, Mr. Dorn," I said, trying to sound normal. I did

not say *I was secretly hoping Rob would pick up, so I could pretend I was calling you.* I kept my cool. I did not babble: *Tell-me-about-Rob-and-does-he-talk-about-me-and-is-he-in-love-with-Juliet-for-real-now*—"I have to ask you a favor."

Rob's dad said the thing all salesmen say. "What can I do you for, Jules?"

"It's Allie," I replied, ignoring the sting.

He coughed. "I'm sorry, honey. But shoot, you're practically twins." I stifled an angry laugh. Even when we were inseparable, we'd never sounded alike. Juliet had a low, husky voice, like somebody who sang in a honky-tonk and bummed cigs from the bartender. Mine was plain, girly, more soprano than I wanted it to be. But I got the subtext: Juliet still called all the time. Mr. Dorn heard a girl and expected the usual. "What's up, Allie? Long time, no hear."

"I need a horse."

"Quarter horse? Thoroughbred?"

With all my might, I tried to force out the laugh I'd quashed. "Pommel horse, I think it's called. You know, that gymnastics bar, the kind they use in the Olympics. . . . "

"Wish it was weighted tires that football guys use for agility training. I got a surplus of those. Pommel horses are not really my area. But let me make a call."

Of course, the next night, while I babysat Tavish, he dropped one off at our house. He'd scored it from Coach Everhart, who taught all the gymnastics to the kids in Iron Harbor, little and big, boy and girl.

I didn't know if Iron Harbor would always be known only as the home of the Tabor Clinic. As David Belle said, there is no limit. The goal is not fixed. It's fluid. You need to push yourself beyond what you mastered. Or else why go on? I decided that I would make my own life as a *traceuse*. A world-famous one. I would put Iron Harbor on the map in a way nobody could have ever foreseen. I would get down. I would get good. I would go places Juliet and Rob could only imagine.

I would mean my amigos no harm. I would just get along without them.

As soon as I saw the pommel horse waiting for me in the garage, I called to thank him. "Mr. Dorn! You're like the go-to guy!"

"Since when am I Mr. Dorn?" he replied with a chuckle. "That's Dennis to you, young lady."

Suddenly, my throat clogged up. I used to have these fantasies of marrying Rob, with Mr. Dorn walking me down the aisle and giving me away, in a church lit by candles at midnight. The especially weird part about my fantasy was someone giving away his son and his son's bride at the same time. Still, Mr. Dorn was about as close as it got, father-figure-wise, in my life.

"You'll be out there again soon, Allie," he said. "Along with your friends."

I opened my mouth, and then closed it. I felt as if all the blood in my body was draining away, pooling at my feet. I heard myself ask, "Are they out there now?"

"Probably," he said. "Torch Mountain, maybe? Though I'd bet on Superior Sanctuary. It's funny. My dad used to go up there when he was a kid. It was a WPA project. I'll bet you don't know what the WPA was."

I actually knew a good deal about the Works Projects Administration and the whole New Deal. (Since sixth grade, we'd never gotten any further in American History than the New Deal.) Rob's dad went on to say that only a few of the buildings were finished but most of them were just rough storage . . . but I stopped listening. "I guess that's why they're so good for Parkour," he finished.

I tried to swallow. My eyes stung.

"Allie? You there?"

"Yes," I finally managed. "Thanks again, Mr. Dor—Dennis. I'll talk to you later. I have to go."

I slammed the phone down on the hook and ran to my computer. Sure enough, YouTube confirmed my worst fears. Someone whose handle I didn't recognize had posted a new Dark Stars video. Rob and Juliet wore black jeans and black hoodies. (Did they have fans now? Or were they just mocking me by choosing a lame alias: "nightclimber"?) They looked like they were having the time of their lives at some Parkour paradise: barracks-type buildings with long, descending stairs and iron railings that turned at right angles every eight steps—and wooden towers with wires and cables strung between them.

It didn't matter who'd posted the video. The message was clear. They'd left me behind and moved on. Two dark stars: together.

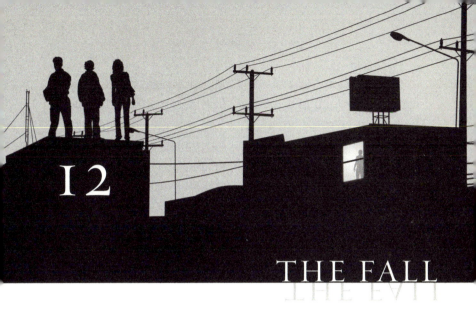

THE FALL

12

THE FALL

The same week that I got my cast removed, we also started school.

For other people, that would have been: *Gah! We're seniors! We rule!* For the Tabor Clinic Few & Proud, it meant that we received a syllabus from the school district and a bunch of books in a box. I made paper covers for them for the last time in my high-school life. A letter with the names of my new tutors was also enclosed. Then an email popped into my inbox—from Nicola Burns. The first yearbook meeting would be at her house. A ray of hope flashed through the darkness of my brain. *Nicola!* Why hadn't I thought of her? When I wrote back, I asked her if we could do something first, hang out and catch up. She didn't respond right away. Finally she replied: OK. No exclamation points or smiley-faces. But that was all right. At this point, I'd take what I could get.

THAT SAME NIGHT, Rob finally texted me. *I get if you don't want to be with me, that way, but why r u not talking to me or J? I miss u. I really do.*

I wasn't sure whether to laugh or scream or start crying again. How long had it been? Two months? Rob had never been so brick-thick before. True, he was the only guy I knew well. (Let's face it: at all.) And having learned almost everything about the guy species from Jack-Jack, I figured there was a certain level with a guy, even an evolved guy like Rob, of not being able to grasp subtlety unless he wanted to (or unless he could punch it or eat it). But even so, by now I wasn't sad so much as furious.

Suppressing the urge to call him right then, and spill everything, I lurched out to the swing set. It was nearly eleven o'clock. I had a feeling I would practice until dawn. I placed my hands on the crossbar when I saw my mother watching me through the screen door.

"I didn't know you were awake," I said.

"You never stopped," she answered, stepping outside to join me.

"I did it while I was healing. I did what the doctor told me to do."

"What you're doing, it's beautiful," my mom said.

"Thanks. It makes you strong, and helps you be alert in an emergency, too. And it's really fun."

She said, "Well, be as safe as you can."

I said, "You knew all along."

"Sure."

"Before I got hurt."

"Yes."

"And you let me."

"What was I going to do, stop you? It's your life, Allie. I just want you to contain the risk."

"That's part of the goal, Mom. The motto of some Tribes is train swiftly; train safely. I got hurt through my own stupidity."

And someone trying to kill me.

"What else is going on?" she asked. Not upset, just curious.

"I . . . I . . ." Before I knew it, I was sobbing again. I shook my head angrily. "Rob."

"You love him." The words were gentle.

I shrugged, unable to speak.

"That's lucky for him. Not so much for you. Allie, sweetheart. I wish I could say he's not worth it."

"He *isn't* worth it!"

"He is worth it," my mother said. "Have you...?" She didn't finish.

"No, but I want to." There was no point in hiding anything at this point. Besides, she knew what I wanted, anyway.

"I don't blame you," she said. "Nothing better for the hormones and worse for the heart than the right boy at the right time."

She could always surprise me. "What do you mean, the right time?"

"Well, you let yourself cry in front of me for the first time in a while. So it's clearly the right time for you. He drives past here ten times a night like a stalker. So something's going on with him, too. But something's not working or we wouldn't be here having this conversation."

I wiped my cheeks. "Don't you want me to wait?"

"No," Jack-Jack said, without hesitation. "I don't want you to wait until the idea of being in love gets all snagged and dirtied with obligations and promises and other people's expectations."

My jaw fell open. "You want me to have meaningless sex at sixteen?"

Mom shook her head and headed back towards the

house. "No, I don't," she said over her shoulder. "Who said anything about meaningless?"

I DECIDED TO wait to call Rob. I wanted to first prove I could do Parkour on my own. The next night, I returned to the roof over the cobblestone alley between the Smile Doctors and Gitchee Pizza. Gideon was not too bad off that night so I alerted him in advance. He came out to watch. True to his personality, Gideon was not at all alarmed at the sight of my leaping from the dentist's roof to his roof, although the insurance liability would have made any other adult lose his lunch and dinner. He raised his fists and cheered for me.

I repeated Juliet's original leap with the twist in the air.

After I clattered down the fire escape, he gave me a large with peppers and anchovies on the house. As I scarfed down the pizza, I debated whether or not to head up to Superior Sanctuary and trace the living crap out of what I'd seen Rob and Juliet do and trace it WAY better than they could ever have possibly imagined—

But then I looked at my watch. It was only 10:11. I was feeling brave already, pumped with adrenaline, so I decided to capitalize on it. I dialed Nicola.

"Allie?" she said, as though my call came from beyond the grave.

My heart immediately started thumping. It was ridiculous. I was more nervous about calling her than I'd been about risking my life only minutes ago. "Yeah . . . I'm sorry. Is this too late?"

"No . . . it's just. . . . Wow. Hi. What's up?"

"Nothing. Well, not nothing. I said I was going to call."

She laughed lightly. "Yeah. But I didn't think you would." What an asshole I was. "So, do you want to do something?"

"Okay," she said.

"Nicola, let me tell you, I'm so sorry for not calling you for so long." I paused.

"This sounds so weird. I know."

"Are you with Juliet right now?" she asked.

"No," I said. "Why do you ask?"

"What happened with you two?"

"Well, I broke my arm."

"You broke your arm? So you're not friends anymore?" When somebody said it like that, it sounded about as absurd as it actually was.

"It's more than that," I said. "I . . . we just have different things going on." Now, Nicola would think I was going to the bench for a relief pitcher. "This has nothing to do with Juliet, actually. I just called to see if you wanted to hang out."

"Okay," she said. "Do you want to go to the Fire Festival?"

"Absolutely."

"Great. I'm psyched. Bye, Allie."

I hung up and let out a deep breath. Gideon smiled at me drunkenly. Maybe that's why he drank so much: he understood that basic social interaction was sometimes a lot harder than risking your life.

FRIDAY NIGHT, POLITELY after dark, Nicola showed up in her mother's convertible: a purple Mercedes. Nicola's mom was a pretty famous travel writer whose stories ran in *The New Yorker* and other big-name magazines. I'd never ridden in a convertible. They're sort of *the* anti-XP car, if you think about it.

"She lets you use this?" I asked as I buckled up.

"It'll be mine next year," said Nicola.

"Seriously? Get out of here!"

"For college. I'm going to the University of Texas at Austin. It's a long way from home."

"I'll drive with you if you go overnight and let me help you drive."

She smirked. "Deal. If you drive the whole way."

The Fire Festival is a generally touristy extravaganza held up at Timbers, the big ski resort on Torch Mountain. It's the town's last excuse for a party before the cold weather really kicks in. It's supposed to celebrate art and food and culture, but I imagine it feels pretty much like any big fair held in any other Nowhere County. There's some fake legend about Native Americans (I'm sure Gideon would scream): Ojibwa deciding to determine who got the first dibs at the caribou by a flame-throwing contest; the Iron Harbor version was more like juggling flaming clubs. There were teams that practiced all year and had the scars to show for it.

I personally would not want to throw and catch a club with an oil-soaked rag on fire. But then again, I imagine they'd think that using buildings and stairwells and any other man-made structure as a perpetual means of death-defiance wasn't too far removed, either. When Nicola and I hopped out of her car, for the first time in a long time, all I could think about was having a *good* time. I thought about the burnt ears of sweet corn I used to eat out of the husks, salting them with tin saltshakers that hung from tree branches by strings. I thought about fry bread, and these little walleye filet sandwiches.

Then I saw Juliet.

Nicola and I had paid our ten bucks and were passing through the banner-festooned archway. In the gaudy light of the food tents, Juliet was standing a few feet from a long line of hungry people. Our eyes met. She didn't smile. She shook her head and sort of wiggled her finger at me, like she was warning me not to approach.

"There's Juliet," Nicola said, and began pulling me toward her.

I tensed. *She must be here with Rob,* I thought, panicking. "No, just leave her for now." I said. I shook free of Nicola's grasp. "I think she's with a guy."

"A guy who doesn't let her talk to her friends?" Nicola said with a laugh.

I didn't answer. I couldn't.

The guy approached her then. He wasn't Rob. If time slowed to molasses whenever I saw Juliet do something outrageously life-threatening, time became solid amber in that instant: frozen and horrible.

Blondie.

He placed his arm around Juliet's shoulder, his back to Nicola and me, revealing the lightning bolt on the back of his head. Juliet laughed, for him, but rolled her eyes at me, frivolously, as if to say: *Men! Can't live with them; can't live without them.*

"Let's go," I said to Nicola.

"What?" she asked. "But we just got here."

"I'm sick. We have to go. I have to get home. Or to a gas station. Whichever comes first. I'm really sorry."

We ran for the parking lot.

Why did I look back? Juliet was far from me by then, at least two hundred yards, but what did I expect? Fear? A mad laughter? Instead, her face opened to me like a prayer, and I got it, in that moment, that Juliet was longing for me, too, just as I was longing for her.

As for Blondie, he followed Juliet's backward gaze, too.

But there was no surprise or alarm. He looked at me the way the opossum had looked at Angie and me that night many years ago, not at all threatening, just communicating what he knew. He had to survive, and if he had to pretend to be something else to survive, he would.

SHORT STRANDS OF questions and suppositions snapped and rolled like a cheap Mardi Gras bead string in my mind. Memory collapsed back and back, to our beginning Parkour, to the cat leap and the descent of that very building on that very night. Was it all planned? In that instant, I remembered the way he pressed against the sliding door on the night we saw the dead girl. That was the first time I had seen his face. Except it wasn't. Not even then. I thought hard now, and it seemed that I recognized him, from somewhere, long ago. Had I seen him before?

I barely heard Nicola when she said, "What's wrong? Is Juliet contagious?"

"It's complicated," I said.

"It always is," Nicola said. "You can tell, if you want."

"I know." Finally I allowed myself to relax. We were sitting in Nicola's convertible. We were safe. "But I don't even know what to say. I don't even completely get why I don't want to talk to her."

"Is it that guy? The older guy? Are you crushing him, too?"

I shivered. "No. But I do know him, though. From someplace. . . . "

"Allie, are you okay?" Nicola asked pointedly.

I shook my head, "I don't know," I said, faking a wan look. "I might have a fever. I've had a headache and I've been shivering all day."

She stuck the key into the ignition. "I'll take you home."

"But I was going to stay over at your house."

"I know," Nicola said as the engine roared to life. "You're white as paper, though. Next Saturday, we'll do something. I have extra shitty AP History and English this semester anyhow, and I have to read two books that are, like, eight hundred pages. You know?"

I knew. They were the same ones I'd already read.

"Next Saturday," I agreed, gratefully. "How's yearbook going?"

"Now *that* is uber-complicated," she said. "In addition to you, we have a stoner, a girl who won't speak, and a guy who shall remain nameless who constantly hits on me. You're the least complicated member of our little team, Allie." She let out a little sigh and laughed. "And there's other stuff. That will take a whole sleepover."

I mustered a smile. "You know me. I'm up all night."

It was weird. I wanted to hug her, and not just because I was freaked out about Blondie. I'd never felt such affection for a virtual stranger before, at least aside from health care professionals. She could never be to me what Juliet and Rob were, but she was funny and smart and big-hearted and she never ever looked at me as if I was a freak.

But could she be just a normal friend? The way I was with her? Was this how Daytimers operated? Did they have normal friends with zero baggage? It seemed as if she wanted exactly that from me—no more, no less. I should have spent more time with her. I should have, in some way, taken better care of her. Yet even then, I doubted I would ever stay over at her house.

Still, when she hugged me goodbye before she dropped me off, I had no clue that it would be the last time I saw her alive.

13

SECRETS AND WHYS

There was no way now that I could keep Juliet's involvement with Blondie to myself. I wanted to tell my mother, and Juliet's father. But before then, I had to confide in Rob. A very small part of me tried to keep another terrible small part of me from myself: the shameful relief that Juliet's companion at the Fire Festival *wasn't* Rob.

As soon as Nicola dropped me off, I texted him: *HAVE to meet NOW*

I heard a ping almost at the same instant my mail took off. *11:30 at the cabin just u*

One hour from now. My whole body trembled as I thought of us, alone up there at Ghost Lake.

THERE WAS POLICE activity just shy of the exit up to the old fire road.

I so wanted to be with Rob that I would have ignored a forest fire, but something about the wreck drew my attention. I slowed as I drew closer to the swirl of sirens, where the police were setting up barricades. A car had skidded off the road and plunged into the ravine below with such force it left the guardrails gaping like broken teeth. I peered over the precipice. Then I slammed on the brakes.

Purple.

At first, all I could process was the color under the glare of floodlights.

The color of crumpled metal that had once been a convertible, now half-buried in mud. I jumped out of the car so fast I left the door hanging open. I ran toward the first officer I saw, Mike Beaufort. "Whose car is that?" I whispered.

Officer Mike held my shoulders as I tried to plunge past him. I gaped down at the cluster of firefighters and cops and medics. "Who was it? When did this happen?"

If I hadn't decided we should be friends, you'd be alive, Nicola, I thought desperately. *It should be me.* Every moment, the stain on my life got bigger and darker and now it was rolling and spreading, bulging and scalding other innocent people, beyond Rob and Juliet and me. And it was my fault—

I stopped. No. That was wrong, and worse, self-pitying. I was innocent. We were all innocent. "It was called in about fifteen minutes ago," Officer Mike said. "The way it looks, the wheels not spinning, the smell of gas . . . it's been a while."

"Was somebody chasing her?"

"Chasing her?" He seemed puzzled. "There are no other tire marks."

"That was her mom's car. She would never have driven it in a crazy way. She was going to drive it to college next year. In Texas."

My hands trembled. I reached into my pocket for my cell phone when I felt a pair of arms close around me from behind. I knew who it was even before I spotted the Washington Wizards logo on his jacket. I buried my face in Rob's shoulder and cried.

THE NIGHT ENDED in Juliet's kitchen.

Rob and I hadn't even knocked. If Juliet's mother or father had been home, I don't know what would have happened. I wish they had been. I wish that Juliet's kitchen had been an open window onto the whole of Iron Harbor, so that every single person in town could hear me as I burst inside and shouted her name. She was sitting at the table, reading. She jumped to her feet.

"Allie! What's wrong?"

"She's dead!"

Rob hesitated in the doorway. Juliet's eyes flashed to him, then back to me.

"Who's dead?" she whispered.

I swallowed. Yes, Juliet was a very, very good and skilled liar. But now she looked frightened. She really didn't know anything about the accident.

"Nicola," I hissed. "Her car is upside down. . . . " My throat caught. I shook my head and squeezed my eyes shut, trying to banish the image from my mind.

"Allie, please. Slow down." She reached for me, and then stopped. All three of us stood there in that little dimly lit kitchen, like chess pieces scattered on a forgotten board. Rob withdrew further into the hall. "What are you talking about?" Juliet pressed.

"Somebody forced her off the bridge. I know it was him! Who is he, Juliet? Please, just tell me who he is."

Juliet reached into her backpack and pulled out her phone, dialing her father. *Where's Ginny?* I wondered. Then

I remembered Juliet's mom spent four or five days at some harvest fair in California every fall, selling her salsa and relish and hand-loomed ponchos. Normally we made a big deal of sending her off. Normally . . . but what about the past few months qualified as normal?

"I'm calling about a car accident," Juliet stated into her phone. Her forehead creased. I could hear the murmur of her father's voice—rapid-fire. She nodded. Then she swallowed. Her face whitened. "No . . . I, um. Allie and Rob are here. They told me. We went to school with her." Juliet paused and then her face clenched. "I'm sorry you have to, Daddy. Thanks for letting me know. I'll see you in a bit."

I felt sick. Juliet's father always said there was nothing he hated about his job except having to walk up to a door where the people inside were having the last good few minutes of their entire lives. It wasn't just XP that claimed lives in Iron Harbor. Kids started drinking in sixth grade and driving at thirteen. Accidents weren't unheard of or even uncommon, although I knew of only two kids who had been killed—two boys the summer after my freshman year.

Juliet turned to me and opened her arms. Before I even knew what I was doing, I fell into them. "Hush, my Bear," she soothed, stroking my hair. "I'm so sorry. I know you were friends. . . . "

Just as quickly, I began to struggle out of Juliet's grasp. "*Your* Bear?" I snapped. "You're goddamned right Nicola and I were friends. And if you care so much, why have you been lying to me? To us? Who is he? Why were you with him tonight?"

She tried to hold my arms. "He didn't have anything to do with Nicola Burns." There was fear in her eyes again, fear I hadn't seen since her ski accident. "Allie, do you know how much I've missed you? How much we both have?" She jerked her head towards Rob. "Is this what it takes for you to come to me?"

"No. Stop it. Stop lying. You know that he tried to kill us, the night I broke my arm. In the parking lot in Duluth."

"No," she said, sounding not just adult, but also old and vastly tired—like a grandmother. "No, that's not true. That was a mistake."

"A mistake?"

"This is all a mistake. It's awful, but not like you think."

"He killed Nicola tonight, right?" I nearly shouted. "Isn't that what your dad just told you? That she's dead?"

Juliet didn't answer. Her lips quivered.

"Right. Dead. All because of me. Because he knows I know! And I saw you with him tonight! It wouldn't matter to him who she was. It was . . . it must be some kind of warning. He wanted to get to me because I'm the only one who saw him with the girl he killed, that night at Tabor Oaks."

She lowered her gaze. "I don't know what you saw that night, Allie."

"Don't say that! Don't say that anymore! You both know that I saw him that night with a dead girl. Her face was covered with bruises. She was gray, Juliet. If you had seen her, you wouldn't be pretending it was all some kind of dream." I turned to Rob. "Tell her! Tell her!"

"I don't know what to tell her," he said. "I absolutely believe you. And after what just happened to Nicola, I want to believe you more. But . . . I didn't see anything, either. And neither did the police. Not that night."

Hot tears stung my eyes again. "So you think I'm nuts, too."

"Not at all. Not even a little."

I turned back to Juliet. "Please. Please if you care at all, tell me the truth."

She kept shaking her head, her eyes flickering over me— as if weighing her options. Would she still lamely attempt to make it seem that Blondie never existed, or, if he did, that she wasn't connected to him in some weird way? Would she insist that her connection with him had nothing to do with how the three of us fell apart? *Let her try,* I thought. I wasn't going to let Juliet make this into a hallucination. My life had become crazy, but I wasn't crazy. I had reached outside the sanctum of the three of us and touched another world, and been touched by it. In some pretty essential ways, in a very short time, I was a different girl. I wasn't willing to be controlled by Juliet for the privilege of her willful, intense, (and yes) sweet friendship.

"Okay," she said. "Okay, Allie-Bear. Do you want to know? Do you want to know things you'll wish you didn't know?"

Very suddenly, *I* was afraid. I don't know why it hadn't occurred to me before to fear Juliet. Maybe because our history together was lifelong, or because even tonight, her sadness was so convincing. Yet it was increasingly clear that if she had been trying to confuse me, she had nothing to lose. My fists clenched at my sides. "Admit that he exists and that you know he tried to kill me."

"He exists, but he didn't try to kill you." Juliet sat down hard on the kitchen chair. "I think . . . or I believe . . . I have to believe that he just tried to scare you. I'm sorry Allie. You're my heart. You're my best friend. I would never be part of anything that would hurt you."

"Who was in the car with him?"

"Me."

"So at least you're telling the truth now. And you say he

didn't try to hurt me. Let me ask you again . . . Juliet, are you insane?"

"He was trying to scare me, spinning out of the garage. Not you or Rob—*me*." Juliet smiled and shrugged, but her face was pinched and closed, and she no longer looked like a kid, but like a crone. "It's this thing he does. It wasn't even bad that night. He off-roads and spins his car on the ice—"

"Nothing you're saying makes any sense," I interrupted. "But say I give you all that. Even if he just happened to be in Duluth with you in the same place that Rob and I had picked to do a course—"

"I knew about what you guys were doing," she snapped. "I wanted to see that. I wanted to show him. He drove me. But believe me, we had no idea we scared Rob so much or what happened to you after the fact."

"It didn't occur to you to apologize?" I said, nearly spitting. "For breaking my arm?"

She stared at the floor. "I was so ashamed. And I didn't want to tell you."

"So, okay. This guy, driving Dr. Stephen's car, tries to scare you and ends up nearly killing Rob and me . . . and you don't even bother to introduce him to us so *he* can apologize. I could call your father right now and have him brought up on charges. You know that, right? You're lying out of your ass right now, but I don't even care. Let's say all of your bullshit was true. How do you explain those girls in the apartment?"

For the first time all night, Juliet looked me straight in the eye. "The girl I saw is fine. And yes, he was the guy with her. But I never saw him with anyone else. I've known him a long time and he's never lied to me."

"You're crazy. You think *I'm* lying about something like that."

"I'm not sure what you saw. Neither is Rob. Neither is my dad. He thinks you might have imagined it. Especially after what happened at Tabor Oaks, when you were babysitting."

I'd all but forgotten that Rob was there, patiently standing near the door, listening to us go at it. The revelation hit me, vivid and terrifying: Juliet knew that I'd called the police the night I'd gone out to investigate the trapped door in the lawn. And she'd decided to tell Rob about it, spinning the whole thing as if I had gone mental. Juliet had decided to sell Rob a sack of garbage, and he'd made the purchase, and he was still halfway lapping it up. *That's* why he hadn't called all summer. *That's* why he'd been spending so much time with her. *That's why* they'd both avoided me after I broke my arm. I was suddenly "the crazy friend." She'd actually succeeded in making Rob doubt the evidence of his own senses. She was a snake charmer. No, she was worse. She was a stranger. In that moment, I truly didn't have any idea who Juliet Sirocco was.

"Allie?" she murmured, "do you really think I'm capable of hanging out with somebody who would do something so horrible?"

I stood there for a moment. "No. Well, I don't know. He nearly killed Rob and me; you've just admitted as much. Basically, you're telling me that there's a key to the lock and I can't even see the door, Juliet. That's not fair."

She nodded. "I know."

"And right now, I am sick to my stomach. I need to call my mom."

"Go ahead," she said.

Rob stepped forward. "I'm gonna go home. Allie . . . call me later, okay?"

I nodded.

"Promise?"

"I promise."

He didn't even glance in Juliet's direction. "Bye," he said.

The front door slammed. Seconds later, the Jeep's engine sputtered to life. There was a thud of tires on the bumpy road outside, and the dull roar faded into the night. Before Juliet could say a word, I dialed home. Angela answered, crying. It all came out in a frantic jumble: Mrs. Staples was with her at our house, because Mom had gone into work in the ER. They were short-handed and a girl from town had been in a car wreck, and she was dead, and they were still getting the dead girl out of the car but the girl's mother accidentally took too many pills when she heard the news. . . .

"Is Nicola's mother okay?" I asked. The words sounded hollow in my ears, as if someone else had spoken them.

"Yeah, I think so, but Mom just called," Angela said, hic-coughing through her sob. "She'll be home soon. I wish you would come home now. She said to tell you if you called."

I swallowed. "I'm at Juliet's. That girl was my . . . she was our friend."

"Can you come home now?" Angie pleaded.

"I'm going to stay at Juliet's. Just for a while—"

"I'm scared you'll get killed in an accident."

"I won't. I promise I won't, Angie. I would never leave you."

"Okay. Will you tell Juliet hi?"

"I'll . . . bye, Angie. I'll be home soon."

I shoved the phone back into my pocket. I felt even sicker. I had no idea what to say. One life lost; another in danger. Because of me. Because of *him*.

"You and Rob," Juliet said, catching me off guard. "Do you love Rob?"

"Obviously," I said. Reacting to her unspoken follow-up, I added, "*You're* the one who's been hanging out with him."

Juliet sighed again, once more sounding old and defeated. She slumped back down at the kitchen table.

"Allie, I want you to hear me right now. I know you're shaken up. You just told Angie you'd never leave her. But you're going to leave her. We're all going to leave our families. We're trapped until then, having blood drawn and giving pinch biopsies and having moles removed and waiting to die, like monkeys in cages."

Now I really was frightened. I'd never heard Juliet talk like this. For a moment, I even forgot about Nicola. "The research with the retroviruses repairing the DNA—"

"Isn't going to happen for us," Juliet said.

"You don't know that. My mother says it's on the horizon."

"She's your mother, Allie. That's what she wants to believe."

I shook my head, mostly for myself. "Juliet, think about what DNA research has changed, in just our parents' lifetimes. There are people who were executed for crimes they didn't commit before DNA testing. There are people who got nailed for murder who would have gotten away with it. . . ." I stopped.

"What?" Juliet said.

I know what I'm going to do with my life. It was an epiphany, the kind only a horrible trauma can induce. I wasn't going to be the female David Belle. No, I was going to stick a pin through insects like Blondie with their own blood and tissue, insects that sucked the life out of friends and turned them into zombies. At work in the dark of a lab, I could wield a sword like Joan of Arc in the sunlight. I had never thought much in terms of my destiny as an adult. It wasn't territory where I was comfortable going. XP kids can think all they want about college online or in person, but usually, the reality is they're going to grow up single and kind of disabled.

I decided right then that I was not. I had reentered my love of the natural world. And I was going to study it, beyond college. I was going to study Biology first, and Criminal Justice, then Forensics. . . . People like Blondie would fear me, their time as predators like an hourglass slowly emptying, one they could not dislodge or turn over.

"Juliet, if I am your best friend, you owe me," I said, returning to the moment. "You owe it to me to tell me everything."

"I can't."

"Then I'm not really your friend."

"No, really, you *are*. It's because I love you that I can't tell you." She stood again and began to tie up her hair in a bun. I was exhausted, by the events of the night, and by the time I'd spent here. I looked at the clock, and it was already past two. What time had it been when I'd arrived? All I wanted was to sleep.

With her hands fiddling with her hair, she unintentionally bared her mid-riff. I glimpsed her tattoo.

"The 'Great and Terrible' Juliet Sirocco," I muttered.

Her hands abruptly fell to her sides, as if I'd caught her stealing something. "If I tell you something, you have to swear to God that you won't ever tell a living person, not even Rob. Even if you think you're doing the right thing, and if you think it's for my safety. I get to decide that."

Slowly, I nodded. "What are you talking about?"

Juliet raised her eyebrows. "Say it. *Swear* it."

"I won't tell anyone," I said. "Not even Rob."

"G.T."

"What about it?"

"It represents . . . my ticket out of here," Juliet said.

"A person? A drug? Are you talking about a way to end your life, Juliet? You said it meant the great and terrible."

"It does, sort of."

"But not completely."

"No. Not completely. And that's all I can tell you right now."

14

ALWAYS

When I got home that night, I found something tucked in my backpack: her little stuffed penguin on skis. Juliet still slept with it even when she came to my house. It was the closest thing to a security blanket she'd ever admit holding onto. (Not surprisingly, she'd named him "Penguin.") He smelled of the only cologne Juliet ever wore, Cartier de Lune. She'd never parted with him.

Part of me melted. The other part hardened. Was this just a cynical chess move on her part, to try to stay one step ahead of me? If she was willing to entrust me with Penguin, it meant our friendship could never be violated . . . right? It meant nothing fundamental had really changed and that she'd felt terrible about the minor things that *had* changed. Or she just wanted me to be her heart again, so I would leave the whole Blondie issue alone until she was ready to confide in me.

I was too tired to think about it. Angie had fallen asleep on the couch. I thanked Mrs. Staples for the emergency babysitting gig and sent her on her way with cash from the drawer, then carried Angie up to bed. I sat in the kitchen, waiting for Mom and eating crackers until I was nauseated and my stomach literally popped out. Glancing in a night-blackened window, I noticed I looked like crap, my unremoved makeup all running in the wake of my shower, my wet hair pulled up on top of my head in a ponytail. I basically resembled the Lorax from Dr. Seuss.

I must have fallen asleep at the kitchen table. When I lifted my head, the kitchen windows were still black. My mouth tasted awful, like dirty socks. I sat up and rubbed my eyes groggily. Mom was sitting beside me, knitting a quilt. As Jack-Jack is not a natural with any kind of needle except the kind you stick in a person, this was very slow going with much quiet swearing.

"What time is it?" I croaked.

"Around four," Mom said. "You looked so peaceful. I didn't want to wake you. And there's no way I can sleep after the night I had."

I bit my lip. "How's Nicola's mom?"

Jack-Jack sighed. "She'll live. That's what matters."

I nodded. I stood and stretched. I filled a glass of water at the sink and sat back down. Mom kept her eyes on her needlework.

"I've been thinking about . . . my future," I said. "I want to apply to colleges that specialize in criminal justice."

"Okay," my mother said. She held up two squares, different colors of purple, to see if they matched in size. "I kind of thought you'd study online."

"Like a bird in a cage?" I said.

"No, like a person with a chronic illness who has to avoid certain situations. Your dad has provided for your education.

You have a fund. I don't want to do anything to stand in the way of whatever it is you want to do."

"You sort of sound like Dr. Andrew right now—the way he talks to me in front of you. I have a theory, you know."

"Oh? Please share."

"He wants to get into your pants."

"Well, if that's true, then I appreciate that about him," Jackie said. "He's handsome and smart and could have his pick of the litter."

I laughed. "Please don't humiliate me by becoming a gold-digging mistress. Gina would do that, but not you."

"Gina would not do that. Don't humiliate yourself by putting down someone who loves you so much."

"Ow! Guilt trip!"

"You are spoiling for a fight, Alexis, and I am not going to give you one. Maybe it's because of your friend's death. Maybe it's because you've had hard times with Rob and Juliet. Maybe it's hormones. Don't take it out on me."

"Let's face it. Things would be easier if I hadn't been born."

Mom slammed her needles down on the table. "You're an idiot," she snapped.

I saw the dark rings under her eyes, purple bruises after a night of dealing with God-knows-what at the hospital. "You wish I didn't have XP," I said. I couldn't stop.

"Don't you?" Mom asked.

"Yes, but I'm not my mother."

"Allie, just give it up. Whatever it is, just let it go. Don't pick away at me like this. Say what you have to say and be done with it. I'm too tired right now."

"That's why you have Angela. She's your backup kid. Right? She's not the same as you, but at least she'ss healthy.

You could get married again. You're young enough to have another normal. . . ." I'm not sure why these words came cascading out, but I was too tired and confused to plug a hole in whatever dyke had held them back until now.

My mom stood. "I'm going to sleep. See you when you come back from Mars."

She stomped to her room and turned up the volume of the radio so loud that the kitchen counter shook. It was possibly the most annoying song in the universe: "The Sound of Music." The hills of Iron Harbor were definitely alive with its overblown theatrical crap. I almost had to laugh. Mom knew exactly how to punish me.

Angie woke up, of course, and stumbled into the kitchen, rubbing her eyes. She asked me what was wrong. I started to cry. Then *she* started to cry, almost out of obligatory duty. I banged on Jack-Jack's door until my hand got sore.

Finally Mom appeared. Her eyes were huge and blotched with her own tears.

"Listen, Allie. Both of you. I wanted another child, *for me*. And yes, Allie, I wanted you to have a sibling because most kids who have what you have *don't* have sisters. I wanted as big a family as I could have without a husband. And you know what? I might want to adopt another baby. And if I do, even if he or she is doomed to die of cancer at the age of four, I'll love that child the same as I love you two." Her voice sharpened. "The way I love you and Angie is not subject to debate. Do you understand?"

I swallowed. Angie and I exchanged a quick glance. I opened my mouth, and then closed it.

"What?" Mom barked.

"Juliet says . . . you only want to believe there'll be a cure. As in, you want to believe in leprechauns."

She sagged against the doorframe. "Why wouldn't I? Juliet is smart, but she's cynical enough for five Chicago politicians. If I could pray, I would pray. Some people see the hand of God in this and it actually comforts them."

I nodded. If I opened my mouth again, I'd probably start crying again. Besides, my mother isn't religious.

"Your grandmother is a practicing Catholic," she mused, staring up at the ceiling and at the same time somehow staring straight through my skull again. "She said that it was wonderful how President Kennedy's mother kept her faith. Because after Mrs. Kennedy's second son, Senator Bobby Kennedy, got shot, old crazy Rose said something like: 'God gave my children beauty and intelligence but not long life.'"

"That's probably the best thing she could say," I said.

"No," Mom replied, her lips tight. "It sounded to me like Old Rose had ice instead of blood in her veins. I wanted to scream in my mother's face: That woman loves God more than she loves her children!" She glanced down. Snapping out of her reverie, she kneeled in front of Angie and me. "Listen. I would rather let the world blow up and everyone in it than let anything hurt you. A God that gave up his own son for other people . . . I have to be honest. I don't get it. I love you too much. I couldn't do that." She sniffled and arched an eyebrow. "Maybe that's why I'm not God."

I reached for her hand. She took it.

AFTER THAT, THE three of us ate a half-gallon of ice cream. My mother didn't even pretend she was going to put it in dessert bowls. She just yanked out the carton and cut the big rectangle into three blocks, which she doled out on dinner plates. Then she slopped on everything in the house she could find, from raspberry sauce to marshmallow fluff.

Daytimers that they were, Mom and Angie started rubbing their eyes once they were finished. As soon as they'd gone to bed, I sat on the screened porch and tried to savor the last moments of darkness. I focused on how I was going to determine Blondie's identity. The fact that Juliet refused even to say his name was the most telling piece of information I'd pulled from the horrible night. She couldn't say who he was because she was afraid.

I could tell Jack-Jack everything Juliet had told me. But I couldn't break my promise to Juliet. Or: Did she want me to break the promise? Did she know I would break it, anyway? There was no way out. I had built the birdcage myself. . . .

The rumble of an approaching car pierced my thoughts. I froze in panic for a second, and then I recognized the sound. I smiled crazily. A moment later, the headlights of Rob's Jeep lurched into view and then went dark.

He flung open the door and hopped out.

I leapt like a cat into his arms.

I kissed him and he kissed me. We fell into the pine needles near the mouth of the driveway. Both of us were sweating, and I was afraid that I smelled and nervous that I didn't have mascara on and hadn't brushed my hair, or come to think of it, my teeth, since the previous night. He said, "You taste like marshmallows."

"I was eating ice cream sundaes."

"Do you want to go bouldering? I brought rope and gear. I thought maybe we could do what—"

"No, that's not what I want," I interrupted.

"What do you want?" Rob said, smoothing back my sweaty hair.

"I want to live," I said. And Juliet's words echoed in my brain: *Everybody dies. But not everybody really lives.* I glanced back at my mom's bedroom. The window was dark. "Right here, right now."

Rob hesitated. "Allie, are we. . . ?"

"I am," I finished for him. "With you. All my life. Always."

15

UP CLOSE

At my four-times-a-year checkup that week, Dr. Andrew asked me if I was sexually active.

It wasn't that I didn't want to tell him, because he'd been my doctor ever since I was a kid. But right then, it felt as though he'd been always watching all of us in Iron Harbor, as though we were little figures in a snow globe.

"Yes," I said. "Just recently."

"You know, there is no one hundred percent safe kind of birth control. Using two forms is—"

"Mom's a nurse," I interrupted. "I could write a book."

Dr. Andrew sighed. "I hope it's a committed relationship, because you're a good person, Allie. I'll leave this issue in your mother's hands." He opened the examination door room.

"Thanks," I said.

"I'm going to pass you onto a family practice doctor for this part of your cares now."

I said, "Okay." But then I jumped off the exam table.

Blondie had just passed by the open door, wearing a white lab coat. His hair was shorter and the streak looked newly foiled, thicker than before.

"What's wrong, Allie?" Dr. Andrew laid his warm fingers on my wrists, his eyes intent with concern.

"I thought I saw someone. . . ." My voice was barely a whisper. "A doctor who passed by. Who's that?"

Dr. Andrew poked his head out. "Tim!" he called, waving. Blondie entered the examination room. "Tim, this is Allie Kim. She rules the nights of Iron Harbor. Allie, this is my son, Dr. Tim Tabor."

Blondie extended his hand. Knowing that mine would feel like a claw of ice, I took it and gave it the sturdiest shake I could.

"Allie, hullo," he said cheerfully.

I forced a sickly smile, my brain a kaleidoscope of awful memories, my pulse thudding loud enough so that I could hear the dull beat in my ears and wondered if he could, too. My eyes roved over every inch of his face. There was something different about it: the chin was square, and the wrinkles around his eyes more pronounced, but the eyes were the same. "You have an accent!" I finally said.

"All those years as a phony Brit." He grinned crookedly at Dr. Andrew. "It'll go away, at least for me. For my wife and our sons, not so much."

Dr. Andrew placed his hand on his son's shoulder. "Tim just got back from London. He was doing a research fellowship in surgical skin procedures. Now he's here in the urbane town of Iron Harbor. Not much like London, huh Tim?"

"It's home, Dad," he said. He gave me a big, genial smile—with no hint that he'd ever seen me before. "You'll have to excuse me. Nice to meet you, Allie."

"Me, too—you, as well," I stammered. I had never fainted, but I recognized the strange sensations I was having as the precursor to some kind of blackout. "Dr. Andrew, I need to lie back down for a moment."

He peered down at me, his eyes narrow. "Are you eating well, Allie? Dieting too much?" He frowned. "Could you be pregnant?"

"It's nothing," I said. I squeezed my eyes shut until the vertigo evaporated. "Really, I'm fine. I'm not exactly sexually active enough to be pregnant."

"It only takes once."

"I've heard that. Let's change the subject. You must be happy to have your son home."

"Two down, one to go," said Dr. Andrew. "My son Marcus is still in college. Undergrad. He won't be a doctor though, like Drew and Tim. He's studying journalism. I know he'll write about all this. He's bitten with the bug to translate the world of science. I think he's having a pretty good time over in New Haven, too." Typical of Dr. Andrew that he wouldn't say the obvious school in New Haven: Yale. "Tim was in London a long time, almost six years. We only saw the little guy once. Now Tim and Drew are running around looking for land so Tim can build a house."

I forced myself to focus on the conversation. "Didn't he look around when he got here?"

"He just got here two weeks ago, Allie."

"That's all?" I almost shouted the words.

"You sound surprised. All they've been doing is getting used to life in Iron Harbor. You know, seeing my dad, who's just thrilled, and Drew taking Tim fishing, like when they were kids, and we had the old boathouse. . . . My wife won't let the grandbabies out of her sight."

My spine stiffened. "Two weeks ago? Did he visit a lot before?"

"Not really. It was hard on all of us. Started work yesterday. I told him to take some time but that's not the Tabor style." He offered a faint, proud smile.

I fell back against the cushions and the crumpled white sanitary sheet. Should I ask Dr. Andrew for the name of a counselor? People with XP have a lot of psychological issues. Maybe this was a neurological issue. Maybe my brain was shrinking up.

Juliet was right.

I had seen her having an innocent conversation with our doctor's son, also a doctor, who'd been in England when we saw Blondie in the apartment last spring. How Juliet knew Tim Tabor was a mystery to me. Why she was in a car with him in Duluth was even more of a mystery to me. Why she thought I was nuts was now, however, perfectly obvious. I *had* hallucinated the second "murder" scene.

But no. Of course I hadn't. Besides, what accounted for . . . everything else? And how could I have had a hallucination of someone I'd never seen before?

"Listen," Dr. Andrew said. "I'll have you see Dr. Bonnie Sommers Olson for your gynecological care, instead of Gina. She's just as nice. I'll set it up for next week, okay?" He lowered his voice. "You are going to confide in your mother, though."

I nodded. "Absolutely."

As soon as he left, I texted Rob and Juliet.
2Nite The Cabin, 10.

"I KNOW WHO he is," I told Juliet that night. "Not just that he exists. I met him."

She stood with her back to me in the clearing in front of the deserted cabin, watching two loons crisscross the flat lake. The very arrogance of her pose, her tiny shrug, seemed to dismiss me. *So what? Big deal!* Rob's Jeep came bumping up the track and he parked next to my mother's minivan. He swung out quickly and kissed me hard.

"So it's official," Juliet said. "You two, I mean."

"Yes," Rob said for the both of us. "What, are you pissed?"

"No."

"Juliet, you told me that's all you ever really wanted." He squeezed my hand. "For Allie and me to be happy together. Let's just get this all out in the open, okay?"

"Yes!" she exclaimed, her voice harsh. "I did! Congratulations!"

I swallowed, not wanting to think about the conversation that Juliet and Rob must have had about me. "Juliet, please just answer me. Answer all of us. We all owe each other that much, right?"

"Answer *what*?" she asked.

"Why are you involved with somebody who is first, married, and second, a doctor—"

"A doctor?" she interrupted. I could see that Juliet was honestly baffled, which only frightened me more. "Who's a doctor?"

"I was at the clinic today for my checkup. I saw him. I saw the blond streak on the back of his head. He was wearing a white coat. His name is Tim. Tim Tabor, Dr. Andrew's oldest son . . . not that I'm telling you anything you don't know."

She shook her head. "I don't know Tim Tabor." She hesitated. "I know Dr. Andrew has a son, or two or three, and that one is a doctor."

Rob let me go. He sat down hard on the ground, thrashed with bewilderment. "What the hell is going on here?"

"Juliet," I said. "Pull the band of your jeans down."

Her eyes glittered in the night. "You're the one sleeping with Rob, dude. Not me. I only bare skin for—"

"She has a tat," I interrupted. "Two initials right above her hip bone. And I know it has something to do with this guy."

"You say," Juliet whispered and smirked.

"What are you so scared of, Juliet?" Rob demanded. "Show me."

"Rob, come on."

"Show me!" he shouted, jumping to his feet. "I know you're lying, and I know Allie is telling the truth! I've seen the tattoo, Juliet! You think I haven't? Enough! I've seen the initials G.T. in weird calligraphy. I'm sick of protecting you. It's the world that ought to be afraid of you, Juliet, not the other way around."

"If you only knew, Rob," Juliet said. "I wish I could scare the world." She turned her back to us again.

"Forget it," Rob muttered. "Let's just get out of here." He reached for me, but I stepped towards her.

Juliet waved me off. She let out a deep, long sigh. "I promise I will find out what's happened," she said, her old, defeated persona taking over. "I can't tell you more than I know. I have never met Tim Tabor, and I swear to God on that. The guy you saw at the Fire Festival, who was driving the car that night, is a friend."

"A friend?" I said.

"He's not bad. He's made some bad decisions."

I laughed. I couldn't help it. "You sound like an abused wife. Next, you'll say that I don't understand him the way you do."

"You don't! But this has gone way further than I thought it would. I wanted to scare him a little, let him know that I was on to him. I knew he was seeing other women." Juliet spoke as if she were talking to herself.

"But the guy's, like . . . old," Rob said.

Juliet stomped from the cover of the trees out into the moonlight. It splashed down around her body like spilled silver. "So what? Don't you ever just want to shake up our lives? Scream? Grab someone by the throat? Make people see us? Does it matter who sees us? When they see us, we're real. When I skied, everyone knew who I was. I wasn't this . . . thing, this *creature*. Oh, the children of the midnight sun! The moon children!" She clasped her hands under her chin and batted her eyes in a parody of innocent bliss. "Poetry! How tragically lovely. What we really are is the human equivalent of cockroaches, scuttling around in the dark. Aren't you tired of that?"

I backed away. "Not as tired as you are. There are things inside me that matter more than what idiots think."

Juliet smiled sadly. "Idiots like Rob?"

"Screw you." I resisted the urge to slap her.

"Yes, screw me, and goody for you two sweet things. The only thing inside me is the night. The freedom to do whatever I please. I want to live with that freedom inside me every moment."

"No one lives like that, Juliet," Rob said. "Movie stars have bad breath. Models have learning disabilities. Athletes have athlete's foot. Nobody is free the way you dream."

She shook her head. "You're wrong, Rob. I was that free when I skied. I was that free when we started Parkour. But it wears off. I'm a drunk, like Gideon. I have to keep chasing that high." Juliet lurched forward and grabbed the arm I'd broken, squeezing hard. "I can't find something that lasts. That's why I have to do this."

"Juliet, don't run," I said.

She let go and took a step back. Her eyes narrowed. "Have you told anyone?"

"No one. I just told Rob, here. Right now."

"Told me what?" he demanded.

"Juliet wants to leave . . . she says G.T. is her ticket out of here." I threw my hands up, hopelessly, towards the starry night sky. "She used to say G.T. meant 'Great and Terrible.' It's what they called her when she was on the ski team. But now I'm pretty sure it means something else."

She nodded. "You're right, Allie. It does. There's a network of the night. There are whole underground cities lived at night. In Europe. Even here. It's not like I'd go to Florida and sizzle on a beach."

"Who's been selling you this crap?"

"People," Juliet hissed. "*Real* people. People who've been outside this shitty little shitbox hole of a town."

"Prove to me that this guy didn't kill Nicola," I said. "Then at least I'll know that someone isn't taking advantage of you. Prove to me that the girls I saw in that apartment are alive."

"I don't know what you saw, Allie. Okay? But I will try to find out! I'm only human. And as for Doctor Who, it's not the same guy. It's some kind of crazy coincidence. It doesn't fit together. Give me a few days to find out. Just a few days."

I stepped over to Rob and looped my arm in his. "If you agree to one thing."

"What one thing?"

"Whatever I say," I told her. "Otherwise, I rat. I tell your father, your mother, my mother, *Rob's* mother, Dr. Andrew and everyone else I know until somebody believes me or locks you up."

Juliet shifted on her feet. "What else can I do?" she asked.

"You can come back to us," I said. "We'll be a Tribe. We'll be three." I looked at Rob and he pressed his lips together, and then he nodded. "For now. Not a couple and a third wheel. We'll be the *tres compadres*, like we were before. Just don't take off."

Juliet took a long breath and seemed to consider her options. "I promise. But, Allie. What are we going to do for the next three days?"

"We'll trace," said Rob. "We'll boulder."

"Exactly," I agreed.

A FEW HOURS later, we were slick with sweat and spent. They'd taken me up to Superior Sanctuary, and I understood now why they'd fallen in love with it.

I also understood something else: Rob had only tagged along with Juliet and made those Dark Stars videos because he was as creeped out as I was by what had happened in Duluth. He wanted clues. And if doing Parkour with Juliet was the only way to get those clues, then that's what he'd do.

You walk up Mount Everest. It is only for the strong, but most of it is walking. You are miserable, cold, oxygen-deprived and in Hell, possibly delirious and frostbitten, and you end up at the height at which planes fly. But not much of the experience is actually "climbing." Climbing a mountain is grabbing onto one part of the mountain and then trying to hoist yourself up to the next handhold or footrest. It means having technical skill, using your boots for traction and an ice pick for leverage—and yes, a rope tied to a trusted friend, so you don't fall.

Bouldering isn't entirely like climbing. It's based more on instinct, on grit and strength. You can boulder up a sheer slab: the side of a city building, a highway pylon, or a wall in your house, if you're Rob.

For weeks, Rob had been practicing, so he could do Parkour with Juliet, to get some kind of insight into what was going on with her. Not that he'd ever, ever admit that to me. The closest I got to a confession was an offhand comment he tossed out as we all headed home in our respective rides to beat the sunrise.

"It's worth giving you up for a little while to keep you forever," he said, in front of Juliet, so she would hear.

As I learned much later, the same never held true for Juliet. We'd given her up a long time ago. And I didn't need a few days to find out what was going on. I found out almost everything I needed to know the following night.

16

IDENTITY

IDENTITY

B efore I went for my clinic visit with Dr. Bonnie Sommers Olson—yes, the woman who was going to give me the whole lowdown on being "sexually active" even though I'd met the criteria of that diagnosis precisely once—I submitted my first college application.

John Jay in New York has one of the oldest forensic programs in the United States. It's one of the few that actually grant a bachelor's degree in forensic science. I'd received the results of my ACT tests: a cumulative 29. (Apparently the broken arm had paid off.) That score would hopefully get me into quite a few places, and I also intended to apply at the University of Minnesota and the University of Wisconsin— both also great science schools. But John Jay was my first choice. Besides, I was almost 100% certain I was the only applicant with my very particular minority status.

DR. BONNIE LOOKED a little like Gina, only minus the gaudy makeup and painted nails and New York accent. She insisted I call her "Bonnie, just Bonnie" as I sat on the exam table. She asked if I was having trouble sleeping.

"Are you asking because it's nearly ten at night?" I joked, a little too defensively.

"Allie, I'm more than familiar with XP," she said. "I was thinking about the girl who died recently. Nicola Burns."

I nodded, though my nightmares were waking: recurring visions of Blondie's distorted, smiling face pressed to the glass at Tabor Oaks. I was almost tempted to ask if she knew Dr. Tim Tabor.

"Are you getting enough vitamin D?" she asked.

All of us at the Tabor Clinic took a hardcore vitamin D supplement because sunlight is its best natural provider. Ironically, vitamin D also helps you with sleep and with a host of other orderly ways of life: another cruel joke of XP. Then she recommended a birth control pill—with a little lower this, and a little less that—and gave me a wad of pamphlets that I handed back, explaining that my little sister had more knowledge of sexual congress just from having dinner every night with our mother. I also told her that vitamin D wouldn't work on me. I was too strung out.

"Let's try some more anyhow," Bonnie said. "What else is going on?"

Well, I think a very dangerous person might be working at this hospital, and he has some weird power over my best friend. Oh, and either directly or indirectly he's sort of ruined my life. . . . I almost started to cry.

"Allie, what's really wrong?" Bonnie asked.

I straightened, regaining my composure. "It isn't about me," I said. "My best friend is involved with a guy who's older. A lot older. But it's not just the age thing. I think he's dangerous to her in other ways."

"Have you asked her to tell her parents?" Bonnie asked.

"No, she never would."

"When you say dangerous, what do you mean?"

"I think he's trying to convince her to run away." Until I'd articulated it, the exact thought hadn't even crystallized in my brain. But it was precisely what I was scared of. G.T.—whatever that meant—was her ticket out of here. *Her* words.

"That's serious," Bonnie said.

"It's even more serious if you have XP."

Bonnie nodded. "Try setting a deadline with her. Tell her that you care too much about her to let her do something that might wreck her life without thinking it over first."

I mustered a smile. "I've done that."

She turned and tapped the desk with her pencil. "Good. Tell her she has to see a psychologist. Maybe not even here. But somewhere. Tell her you'll go with her." She began to fill a prescription pad. "It's a small town."

"It is," I agreed.

"The Nicola Burns tragedy has been hard for all of us," Bonnie stated, snapping on her gloves. She told me to complain if anything pinched, then she started the exam.

"Yeah." My eyes began to sting. "Nicola . . . She still wanted to hang out when I ignored her for, like, a year. I avoid Daytimers."

"That's what you call them?"

"It's supposed to be contempt. But it's envy."

"That makes sense." Bonnie laid her palm flat on my belly and tapped her finger against her joints. "Everything feels fine here." The tapping made a hollow woodblock sound. "You're using two forms of protection?"

"You betcha."

"Let's have a little blood."

"They test me for everything but Ebola."

She laughed. "You know better than to deny a doctor a little blood."

For some reason, that set me off. I pictured Blondie, wandering these very halls. I started to cry. I hadn't done so much crying since I was six.

Without a word, Bonnie folded me into her arms in a way no one except my mom ever has. She held me for two or three minutes, maybe even longer. I leaned against her, breathing in the smell of antiseptic mingled with shampoo and that over-dried hospital laundry scent I'd grown up with. Finally the tears stopped coming. I drew in a deep shaky breath and sat up straight again.

"I'm going to give you my cell phone number," she said calmly. "Call or text whenever you want. I'm serious. It's good to have another adult who isn't related to you in your life. Or just another human being."

"Thanks," I said.

"I'm speaking from experience," Bonnie said. "I'm having my own issues. I barely know Nicola's mother. But every mother I know can empathize with how she reacted, even if she wouldn't do it herself."

I almost started crying again. Bonnie thought all this was about Nicola. I felt horribly guilty that it wasn't.

"I do have a mother who says she loves me more than God," I offered.

"And I believe her," Bonnie replied, her voice soft. "I'll let you skip the blood test for now. But not for long."

I nodded, slipping off the exam table, embarrassed about the crying, embarrassed about telling this stranger that my mother loved me more than God. The office blinds were parted just a crack, and in the harsh glare of the parking lights, a flash of red caught my eye. My heart seized. The Alfa Romeo convertible was pulling up to the clinic entrance. I forced myself not to squint or stare. Instead, I took a slow breath and let it out slowly. If I had a meltdown, I wouldn't find anything out.

"Hey, look! That is some car," I said. "Does it belong to Tim Tabor?"

"No. His cousin. You know, the coach?"

My head began to buzz. "The coach?"

"Yes, the ski coach. At school."

"At school?" I repeated.

"Well, not exactly. The team has kids from all over . . . you know, the team I can't afford my younger son, Elliott, to be on." Bonnie flashed a crooked, apologetic grin. "The one that wins championships all over."

"The jumpers," I said. "He coaches freestyle jumpers."

My new nurse friend's face brightened. "Exactly. You do know him."

"Not . . . exactly." My brain shut down, mostly out of guilt. *Juliet never once mentioned the name of her ski coach. Why would she? I never wanted to talk about skiing. I only wanted her to stop, so she could hang out with Rob and me. And then my wish came true.*

"Garrett," Bonnie said. "That's his name. When I hear about what those kids do, I think they're an orthopedic ward waiting to happen. So it's a mixed blessing Elliott is missing out."

"You should see the things *I* do at night," I forced myself to say. "I think I saw Dr. Andrew's son driving that car, the one who has the white highlight in his hair?"

Bonnie laughed. "No, it was Garrett. Tim, the doctor, has a streak too. But he drives a little Toyota."

I stared at her. "He has a blond streak? The doctor?"

"It's not a fashion thing. It's a birthmark, a place where there's no pigment. It's called poliosis. It's as common as eye color. From the Greek word for 'gray.' That woman who hosts that show about bad clothes, I can't think of her name, has one that goes right down the front of her hairline. That's where they are most common. But they can develop anywhere, and anytime in your life. It runs in the Tabor family. But it's not like I have to explain genetics to you."

My mind whirled again. I blinked several times. "It's not a sickness? Like XP?"

Bonnie shook her head. "No. According to the doctor he's dating, Garrett's very healthy indeed." She slapped her hand over her mouth and laughed. "Now I'm gossiping. Time to leave, young lady!"

MY MOTHER PICKED me up in the circle drive. We drove slowly past the red sports car. I asked her if she knew Garrett Tabor.

Garrett Tabor. G.T. G.T. G.T.

She looked surprised. I think she was all set for a heart-to-heart talk about the import of my doctor visit in the wake of what had happened with Rob. Not that I'd told her, but of course she knew. She was Jack-Jack. I wasn't ungrateful for an excuse to postpone that little chat. You can have the most open-minded mother on earth, but there are still going to be things that are uncomfortable.

"Well," my mother said. "I know who he is. He's an ass-hole."

I almost smiled. The wonderful thing about my mother: she is so socially reticent on delicate subjects. "How so?"

"He's screwing one of the residents, and I mean that in every sense of the word," she said. "Anyway, he's Dr. Stephen's son. Why do you ask?"

"He's a ski coach," I said.

"Right. Oh . . . he coached Juliet! That's why you're wondering. For a while, he coached in upstate New York someplace. Now he's back here full time."

"So he's really an asshole, huh? But Dr. Stephen is so nice."

"Good people have rotten kids. Look at my own fate."

"Ho, ho. Ha, ha. Tee hee."

Mom chuckled, but her grip tightened on the steering wheel as we rounded the corner onto the road that led home. "Can you keep a secret?" she asked with a conspiratorial grin.

"Jack-Jack, please. I'm insulted."

"He's definitely sleeping with Dr. Olson's friend, Dr. Wilenbrand." Her voice dropped to a stage whisper. "But he's also sleeping with Gina."

"Gina? She's older than he is! Lots! And you told me she wasn't a gold-digging mistress!"

"That's not illegal," Mom muttered.

Still, I thought . . . Gina was a single mom with two daughters older than Angela, but younger than me. In past summers, Gina and Mom spent vacation time together between the dark and the light, bringing out sandwiches and sunscreen for all us little girls so we could splash in kiddie pools. On the other hand, maybe it did make sense. More than once, Gina had announced (after a few beers) that she wished she'd never met her husband, and that she wished he could have just mailed her his sperm to produce Regina and Ronnie.

"Maybe Gina thinks she could end up with a piece of the Tabor pie," Mom said in the silence.

I stared ahead at the road. "I can't believe Gina would be with that guy. She's so strong and tough. . . . " But so was Juliet. Had Juliet really gone all the way with him? You don't tat a guy's initials on your belly because he helped you master a triple twist.

"It's worse because Lauren Wilenbrand works with Gina and me, and Lauren's about twenty-eight years old." Mom sighed. "I guess people see what they see."

17

BOLDER

BOLDER

Instead of going to Nicola's funeral, we decided to make a Dark Stars video in her honor. We couldn't have gone to her funeral without attracting an offensive and inappropriate amount of attention, anyway; like all funerals, the service was held when people were generally awake. That's one thing you learn hard and fast about XP: nobody is ever really equipped to deal with a ski mask, sunglasses, umbrella, and layers of (hopefully) reflective clothing at a midday gathering. But any guilt dissipated as we approached Watching Rock in Rob's Jeep.

I will say this: for the first time in a very long while, we were the *tres compadres* again, united by a single purpose. We weren't just going to boulder tonight. We were going to boulder in a way that made Parkour and David Belle look soft. We would live hard and fast for a girl who no longer could. And for the first time in a very long while, I truly didn't care what Juliet was thinking. She was here. With us. For Nicola. At least I hoped. That was all that mattered for now.

Watching Rock is tall, thirty feet at its flat top, overlooking Lake Superior. The legend is that its name derives from a lonely woman who stood waiting for her absent husband, a merchant seaman off gallivanting in Canada. There are three outcrops, like tongues, that extend out at three different levels—one about six feet up, one about five feet above that, and one close to the summit.

We laid a pile of narrow gym mats (again, courtesy of Rob's father) around both the lower shelves, but there was nothing we could do to break our fall for the topmost. It jutted directly above a sloping, rocky incline.

There was some kind of unspoken agreement with Juliet that these few days would come and go without question, so long as she didn't leave us. It was a pantomime of our friendship. Still, Rob and I pretended to be only friends, and Juliet played her part as the wild girl who'd try anything. We all tried to "feel it," and eventually, we did become transfixed. Rob began to talk about next summer and how we could check out the Precambrian volcanic outcroppings along the shore, and then drop fifteen or sixteen feet into water that had been a mastodon's swimming pond.

I let him talk. I just hoped there would be a next summer for the three of us. At the base of my mind was the solemn unspoken thought: tonight was our only tomorrow, and we would bet the limit on every hand.

"Speaking of volcanoes," Juliet said, "how about we light a fire?

We decided to light a flame for Nicola, to honor her. You weren't supposed to make a fire on public land without a permit, so maybe it was some sort of weird rebellion. Still, it helped me feel not quite so bad about missing out on Nicola's funeral. When the little campfire was lit, we turned on some tunes and danced around it. Juliet was wearing some kind of big old velvet hat, and I'd pulled out my fake-rhinestone-beaded inside joke of a ski mask, an atrocity that my Grandma Mack knitted for me two Decembers ago. It was some kind of confused homage to the Dolce and Gabbana ski mask that was hand-studded with Swarovski crystals, the one that cost a few hundred bucks. (The idea was that I'd "sparkle" during the wintertime if I ever had to go out during the day.) Like all hand-knitted things, it was heavy and itchy and hot.

Juliet must have seen me fidgeting. Before even putting it on, she tossed me her plain black ski mask, spun from the lightest, warmest stuff—which probably cost three times as much as mine, anyway.

"I should have the gaudy one, Bear!" she said. "Remember, you're the one who doesn't approve of labels. I'm keeping this one. It matches me."

I had to laugh. For that brief fire-lit moment, Juliet was once again Juliet.

"That's my best friend," I heard myself whisper to Rob.

"I thought I was your best friend," he whispered back.

I felt a pang and squeezed his hand while Juliet pulled on my mask.

BOULDERING IS JUST like Parkour, of course: it's not you "against" an obstacle; it's you in harmony with it. The challenge is linking destinations together in the most creative way possible, the tradition being that everyone waits for each member of the Tribe before moving on to the next challenge. The patience comes when you're all hyped up and still have to summon the will to encourage the others.

Juliet went first, scaling Watching Rock's lowest outcropping with such speed and agility that anyone else would have thought she'd been an expert her whole life. We forgot to film her she was so beautiful, twirling in a victory dance, punching the air with her gloved fists. We prepared to follow. Having been so close to an open flame for so long, we were sweating hard. But the night was forgiving, warm and moon-bright, everything awash in silver that reminded me of old coins.

"Shit, the camera," Rob said. "Let me—"

"Hey!" Juliet's cry pierced the air. An instant later, she tumbled end-over-end to the ground. Her head, neck, and shoulders thudded on the bouldering mat. Her waist hit the bare earth. Around her thigh, I saw a thick darkness spread like wings across the dirt.

"Juliet!" I sprung towards her, skidding on the pebble-strewn slope.

The gash at the back of her leg was bleeding freely. What happened next seemed to pass in stop motion: Rob and I made a chair of our arms to carry her to his Jeep. I sat with her while he gathered up the mats and lowered the rear seats. I scrambled into the back with her. Tough as she was, Juliet cried and clung to my hand all the way to the hospital. Rob called her parents.

Twenty minutes later, we screeched up to the ER.

Officer Sirocco met us there, along with a familiar nurse who helped Juliet lie facedown on a gurney. "You guys are keeping this place in business," the nurse muttered to me. I was grateful. The good nurses never panic about anything. If I had been carrying Juliet's severed leg in my hands, she would have made some joke about people who can't keep it together. From my perspective, it looked as if Juliet was gushing blood like an oil well, but the nurse asked if Juliet felt cold or was sleepy, and Juliet screamed "NO!"

The nurse grinned. "Good girl."

And then they were gone. Rob and I waited in the lounge, mindlessly consuming a bag of taco chips. After a while, my breathing evened. Rob took my hand and held it gently, and when I looked down, I perceived how we must have looked to the rest of the people in the room. We were filthy, caked with dust and streaked with dirt and blood (and taco chips)—and, *oh, right* wearing ski masks like terrorists or bank robbers. In that instant, we both pulled our ski masks off our heads, in unison, as if we were synchronized swimmers. I was going to suggest we either leave or wash up, when the same nurse appeared and told us that Juliet had been given some light sedation. A surgeon was about to stitch her leg.

"She asked for you, Allie," the nurse said.

I glanced at Rob. He shrugged. "Go ahead. I'll wait for you."

I followed the nurse down that familiar mint-green corridor. Juliet lay flat on her belly in an emergency cubicle, her father at her side, with layers of blankets over her arms and back. Only a grim section of her leg was exposed, a crooked nasty gash running from just above the back of her knee to her left butt cheek. I kneeled down by the foot of the table and patted her grimy sleeve.

"Leave for a minute, Dad, okay?" she whispered.

"I should wait for your mother, anyway," Officer Sirocco replied in a toneless voice. He shot me a stare that I couldn't read, and then pulled the curtain shut behind him and the nurse.

"I won't do it anymore," Juliet hissed at me between clenched teeth. "I promise, Allie. I'm afraid, and I won't do it anymore."

"Do what?"

"Any of it. I promise. Just be my friend and stay with me, no matter what."

I nodded. "I'll always do that, Juliet."

"No matter how it seems."

"Forever, Juliet." I swallowed. I felt sick. I wondered how I could have ever been scared of her. For the first time ever, I saw her as the victim she was.

"WE'RE PARANOID," ROB said as he drove me home. "No one could have put anything down that could have hurt her. Not while we were actually climbing. No one could have known she would fall."

I nodded. "That's true. I just feel weird. And I feel like our weirdness is spreading all over everything."

Rob drummed the steering wheel. "Do you want me to take you home?"

"No," I said. "I want to stay out. And up. With you."

We ended up back at Watching Rock. All we found on the rock where Juliet was cut was a sharp tab from a soda can, wedged into a crevice. We couldn't be sure anyone had put it there on purpose. That, and the mat we'd forgotten in the mad dash to get her to the hospital.

I'm still not sure what came over me. I mashed my lips against his almost as soon as we were out of the Jeep. He pressed against me. Seconds later we'd collapsed on top of the mat, and I caught a glimpse of the starry October night as I shut my eyes.

The first time we'd been together, there had been a rush, an urgency, a fumbling sort of frantic-ness that blotted out most of the memory of the actual event. Honestly, I didn't remember much except the pounding of my own heart and a vague hope that the contraception had worked. But tonight, after the initial hungry attack (mostly on my part) there was sweetness and slowness and tenderness that I knew I would remember as long as I had a memory. I had a fleeting thought that I finally understood the term "making love" because that's what it was: love in the purest sense, wishing someone else well, wanting him to have the best, your best and every best.

Afterward, I was conscious only of *his* heart pounding: a gentle drumbeat. I lay against his bare chest. Wrapped in the darkness and the filthy blankets, exhausted by the night's weird drama but still consumed by the closeness of Rob, *this boy,* my dream realized and tangled up in me in every way, my lids grew heavy. The last thing I remember was him mumbling something about setting his phone for four, so that we'd beat the early hikers and the sunrise.

WHEN MY EYELIDS first fluttered open, I thought that I was dreaming. The glare was intense. I half sat up, and was hauled back down by the blankets swaddling Rob and me.

"Rob, help! Oh shit! It's morning!"

Panic opened a vein of adrenaline in my lower belly. It was past sunrise: after seven, easily. Fingers trembling, I moved quickly to pull on my black turtleneck and pants and haul one of the blankets over my head, while Rob did the same. The times we'd been caught out unprotected in daytime were times we could count on one hand. The light itself was crackling, trippy; for a Daytimer, I imagine it would be like waking up underwater. We lowered ourselves to the ground, Rob grabbing his sunglasses out of his backpack. His disembodied voice struggled to keep me calm, insisting we would come back later for the mats; the important thing was to get into the car and home because our parents would have the cavalry out by now.

"Why didn't your phone work?" I gasped, crawling quickly toward the Jeep.

"Who knows? Don't worry about it. Get in and we'll get the blankets up on the windows." His exposed fingers slithered up to the door handle. The car was locked, the keys visible in the ignition, my backpack with my own phone visible on the seat.

"Did you lock it?" he hissed, feverish.

"No! Obviously. No way."

"Get under the car," he commanded. "Just lie still."

Before I could protest, he shoved me under the car and scrambled under after me. Fortunately, the Jeep had a high carriage and plenty of room. He snatched up his phone and scowled. "Well, that explains it. The battery's dead. We just have to wait."

"Jesus." I fought to keep from squirming. Joggers or hikers would probably come by. It was a beautiful October morning in a popular park.

"Holy shit," Rob said.

"What?"

"My battery isn't dead, it's gone. Somebody must have messed with it at the hospital, or . . . maybe while we were sleeping? You didn't—"

"I fell asleep!" I rolled over so I was facing him. In the shadows, his red-rimmed eyes looked as frightened as mine must have. "Who came last night? Who saw us?"

"Allie, you have to tell me everything. I know you and Juliet made some kind of pact, but something happened while we were asleep."

I couldn't keep it bottled up inside any longer. It wasn't

fair to Rob, either. And so I told him everything. I started with the trap door in the lawn outside Tabor Oaks, and the text I received. I told him how I called the police. I told him about Juliet's tattoo, and the hair-twin Tabor cousins, and how I suspected Nicola's death wasn't an accident after all . . . and now this.

Helpless, we lay under the Jeep, holding hands and praying. It seemed as if hours passed, but maybe it was only minutes until we heard a sound. Voices approached, scuffling footsteps—and a tiny face suddenly appeared behind Rob's head.

A puzzled little girl, younger than Angela, said, "You are not supposed to play under the car." Then she stood.

Another pair of feet joined her, parallel to her tiny hiking books. "Dad, those big kids are playing under the car."

"Go over by Mom and Lacey," a man's voice stated. "Right now."

Rob loudly cleared his throat. "Sir, please," he called. "Please. I apologize, but I need your help. Just dial this number." Slowly, Rob recited his father's cell phone, one digit at a time. "My dad will answer. He will tell you that everything I'm going to say is true. My friend and I are under this car for a good reason. We have Xeroderma Pigmentosum. XP. It's a rare genetic—"

"Yes," the pair of hiking boots interrupted. "My name is Marty Brent. We're from Chicago. I'm here with my wife and kids. We're cycling, and I seem to have found your son." The man paused. The shoes shifted slightly from their shoulder-width stance. "Are you Rob Dorn?" he called down.

"Yes, I'm Rob and this is Alexis Kim. We can't come out from under here."

I stole a lightning fast peek, anyway. I saw the lady with

the little girl and the baby, and the bikes, and the molded plastic helmets, and restraining devices with rounded aluminum tubes, and thick mesh straps, and the saddle bags and backpacks and bottles. I remembered that I used to think that parents were selfish when they did things like this: stuffing kids into snowsuits to go sledding, or bundling them up in life jackets to go rafting, or saddling them up on mountain bikes. I thought they did it just to prove that even though they had kids, they didn't have to give up doing the things *they* loved.

Maybe it takes actual sunlight (mixed in with a corresponding dose of panic) to have a true *a-ha* moment. But only then did I truly get Jack-Jack. Parents—the good ones, anyway, never did anything for themselves if their kids were involved—no matter how weird or unfathomable. Jack-Jack stayed up knitting even though all she wanted was to sleep; Dennis Dorn, Rob's dad, collected NBA jackets for his son in every imaginable size and design; Tommy Sirocco kept Nothing Town safe in its Nothingness. But on top of that, they only wanted to be merchants of nostalgia, *for their kids' benefit*. Right now, Marty from Chicago was lamenting this strange turn of events. He was happy to help us, but he was pissed. He wouldn't be able to provide a fun experience his kids would look back on, even only in a photo, as a bright pin on the psychological map of devotion.

That was what it must mean to be a parent: the never-ending celebration of a bond, no matter how tenuous and fleeting. It was the sole reason parents made such a huge deal out of documenting everything and anything. And there was a paper doll chain of all those parents, from Rob's parents to Juliet's parents to my mother to Marty, joined together: a magic circle of protection around their kids, *anybody's* kids. But the circle wasn't magic. Nothing could protect their kids from the world.

Besides, we kids couldn't wait to bust through that paper-doll chain, ripping it to shreds on our way out.

"Your dad's coming," Marty said. "But he sent an ambulance. Don't object, I know. You probably think it's dumb. But he's worried, and I would be worried. They called the hospital and apparently your friend was already in there, and naturally your parents thought you were hurt when you didn't come home, before sunrise?"

"It's how you live, when you have XP," Rob said.

"I'm sorry," the guy said. "That's a bummer."

"Don't be sorry. We should be thanking *you*. We just got caught by the sunrise. We came out here to make a video for a friend," Rob finished awkwardly. "She had it way worse than we do."

Nicola.

Right. In theory, we'd come out here for her. I tried to justify how sick and ashamed I was by desperately thinking that my recent epiphany explained everything: *No, we weren't creating this video tribute (that never happened) for you, Nicola; we were creating it for YOU, Mrs. Burns, who tried to take your own life after learning you would never see your daughter again . . .* but that line of thinking only made me want to vomit. There was only one reason we were trapped under Rob's car right now. We'd only come out here for ourselves.

Rob shifted on his side in the gravel and rolled over so he was facing me again. A faint, sad grin played on his lips. "Allie, when we're older, we should open a night water park, completely lit with solar fixtures from below."

"Instant millions," I said. "In Las Vegas."

The sound of sirens whooped, at first far away. Then, there they were, the paramedics around the Jeep, debating what to do, at least for the two minutes it took Jackie to arrive in her all-terrain minivan.

"Why are you standing there?" Mom barked at the multitude of booted feet.

"We're assessing effective transport," a firefighter said.

"Use some of those tarps to make a canopy and give them both Hazmat equipment to put on while you get them to the hospital. That sun is lethal."

"We aren't carrying biohazard suits, ma'am."

"Give them turnout gear, then, ordinary fire suits and helmets."

My mother squatted down next to me and lifted the edge of the blanket "What the hell are you idiots thinking?"

"You're all heart, Jack-Jack."

"Is it the full moon? First, your poor friend Nicola, and now Juliet's in the hospital. There's been about a full decade of weirdness packed into these past few days. How do I explain this?"

"You mean, what will people say?"

"No, *Allie*. It's just you live almost seventeen years with a person and, suddenly, in one night, her best friend is in the hospital and she's trapped under a car with her boyfriend."

"Adolescence?" I offered.

Mom's face twisted into a grimace and disappeared. I felt Rob's fingers intertwine with mine. Then I closed my eyes and let the paramedics take over.

18

CONFESSION

CONFESSION

I was lying on a bed waiting for the okay to shower when Juliet appeared. She wheeled into my room, her leg extended on a padded board, a pole with an IV at her side.

"You have that syndrome that chronically sick kids get, like overdeveloped conscience syndrome," she announced.

"You made that up."

Juliet laughed. "I did. You have it though. You always feel like you're inconveniencing somebody."

"I am always inconveniencing somebody. I'm an inconvenient person."

"But you're not. We didn't ask to be born this way, Allie. The world owes you one. Not the other way around."

Bonnie came in and drew the curtain so that I could undress and shower. "Juliet, you need to leave. Jackie Kim's orders."

"Allie doesn't have anything I haven't seen," Juliet said.

"I'm sure she wants her privacy," Bonnie said.

"Actually, I'm fine if she stays," I said. "Tell my mom. It's cool."

"She's my best friend," Juliet added. "I saw her boobs before she had boobs. Not that she really has boobs now."

I swallowed, watching Bonnie's face soften as I remembered the first time Juliet and I got bras. It was one of the summers when she had a month or six weeks off from the hours and hours of gym work and indoor running that was necessary for ski jumping. My mother took both of us to the mall, at night. (We didn't have to wear full gear, just sunglasses, ball caps and long-sleeved shirts, so we looked only like lepers instead of aliens). Juliet wanted a push-up bra that wouldn't adapt to the style. *They're too far apart,* Juliet had told my mother. "*What's going to happen to me if they don't grow and they stay pointing different ways? I'm going to have to get one stick-on cup for each one.*" We ended up buying every conceivable bra, training and otherwise, just to be safe.

"I'll give you twenty minutes," Bonnie said.

I slipped out of my clothes and tossed Juliet her ski mask, which had been stuffed into my back pocket since last night. I gratefully spent the next twenty minutes rinsing the grime from my hair and teeth and every cleft and crevice of my body, before dousing myself with the hospital lotion that reminded me of home, since my mother used vats of the stuff. For me, it was like Vicks. Nicola told me once that when her older brother went to college and got a cold, rubbing Vicks on his chest for a cough made him homesick. . . .

I examined my scratched and blotchy face in the mirror. In my own home—in my own context—I never saw how truly pale people are who are never exposed to sunlight. My skin was perfect, but looked like the unblemished petal of a funeral-parlor lily. Blush might have helped, but there was no makeup called XP, for X-tra Pale. Searching that pale face, with its eyes in a state of perpetual alarm, I didn't even recognize the real Allie. I didn't know where she was. But the real Juliet was waiting outside. I pulled on my hospital pj's.

Afraid as she had been, how much could Juliet know now? Did she know that someone had screwed with Rob's phone?

I reentered the room, my burden of questions caged in the back of my throat, just as Rob waltzed in, waving a DVD. He wanted to make us whole again, or as whole as we three could be. I almost had to laugh. The DVD was "The Best of David Belle, Volumes I-III."

"Let's commence the theater portion of the entertainment, ladies," he said, cleaned up and looking normal except for the purple hollows under his eyes. "Allie, your doctor said we could hang for another couple of hours. . . ." He broke off, seeing Juliet's tight lips.

We were all on edge. Who wouldn't be? My mother was right about a full decade's tragic weirdness packed into less than a week. But also, we just weren't used to being awake during the day. It made everything feel strange.

"I have popcorn and ginger ale being delivered—although not beer, which my father frowned upon for some reason," he said. "Cheesy popcorn for you, Juliet, if you share."

He paused. "Can I see your wound?"

"That would involve seeing part of my ass, and that's off limits to mere mortal eyes," Juliet replied.

"Not what I hear," Rob said. "I've heard it's a staple of cyber-assity."

"If you let me keep all the cheesy popcorn, I'll show you," Juliet said.

"Juliet, I'd rather have the popcorn. I've seen your fabled ass covered and uncovered since you wore your big girl Huggies, and it's not one of the seven wonders of the ass-ential world."

"Rob, you wound me even more!" Juliet cried. "If there were an Iron Harbor Parade of Asses, it would be on it, at position one or two."

"What about Caitlin Murray?" Rob asked.

Together, Juliet and I said, "Seriously?"

Juliet added, "That ass has all the stability of, like, Nerf. . . ."

Then I ruined it. Maybe even on purpose. I wasn't sure. But I couldn't put on an act anymore. I said to Rob, "Did you get sunburned at all?"

He shook his head. Without a word, Juliet started wheeling past him. We both watched her disappear into the hall. "Wait," I whispered.

I jumped after Juliet and clamped my hand down on her shoulder.

"You're together," she said. "It was a dumb promise." She smiled, not stopping, and waved one hand. "No, Allie-Bear. It was dumb. When you care about someone, and you've done it, you can't just stop. It's fine. It lets me off the hook."

"No, Juliet. That's not it. It's way more important that I talk to you than him."

I ran back to the room where Rob was now greeting his dad, displaying the DVD and assessing the bags of junk food. "Rob, I have to talk to her for a while," I informed him. "I'm sorry. I'm sorry, Mr. Dorn. I mean, Dennis."

Rob nodded. "I get it. Come on, Dad. We'll go to my room. The view's better. My sun-block shade has graffiti."

The four of us laughed uncomfortably. Rob's dad, looking far older than his fifty-something years, closed the door behind them.

I turned to Juliet and sat on the bed. "We're alone. We have two hours."

"I have to tell you things you don't want to know," Juliet said. Her ski mask still lay perched on her extended leg, seeming to mock me, us, the whole situation.

"I already know more than you think I do. I know about my mom's friend, Gina. And about the doctor, Lauren Wilenbrand."

Juliet's eyes bored into mine. "You see how that works?"

"What do you mean?"

"Dr. Andrew is Gina's boss. Dr. Andrew is Lauren Wilenbrand's boss. Gina is training for a certificate as a nurse practitioner in genetic disease. Lauren wants to be chief resident. Garrett's so good at this. He doesn't have to just keep secrets. He's the puppet master. He gets women to keep secrets for him. It's all to their advantage. Me, too." Juliet raised her own hospital scrubs, pointing to her tattoo on her belly. "I'm worried, Allie-Bear."

I nodded, suddenly thinking of Nicola again, suddenly angry. Afternoon sunshine threatened us from a tiny crack in the blackout shades. "In hospitals, this is the time most people die," I finally muttered.

"I thought they died just before morning," said Juliet.

"That's all night is, just before morning," I said. "People start dying right after dinner and they die all night."

"True enough," Juliet agreed.

"So you owe it to me to tell me everything. I'm not going to leave you. I just need to know. From the beginning."

Juliet wheeled herself over to the end of my bed and let out a deep breath. "First of all, those years when I was competing, they were years without rules," she began. "So I went from a life that was *only* rules to total freedom. Or as much freedom as I could have. My mom couldn't come with me every time. It cost too much. When she didn't, well, like everyone else, of course, she trusted Garrett. Before he was a coach, Garrett trained to be a nurse. No big shocker, he's a Tabor. But he's also an RN. Did you know that? Who better to manage your daughter and be sure about her cares and precautions?"

I couldn't answer. I couldn't even really focus on her specific words as she went on and on. She barreled right into their relationship. The first time they had sex, Juliet was fourteen and a half, in eighth grade. A year after we'd gone to buy our first bras, a year after she began having her periods. As she spoke, I wanted to give Penguin back and embrace them both. I wanted to hold her like the child she still was.

"No one knew what we did," she said. "Because of XP, I always had a private room, so that no one could jump up and open the drapes on some beautiful snow-blinding Utah slope. Garrett did a bed check every night. He was never intrusive, but nobody tried to stuff their beds with pillows and sneak out for beers. We were all too competitive."

It began with the massages he gave Juliet to keep her from cramping up. They simply grew longer and more intimate. Garrett made sure his suite always adjoined hers. What hotel wouldn't want to provide for the little wonder girl who gutted her way through the hills in the sky despite her grave skin disease? To the Juliet she was then, this was a love affair, the best way to break out of the prison built by our genes. What she was describing to me now was in fact the rape of a little girl. She didn't articulate it as such because he still had hooks in her. Juliet said that there was nothing between them sexually anymore, and there hadn't been for years. But he enticed her with freedom.

Later that fall, in November, Garrett Tabor planned to take a break from coaching and join Stephen and Andrew on a research mission in Bolivia. Now that Dr. Andrew's sons were both on staff, he could take a break for research, too, which was his real passion. Dr. Andrew was insanely certain that using retroviruses to implant normal DNA into our lousy DNA would basically get our genes to repair themselves. That's making a very long story very short. The most famous retrovirus is HIV, the one that causes AIDS. AIDS used to go so fast and just gallop through people and kill them because how quickly retroviruses mutate. You'd be treating one thing and the cells would change and you'd be facing another strain of virus. That's why something awful can turn out to be so useful. The retroviruses can cause cells to mutate *back* to the way they were before they changed into the light-sensitive mutation that causes XP. And then, all the new cells after that would be normal, at least theoretically. They could even do it on unborn babies.

They can do this with animal cells in the lab now, easy as peanut butter and jelly. Vets use this kind of treatment all the time for horses who rip ligaments racing or jumping. So the work Dr. Andrew and his brother and his son were doing with XP could someday, many generations from now, lead to a world with no sickle cell and no Huntington's disease and no cystic fibrosis, the killers of the young. When I thought of it in that way, I felt not like an experimental animal, but proud: a pioneer, like Juliet had made me with Parkour.

"Even if they can do that, and say they can, what about cancer?" Juliet said.

"You're going to get squamous cell cancer sometime in your life. That's the nature of the beast. Big deal," I said. Squamous cell skin cancer is gross and it leaves a scar where they remove the superficial skin, but it's not usually a lethal type of skin cancer. Some XP people have them all over. I've never had one. Rob had one, on his shoulder, despite his face getting all those huge blisters when he was a baby.

"I mean melanoma that goes all the way."

"If they get it early, like Rob, it's completely curable."

"But you'll get it again, somewhere else on your body."

"Juliet, you have to die of something!"

"Whatever." She turned her back to me and continued in her detached monotone. According to her, even Dr. Andrew wouldn't reveal the specifics of some genetic mutation among the children of certain families of one "tribe" in Bolivia. But it meant that, although they suffered the same symptoms of harm from sunlight as every other XP kid, they didn't develop melanoma. Finding a way to make XP a chronic illness was one giant leap in eradicating it. If people with XP could live the same way as people with diabetes or high blood pressure, they could have real lives.

Hearing all this, my heart thumped with excitement. But it also thumped with fear, because something else was clearly on her mind. That was when she dropped the bombshell: last October, Garrett had promised to take Juliet with him when he joined the research team. He promised to make her first among equals in the study—although, by virtue of being Dr. Andrew's patient, she'd have been in the first pool, anyhow.

That was how they reconnected.

"But weren't you going out with Henry LeBecque?" I asked.

That was a front, she explained. Besides, Garrett's father and his uncle would be there, safeguarding her.

I stared at her, not sure what to believe, not sure how much *she* believed. "You considered it? What about your parents?"

Juliet scoffed. "No! What works with them is: I don't bring anything up until the last minute. Then, they won't stop me. With this, I could say it's for credit, for college, or something. Besides, I can't tell anyone. Which means *you* can't tell anyone, either."

I chewed a nail. I wasn't sure how to respond to any of this. But she kept going.

In the past, Juliet's disappearances, her sabbaticals, her so-called "periods of reflection" had all been stolen time she spent holed up with Garrett. Sometimes, she even used the all-purpose, fail-safe excuse; she said that she was with me. I felt sicker and sicker. Was I suddenly her therapist? It was a job I didn't want. But I listened anyway: to tales of Juliet and Garrett Tabor traveling to Minneapolis, sleeping in blackout rooms where waiters brought them caviar and champagne at midnight. These hotels, Juliet said, were frequented by foreign businessmen; the staff had a policy to avert its eyes from unusual couples. Tabor told the desk that Juliet was his daughter (Juliet was always swathed in expensive scarves and huge sunglasses); no one could have believed that a father shared a bed with his college-age child. So he was careful to get a double-king room. Even then, the relationship had been much more than sex: *One Thousand and One Arabian Nights* in reverse, with a harem of one. Garrett told Juliet of cities, like Las Vegas (which might as well be Jupiter to Juliet and me) where lives were lived on the reverse clock, like our own lives. They could be happy there, together—

"What about the women his own age?" I finally shouted. "What about the Daytimers? Like Dr. Wilenbrand. Like Gina—"

"I know about them," she interrupted. "They're a front

for the sake of his family. Like Henry was for me. Don't you see that? We had to keep up appearances."

"What about your *dad*?" I said. "How could he not know?"

"He sees what he wants to see. When it comes to me, he's no detective. He sees you. He sees Rob. He sees how you have my back. He sees our cozy little world of three, doing crazy stunts at night, but never getting into any real trouble."

My jaw clenched. Jack-Jack was right again. People do see what they want to see.

"I haven't been with him that way in a long time, I swear. But I can't give him up. I told you the truth." She sighed, that defeated adult-stranger sigh I'd gotten used to hearing. "He's Garrett Tabor. And I was a kid. He treated me like an adult. He treated me like an equal. Also, it was like being with a genie. You made a wish for an escape, and there it was."

"What about what we saw at Tabor Oaks?" I demanded.

"We only saw him once, Allie-Bear. I'm not sure what you saw that other night. And I've been over it with him. He made a bad choice. He picked up some woman in Duluth and brought her back to his dad's apartment. He was lonely. He was confused. He swore it was a one-time thing. . . . But still, you're right. There's too much. I mean . . . Nicola Burns. No one will ever forget that. It changes everything, forever. It made me start to think about my life, and my mother, and what I've done to them that they don't even know about. I was only fourteen, Allie."

"But now you're almost seventeen."

"And then maybe I can be with him. You know, legally. I mean, it happens. People used to get married when they were thirteen."

"Listen to yourself right now," I said.

We were silent.

"My leg hurts," Juliet said.

"I'll go find a nurse."

My head felt as if it were about to explode. I was grateful for the chance to bolt out the door, to stretch and jump and run in place, to punch the flat of my hand with my fist because I couldn't take a bat to the walls and the windows. Tabor. *Tabor. Tabor.* . . . The name was everywhere I looked. This hospital was called Divine Savior, but our wing was The Tabor Clinic. Our savior was Dr. Tabor, the founder.

"My friend Juliet is in pain," I told a nurse who was unfamiliar to me.

"Are you Jackie Kim's girl?"

"Yes. I'm Allie. And I don't know if you can give me some Tylenol? I don't know if it's in my orders. But I have such a headache, I'm afraid it's going to make me sick. . . ." Which it did. All of a sudden.

I ran to the nearest washroom.

Garrett Tabor had killed Nicola. I knew it as sure as if he'd pointed a gun at her and fired. Only *he* knew where that poor dark-haired girl was now, the girl he left stripped on the floor like a broken doll. He would have been happy to explain to Juliet how killing Rob and me would have been an accident.

I never got another chance to speak to Juliet alone that night. As it happened, I ended up getting a shot for my first migraine—orders from Dr. Lauren Wilenbrand—along with an order to lie with cold packs over my eyes for the rest of the afternoon.

ACCEPTANCE
ACCEPTANCE

When I got home from the hospital, I found my early admission acceptance letter from John Jay. Because of my bad genes and my good grades, I had even received a tiny scholarship: $4,000 per semester if I maintained a 3.0 GPA or higher. Apparently, mine was also the first letter they sent out. They really seemed to be chomping at the bit to accept me. I'd be starting in September, eleven months from now—but there was the option of starting in January, too. I decided, why not? All my classes were AP anyhow. I wrote to my advisor, Dr. Barry Yashida, to ask his advice.

Casually but elaborately, as I passed through the kitchen from the shower, I let the scholarship letter drop on the counter where my mom was chopping vegetables. When I came back out, fifteen minutes later, she was wiping her eyes with the back of her hand. Jackie Kim is not easy to tears.

"Onions?" I joked.

"No, age. Being old enough to have a college kid rocks my world."

"Time for that Ethiopian baby, huh, Jack-Jack?"

"Alexis," she said. Our eyes met. For the first time, my mother had acknowledged that I actually might go away at some time, live apart from her, have a life of my own. "I'm proud of you."

"I think my porcelain skin tone had something to do with it," I said.

"Stop!" She swept me into a hug. "Let me enjoy this moment."

"Okay," I said. I shut my eyes, letting myself enjoy the moment, too.

"I'm glad you're not going away right now, though."

"I know," I said, not quite agreeing. We turned our focus to the stir-fry.

Angie burst in with plans for her Halloween costume. Naturally, she was going to be David Belle, which meant she would look like a guy in a T-shirt. I texted Juliet and Rob, both of whom instantly texted back *LOL!!!!* and insisted on helping her prepare. And that set the tone for the next few weeks. The tres compadres, somehow united again.

IN A PERVERSE way, that build-up to Halloween was a sort of premonition of longing for the past, the kind I'd first understood trapped under the car with Rob. I'd spent so much time worrying about the future I'd rarely focused on the preciousness of *now*. I'd made a very conscious decision not to discuss Garrett Tabor with Juliet anymore until she was ready. And I let Rob know that I wanted to cool it a little on the intimacy front.

Naturally, he thought it was because I was scared of losing him when I went to John Jay next year. He was right, but it was more than that. I couldn't be with him until the

Garrett Tabor issue had resolved itself completely, until I knew for certain that Juliet would be all right. And Rob, being the person that he was, buried himself in creating a tribute video for Mrs. Burns in honor of Nicola, cobbled together from the existing footage that we had. He never heard if she received it; she never thanked him. But it didn't matter. She was alive. She was surviving, for now.

When the three of us were together at night with Angela, we were one again. Or at least we were one in playing our respective roles. But it was enough. All the annoying and hideous things that Angela did suddenly made me laugh. In them, I could see me and Juliet—one minute jumping out of trees, the next minute threatening to chop off her hair so she looked "more like the King of Parkour," and another minute talking back to Jack-Jack because Mom wouldn't allow her to trick-or-treat past ten at night.

The morning of October 31st, maybe an hour before dawn, Juliet reached into her pocket and handed me an old picture of us in our Halloween costumes: me as her penguin (yes, I loved her so much that I dressed as her stuffed animal) and Juliet wearing oversized ruby slippers, holding hands, knowing that trick-or-treating would be limited to a few homes who stayed up late just for us. Beneath it was a scribbled quote from Henry David Thoreau. *I have traveled a great deal in Concord.*

Juliet missed nothing; she just didn't tell everything she knew.

"Thanks," I murmured.

"Can I stay over?" she asked quickly. Angie and Mom had been asleep since midnight. Rob was pulling out of our driveway. I nodded.

She borrowed a pair of pj's. We slipped under the sheets, huddled on one side of my big bed, as we'd done hundreds of times before.

I waited for her to speak.

"That's really cool you got into college," she said. "I'm happy for you."

"Yeah . . . I've already started, in a way."

"What do you mean?"

"Reading," I said. "And writing. Just to get a head start. I might try to graduate in December. I have the credits."

I debated whether or not to tell her more. Although some assignments were ordinary, others were instantly fascinating and demanding. One instructed us on the fundamentals of criminal research, the ways that experts used field notes and different kinds of observation to tighten the loop on criminals. Another discussed the ways in which traditional constants of human nature and behavior, in the anthropological sense, were some of the most reliable tools in modern criminal investigation.

In the past two weeks, I'd learned one fundamental lesson: the world changed, technology changed, but people did not.

I discovered that I was born to love this discipline. Seriously. All I lacked was the ability to go outside. But my freshman-advisor-to-be, Professor Barry Yashida, even wrote me a personal note. Not every investigator works in an urban lab, he assured me. One of his students was confined to a wheelchair and a computer speaking board by cerebral palsy, and, though she never left the first floor of her house, she was a full-time, respected LAPD officer in their major crimes unit. I didn't think I would ever have that kind of future. But it was encouraging to hear. I would begin online in January.

Meanwhile, I learned more than I ever wanted to about serial killers, even after my brief summer research. For instance: Bellevue, Washington, seems be serial killer central.

You would probably find half the missing persons in America, there or at least their skulls. Also, until they fell apart, serial killers compartmentalized. In their "professional" lives, they took strays, prostitutes and addicts and homeless women and runaways: the earth's restless whose last known address was a street corner. Tony Costa, who cut up girls and buried them in the woods on Cape Cod, had at least two wives . . . and three kids. Charles Manson was expert at spotting needy throwaway girls. But for every rule there was also an exception. For instance, Ted Bundy was different: his victims weren't the lost. They were nurses and university students and school kids. He could look preppy and speak with intelligence. People trusted him.

People trusted Garrett Tabor, a doctor's son, an inspiration to young athletes.

I'd also started the readings for a psychology class that explored masculinity in American culture. They were drawn from fiction and non-fiction as well as scientific studies. Each text, in its own way, considered what it means to be an American man and how women and their thinking influenced the idea of maleness. One of the sections touched on sexual deviance, and the prevailing theories of why rape and sexual battery, or any kind of battery, had nothing to do with masculinity. Yet somehow they were almost exclusively an enterprise of men rather than women, and directed at women and children. Myths about the ways that a woman's behavior "provoked" men to sexual frenzy were just that, although the ardent sexualizing of pre-adolescent female children was no help. Most rape victims were not glamour queens. They were helpless or believing, friendless or unguarded.

One observation throughout the literature troubled me in

particular. Almost always, within twenty-four hours before a murder, something had happened to upset these predators. Some incident affected them profoundly and emotionally, the kind of thing that screws up your radar. If your ability to sense things that are out of whack is your greatest camouflage, then distress strips it away and exposes you. Preoccupied people are people at risk. They wreck their cars. They wreck their lives. And those who hunt predators know exactly how to spot them. . . .

"Allie-Bear?" Juliet prompted in the charged stillness. "You were saying?"

I forced a laugh. "Right. Like I was saying: college but not college. All the work and none of the perks. No gorgeous guys and sororities and that stuff. Not yet."

"You wouldn't do that shit if you could, Allie."

"But I want the chance to refuse."

"Why'd you choose geek college then?"

"Geek college?"

"Choose to go to school for four years to be a little lab mouse comparing two pubic hairs under a microscope?"

"Because it matters," I said. "Two hairs can mean the different between a bad guy getting caught or getting the chance to do it again."

Silence dropped like a stone between us.

"Promise me you'll never see him again, Juliet," I whispered.

"I . . . can't promise anything." She squeezed her eyes shut. "I know you could never understand. He wouldn't have gotten to you. You're different."

"I would have been too afraid. You've never been afraid."

"No, you have common sense. You do. All I've ever been afraid of is missing out on something. You know, of dying."

"Without ever having really lived," I finished. "Juliet,

you're living now. You're being brave to shut him out. Especially if he really is dangerous."

"My father's the sheriff," Juliet said, almost automatically.

"His father's the freaking medical examiner," I snapped back.

"Exactly," she said, her voice suddenly cold. "Who could be better at making every trace of somebody disappear?"

I stifled a gasp. Not for nothing was Juliet a detective's daughter. The idea of gentle Dr. Stephen, with his awkwardness and golf ties, colluding with his son in a girl's murder and the accidental death of a teenager, was so far beyond the level of possible that not even *I* could boulder up there. But maybe that was a mistake. Juliet always pushed farther. That was her strength.

For maybe another hour, I lay there until I noticed that Juliet's breathing had grown loud and steady. I pivoted to glance at her in the moonlight. She was asleep. Penguin was tucked between her right shoulder and her head. The G.T. tattoo poked out from beneath the bottom of her borrowed pajama shirt, gently rising and falling with her breath. Hatred like venom seeped outward from my stomach.

I won't let you hurt her anymore, I thought.

There was no way I could sleep, so I decided to text Rob. When I fumbled for the phone in my jeans, I saw that there was a text waiting for me. From BLOCKED.

Tonight, 11 P.M. Nicola Burns's grave. To clear the air. Just you. You're smart enough to keep this to yourself.

20

TROUBLED

TROUBLED

Funny: last Halloween, I'd visited the cemetery, too. Only then, I'd been the one pulling the strings, setting up the villain to pay for what he'd done to Juliet. Amazing that I'd even harbored such ill will toward Henry LeBecque. He may have been a weenie, but he was no monster. He was a lost and confused kid. He was even honest. Instead of pushing him into an open grave and giggling at the thought that he might have pissed himself, I should have been trying to repair his relationship with Juliet.

Nicola's grave was the freshest in the lot, of course. It already looked like one of those graves you see on the news: festooned with flowers (some wilted, some still blooming) and photos and empty bottles and other detritus of a life snuffed out, items that only assume value and meaning when one of their shared possessors is no longer there to possess. I kept spinning in circles, partially to keep warm, but partially so Garrett Tabor wouldn't be able to sneak up on me.

I wasn't all that scared, though. The whole night had been such a royal fiasco that I was too ashamed to be scared.

First, neither Angie nor my mother could figure out why I didn't want to go trick-or-treating with them. I feigned exhaustion (who wants to argue with an XP kid over *that*) and it helped that I'd had a fight with Rob. Or what they'd perceived as a fight.

As soon as the sun had safely set, he'd texted me that he wanted to show me a surprise. I told him I couldn't. Then he texted *SCREW THE SURPRISE* and sent a series of photos of the cabin up by Ghost Lake. He and his dad had renovated it. I got the full-on real estate section treatment, a slideshow tour of our new romantic getaway: new glass windows, a little electric generator for lights and heat, a queen-sized bunk built from natural logs into one wall, piled with a thick mattress and pillows and a gigantic patchwork quilt. There was a log table, stools and shelves that held canned foods and candles. And of course, workout equipment for Parkour.

We were only seventeen. Rob's dad had helped his son create a place of our own.

First I burst into tears. Then I called him and told him I had a mission, just tonight, but that I loved him and our cabin like crazy. He asked if it had anything to do with Juliet. I told him I couldn't tell him. "So it does," he said.

Only then did I notice Angie and Mom standing at the bottom of the stairs, Angie all decked out like David Belle— which just made me cry again. Whatever. The (feigned, or not) adolescent freak-out had done its job. Everybody left me alone, and I was able to sneak off in the minivan.

I glanced at my phone, half-praying Rob would call. Or my mom. Or Juliet. It was already 11:15. Maybe. . . .

My ears perked up. There was a distant rustle in the

cemetery's blanket of autumn leaves. A moment later, he swept into view. He didn't look remotely threatening. He simply plodded with his head down, his hands jammed in his coat pockets, his icy breath producing little moonlit clouds.

Crunch, crunch, crunch went his boots. I thought of the tide. *Now? Now?*

"Thanks for coming, Allie," he said, keeping his distance.

I nodded. It was the first time I'd heard him speak. His voice was measured, slightly more high-pitched than his relatives, but resonant. Even at night, I could see now that he was not an exact clone of his cousin, Tim Tabor. His face was thinner, almost gaunt. His shoulders were broader. His hair was more closely cropped.

"What do you want?" I demanded.

"For starters, I want you to know that I didn't hurt Nicola. I feel terrible about it. I feel terrible about what happened to you and your friend back in Duluth. I was joyriding. I'm a nurse, Allie. I should have stopped and checked on you. . . . That was just stupid. I just didn't want you to drive Juliet away from me."

I'd planned for a quick getaway. My anxiety fueled my focus, just like in Parkour. My mom's minivan was parked at the opposite end of the cemetery, at the back entrance. He'd come the way I'd expected, through the front, which meant that if I suddenly turned and ran, it was a straight shot past Nicola's grave and downhill and to my car. I'd even prepared a note on my computer, so that if anything happened to me, Juliet's dad would find it. Worst case: I would phone Officer Sirocco if I had to escape. His number was cued up. It was just a matter of touching the screen.

"I don't believe you," I forced myself to answer. "I saw what you did at the apartment. I saw those girls!"

"There's only one girl, Allie, and you can see her any-time you like. She lives in Burnt Bluff. I can call her and you can talk to her." He reached into his pocket (I flinched) and extended his phone. He clicked the speaker button. I could hear a ring tone.

Then a woman's voice: "Gary? Is that you?"

"What does that prove?" I shouted.

Garrett Tabor whispered, "I'll call you later, sweetie," then shut the phone.

"That could be Gina. Or Dr. Wilenbrand. That could be anyone but Juliet."

He sat down on a stone bench. Slowly, he ran his fin-gers through his hair and seemed to massage his forehead. "I don't expect you to understand. I love her."

"Her? The woman you just called sweetie?"

"Juliet."

"You *love* her? You're old enough to be her father. You tried to ruin her. You tried to make her into your own per-sonal slave. Like that woman you just called."

His face changed then, like ice melting in a hot pan. All the fake sincerity slipped and there again was the empty face behind the balcony glass. I backed towards Nicola's grave. My fingers moistened. The phone slipped to the bottom of my pocket. "I'm . . . I'm going to be a criminal justice student," I said, and the words sounded ridiculous in my own ears. "I know about hair and fiber evidence and other evidence, too."

He smiled and stood. "That's great. So do I. Raised on it, you could say. But we weren't talking about a crime, because none has been committed."

"You stole the battery from Rob's phone," I said. I forced myself to meet his unreadable gaze. "You stalked two kids and jeopardized their lives."

"You can believe all you want to believe, Allie," he said. His voice remained a polite monotone, a stark contrast to my scratchy quaver. "But no one is supposed to use a public park as a private playgound."

I shuddered. *My God. He really was there. He really did do it.*

Without thinking, I whirled and sprinted toward the minivan. He was faster than I imagined he would be, but he gave up the chase fast. He was smart, no doubt about it. I was sweating as I vaulted over graves and sidestepped tombs. In seconds, I was at the back lot, the minivan eerily vulnerable there in the gravel, alone. My fingers shook nearly uncontrollably. I pressed the unlock button and slammed the door shut and jammed the key in the ignition and struggled to *start the goddamn car—*

I held my breath. He was probably revving up his own car right now. I had to get home. I had to put distance between him and me. I jammed my foot on the gas. At the mouth of the highway, I stopped, forcing myself to breathe again. Checking to make sure that I had enough gas and that the doors of the car were all locked, I heard a car motor. *Shit.* His headlights swept through the trees.

As I swung out onto the highway, only three miles from my own driveway, the Alfa Romeo fishtailed out from the path behind me

What if I led Garrett Tabor to my house, where Angela and my mother were getting ready for bed? Now was the time to call Juliet's dad. Why hadn't I called him earlier? When I frantically snatched for my phone, it bobbled in my hand and it dropped to the passenger seat, vanishing on the floorboards. *Stupid, stupid, stupid. . . .* The headlights bore down upon me in my rearview.

No choice but to gun for downtown and scream for help. Then I saw a light. Of course. *Thank God.* Gitchee Pizza.

Throwing the car into park, I leaped out, and grabbed the handle of the glass door, shouting, "Gideon!"

The doors were locked.

The red convertible screeched to a halt beside me. Garrett Tabor jumped out. I ran down the alley for the fire escape, muscling up onto the lower rung and tucking my feet as he lunged for my legs. I darted up the ladder to the roof. If only I had my headlamp. . . .

I winced. There was a piercing staccato explosion. Then I froze, my legs turning to jelly. I knew that sound. It was a shotgun blast.

It reverberated throughout the darkened streets and buildings. Well. Apparently I really *hadn't* learned that much from my brief foray into the minds of serial killers. Garrett Tabor was going to defy expectation. He planned to dispose of a victim with a shooting. Which meant I wouldn't die at the age of thirty after my toxic skin finally gave up on me; I'd die at the hands of a monster on the very roof where I last remembered having real, honest fun with my two best friends.

"Get the hell off my property," Gideon's voice yelled.

Falling to my knees, I peered over the edge of the roof. Barely visible at the mouth of the alley was Gideon Brave Bear. He swayed slightly but lowered his barrel towards the bottom of the ladder, where Tabor had dropped himself. Gideon cocked the gun a second time. My shaky lips formed a smile.

"There's a girl up there on the roof," Tabor said urgently. "I don't know what she's trying to do."

"None of your goddamned business," Gideon said calmly.

"She's a teenager. She's troubled."

"Allie?" Gideon called. "You troubled?"

"Yes!" I shrieked in relief. "I mean, no! I mean, I'm *in* trouble!"

"Not anymore. This guy is leaving now." He lurched forward and raised the shotgun to his eyes, squinting down the barrel. "Aren't you, friend?"

Tabor stared back at Gideon. Then he chuckled. With a glance up at me, as amused as it was menacing, he shrugged and marched out of the alley, sidestepping Gideon and slid into his car. "Well, she's your problem now."

"Always has been." Gideon kept his wavering sights trained on the Alfa Romeo until it disappeared around the corner.

Only long after the engine had faded completely, only after the other familiar night sounds had settled over Gitchee Pizza . . . actually, to be completely honest, only after I heard the loon was I able to muster the strength to leave the roof.

I scrambled down the ladder and rushed into Gideon's thick arms. I held him tight. The shotgun clattered at his side. He stank of whiskey and cigarettes and garlic. No combination of awful had ever smelled better. I'm not even sure how long I clung to him, but he finally had to extricate me. "Feel like a slice on the house?" he slurred.

I stood on my tiptoes and pecked him on the cheek. "Rain check," I murmured.

Before he could protest, I scurried for the minivan.

"Thank you, Gideon!" I shouted as I slammed the door. I couldn't make eye contact; if I did, I might cry. Instead, I drove. I made sure I was halfway home before I dug for my phone. I couldn't explain the situation to Gideon, but I didn't want to endanger him in case Garrett Tabor did decide to return with his own gun. I hopped out and threw open the passenger door side, digging under the chair like a squirrel. When I finally found the phone, I realized my eyes were bleary. But it was only 12:05.

I had three texts waiting.

From Rob, at 11:25: *Can we talk? Is Juliet w/ u? Can't find her.*

From Juliet, at 11:59: *Meet me at Lost Warrior Bridge at 2 A.M. Don't tell anyone but Rob. Need to trace. Will explain. xoxo*

From BLOCKED, at 12:01: *Don't worry, Allie. The wait is almost over. I'm gone as of tomorrow. Forget about me and everything you think you know.*

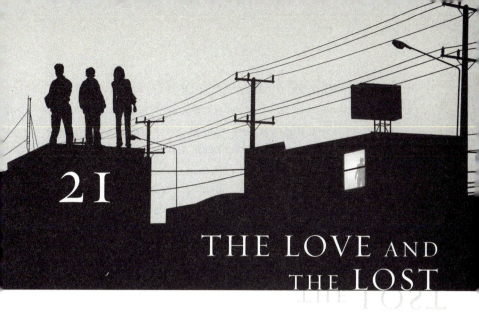

21

THE LOVE AND THE LOST

Rob was waiting for me at Lost Warrior Bridge. Juliet must have texted him, too. It was 1:47. He didn't say a word, just hugged me close.

Lost Warrior Bridge was, in fact, a recreation of something that archaeologists claimed dated back a thousand years. Back to the time of Gideon's forefathers. Apparently the original bridge had also been built of logs drilled at both ends and joined with thick strands of rope, the ends knotted and crisped under flame to hold fast. It was supposed to be a sacred place, like a museum. But Daytimers still jumped on it and wore it away further, despite its antique beauty.

I'd never actually stood on Lost Warrior Bridge. It was a good hour from Iron Harbor in the opposite direction of Duluth, and the prospect of driving so far to see a bridge recreation (closed to the public at night) was always met with quick dismissal from Jack-Jack. But for some reason the way people treated it had always rubbed me wrong, the way they were so dismissive of history. When I first realized I was falling in love with Rob, he'd asked me, "Do you really think the fake bridge was built to last forever, Allie? The kids who mess with it are part of history, too. For all we know, the original bridge was fake. It might have been a tourist attraction for the Gitchee Tribe."

He was right. For all we knew, everything was fake. The passage of time stamps a label of authenticity on even the worst bullshit. "History is written by the victors," Winston Churchill is said to have claimed in his fight against the Nazis—and only now did I understand why Professor Barry Yashida had chosen to include that quote in my pre-John Jay literature. Winston Churchill could have been speaking about criminals who get away with it. If he'd even actually *said* it. Even that was subject to debate.

Rob stepped away from me and jabbed his finger at his phone. Then he held the screen up to my face. I found myself watching a taped news segment about the imminent departure of the Tabor XP Research mission to Bolivia.

First there was a wide shot of crates full of sunglasses and gear and the wacky sun blocker some people wear because they just want to experience walking down a beach, even if it's with an umbrella and a ski mask on. All winter, the Tabor XP team would not only perform surgical excisions, but collect tissue samples from those few who managed to outlive the condition, if not outrun all of its complications. Dr. Stephen would be absent from his duties only for a few weeks, but Dr. Andrew and his nephew, "a nurse, Garrett Tabor," would be there the whole time.

The newscaster finished with, "They're leaving first thing tomorrow, November first. We wish them all well."

Rob shoved the phone back into his pocket.

A car was coming. Before he could speak, Juliet pulled up

and leapt out. She wore the bodysuit with the blue glow-in-the-dark stars on it, our original Dark Stars uniform, faded now from too many spin cycles in the washer.

"I need to do this, okay?" she began. "And I need to go first. Plus, it'll be a great trace. The last one of our year."

She outlined the plan: to leap from the exterior platform of the bridge to the bank beyond. A sign warned that the suspension wires were electrified but, like most warnings in our county, its expiration date probably preceded our actual birth date. Nobody had been electrified here, ever. It was a long jump, more than fifteen feet. But the angle was downward, and if you missed, it only meant hitting deep water after a drop of no more than twenty feet. The current was fast, but not too fast for us. If it did catch us, we'd be swept towards Lake Superior.

Juliet began to stretch. She took deep breaths.

The wide stretch of flat beach where she would make her landing, where we would all make it, was plainly visible in the moonlight. My thoughts were racing too fast to ask Juliet why we were doing this particular thing. Was it because she planned to leave with Garrett in the morning? On the sole basis of wanting to trace, it seemed to be very un-Parkour, without reason or destination: just a show-off way to pass time.

"Here I go!" Juliet cried.

She scaled the bridge railing and balanced there. Then she deftly whipped her long blond mane into a hair band. It was all off, and at the same time awfully familiar. She stood poised, her legs bent, her headlamp forward. I opened my mouth to shout for her to wait, but she paused before I could utter a peep. She shimmied back down through the cables and planks.

"Tribe," she said.

Rob and I glanced at each other.

"*Tribe,*" she insisted.

We all touched fists, the way we did when we first began last spring, just a few months ago, but so much longer. She put her hand on the back of my head and said, "I love you, Bear."

"I love you, too. What's wrong?"

"Nothing. I just think people should say that."

"Me too."

"I'm proud of you being in college. I'm proud of how you think you really can stop bad people."

"Juliet—"

"Maybe you can't stop them until after they do what they do, but you can stop them. *You* can. You're going to college for it! Rob, aren't you proud of our girl?"

"I haven't even started," I muttered. "Why am I getting the graduation speech right now?"

"It's not a graduation speech. If I were giving a graduation speech I'd say that everybody dies, but what the hell? Been said." She nodded towards Rob. "Please give this man a big smoochella."

"You give him a kiss yourself. What the hell is going on?" Uneasy, unidentifiable thoughts were smacking against my mind fast as bugs on a windshield. "Juliet, I don't like any of this. If you're planning something, you need to tell us now."

But she was already up and in her stance. Then she leapt. This time her stars truly were dark; I could only see her silhouette. I heard her land solidly, well past the lip of the beach. It was so dark over there that I could barely make out her shape—but it was in motion.

"Juliet?" I called feebly.

"Get out of the way!" Rob shouted after her. "I'm coming, too!"

There was no answer.

"The woman of mystery," Rob muttered as he prepared for his jump. We heard a hard splash. I caught a glimpse of something big and light-colored hitting the water in front of the beach. There was another splash, upstream. Then there was a scream.

"Juliet!" Rob shouted.

A light seemed to shimmy far back among the river birches, followed by a snap of wood and a crunching sound. Without a word between us, Rob and I ran for the Jeep and sped towards the real man-made bridge, brights on, searching for the first road that would take us to the beach. Excruciating seconds crawled past as we screeched down a gravel road. What if she had fallen after she landed and hit her head? Tripped over a root and rolled into the water? Why hadn't we scouted the place, as Parkour and good sense dictated? The current was fast. Was she unconscious?

When we could drive no further, Rob and I jumped out and scrambled down a steep, well-worn track to the spot where Juliet had landed. With his Maglite, Rob swept the shore. There were the prints of the soles of Juliet's new La Sportiva shoes, along with a deep pattern in the gritty sand, as though something had been rolled to the water.

Like fools, we screamed her name. Miraculously, for the first time in all the years we'd been outside at night screaming, we actually woke someone up.

A grizzled man in longies and a flannel shirt came crashing through the brush. "Are you kids drunk? People are asleep up there!"

"My friend jumped off the bridge!"

"Holy shit," the guy said. "Well, why are you screaming? Call 911!"

TOMMY SIROCCO WAS the first to arrive, accompanied by Mike Beaufort. Tommy pulled Rob and me aside as Mike investigated the beach. He wanted to know "everything."

We knew what he meant.

And as he listened to everything that Rob and I had to say—about the girl in the apartment and the near miss at the parking garage, and Tabor chasing me through the cemetery, Juliet's father's face looked like it was aging in fast-forward . . . his skin loosening as though moments were years, until it hung slack, too big for his face, drawn down by anguish and time. Finally he reached for his pen and pad. Other cops began to arrive. While the officers and the fire and rescue units set up lights, Tommy carefully wrote everything down.

Still, taken all together, I knew what we'd told him added up to a story that proved nothing at all. That was because I'd left out the crucial element. I didn't tell him or Rob about the real relationship between Juliet and her former coach. I chalked it up to a "crush." The word sounded even more pathetic spoken out loud than it did as an excuse in my brain. *Crush?* It didn't matter to Juliet's dad, though. He got it. The fact of Garrett Tabor trying to influence Juliet to run off was enough.

"Why did you let her do it?" Tommy said finally.

I felt sick. "They're not leaving until tomorrow," I insisted. "I mean . . . today. This morning."

He shrugged. "There's nothing we can do. To stop a plane from taking off, you have to get passenger manifests from airlines. You have to be able to prove somebody's involved with something. It would take more than Gideon taking a pot shot at someone who was ostensibly trying to help you." He studied my face. "Do you know more about this than you're saying?"

I shook my head. My stomach squeezed.

"You suspected something before. And you didn't tell me before now?"

"I thought it was over or I would have," I pleaded, tears stinging my eyes.

Tommy steeled himself and sighed. "Allie, please forgive me. I know you couldn't have stopped her."

"How do you know?" I said, through tears.

"Because I never could," Tommy said.

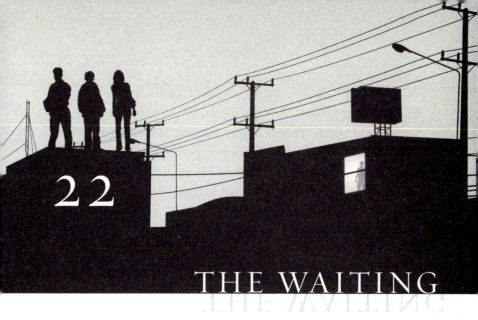

22

THE WAITING

Three days passed in a surreal blur. I spent every night alone in my bedroom, texting with Rob as he watched the same news stories unfold. First, dog handlers brought huge Saint Bernards and bloodhounds, tracking dogs, cadaver dogs. The dogs circled the place where Juliet had landed. So the firefighters and deputy sheriffs began to dig into the sand. They dug down to rock, a depth of more than three feet. They found nothing at all. Not a fiber, not a shoe, not a water bottle . . . not a trace.

Officially, the search of the river now was a recovery instead of a rescue. I refused to believe it, or acknowledge what that implied. Juliet had vanished for a reason. She hadn't ended it all.

Then the call came. The police wanted me for questioning.

IT WAS COUCHED as "a chat." My mother needed to be present, as I was a minor. Naturally, the "chat" would occur at night, to ensure my comfort and safety. I wouldn't be talking to Officer Sirocco, either. I'd be talking to another detective, Deputy Sheriff Sonny Larsen. She was built like a linebacker (six feet tall, all muscle, with blazing blond hair), and had the gruff voice to match. From Deputy Chief Larsen, I learned that Garrett Tabor had received an invitation too.

"He'll be joining us momentarily," she said as she showed my mom and me into a concrete block waiting room, well-stocked with magazines describing weddings of celebrities who had been divorced for years. From behind the room's only other door (closed), I heard a voice I recognized too well, but couldn't make out the words. Garrett Tabor didn't sound stressed at all, though. He sounded calm.

A few moments later, Deputy Chief Larsen reappeared. "Hello, Miss Kim," she said. She nodded towards my mother. "Mrs. Kim."

"What's Sonny short for?" I asked.

"Sonny," Deputy Chief Larsen answered, without humor.

"Did your dad want a boy? Or did he think you were very optimistic?"

"I'm sorry?" she asked, turning her beady eyes on me.

My mother swatted my arm. "Alexis, stop."

"I mean sunny. Like the sun. Optimistic. Did your dad think that?"

"You'd have to ask him," Officer Larsen replied.

Are you alive? I wanted to ask. *Or battery-operated?* She asked me for a rundown of the night Juliet disappeared. I told her about Parkour. She asked me to elaborate on our plans (illegal, she pointed out) to jump the bridge to the bank. I gave her a timeline. She asked me about Juliet Sirocco and how I knew her. I described our friendship and its duration. I also added that I had a written statement.

I didn't add that what I added next I'd learned from John Jay: as soon as the police call came, I detailed every moment of my very unpleasant encounter with Garrett Tabor at the cemetery, including the mysterious texts. Now that my mother knew everything, she was as outraged and terrified as I was.

Deputy Larsen examined my statement for several long minutes. She read it once, twice, three times. Then she glanced up. "Thank you for being so very thorough. Now, I think you and your mother and Mr. Tabor owe each other a conversation." She stood and knocked softly on the door that adjoined the two offices. "You can come in now, Garrett. Sorry to keep you waiting."

"I'd rather talk to Allie alone," Garrett replied.

My mother shook her head furiously. But I gripped her arm. "It's fine, Mom. We're in a police station. Nothing bad can happen."

"Alexis Kim—"

"Trust me, okay?" I whispered. "You know how you hate the word 'conventional'? Well, this is not a conventional situation. You understand?"

She nodded, seeing through my skull. He'd be less guarded if I were alone. He'd try to threaten me if it were just us and the police, somehow in some subtle way, even though he knew he'd be observed the entire time. He might even crack.

"Fine," Mom said. She shot the cop a cold stare and headed back out to the waiting room. Deputy Larsen closed the door, and the other flew open.

Garrett Tabor looked surprisingly well-rested for some-one who had just flown to and then flown back from Bolivia. He was even wearing a suit. Black: for fake mourning. "Hello Allie. I'm sorry you're going through this," he said.

Really? I almost laughed. He'd chosen the lamest possible script. I said nothing. I stared at Deputy Chief Larsen.

"I have nothing to say to this man," I announced. "You can read my statement. If anything is wrong, I'll point it out."

So she did. She read it aloud. "The witness is Alexis Lin Kim, age seventeen, a resident of 1814 Oxford Street in Iron Harbor, Minnesota. The witness swears to a close relationship with the missing woman, Juliet Lee Sirocco, age seventeen, whom she has known since they were four years old. On October 31st, the witness, responding to an unidentified text, arrived at the Torch Mountain Cemetery. . . ." Deputy Chief Larsen didn't even look at me. She read on and on, for at least five minutes: about the chase, Gideon and the gun, about Juliet and Rob, and finally about Juliet's disappearance at Lost Warrior Bridge—all concise, incident-by-incident reportage.

"Are those the observations you want to present here today in this interview?" she concluded.

"More or less," I said.

"Which is it?" she asked. "More or less?"

I felt like Alice in Wonderland. "It's accurate!" I said, too loudly.

She glanced at Tabor, who nodded. "I have a statement I've prepared too, with my lawyer," he said, pulling an envelope from his inside jacket pocket. "I've detailed the chronology of my relationship with Juliet Sirocco as her athletic coach, and later as a friend and mentor in whom she confided. Juliet was a spirited young woman and the kind of competitor any coach values. But she was also deeply troubled."

Troubled. I sneered. The same BS he'd tried on Gideon. "She was deeply troubled because you got your hands on her," I said.

"Please, Miss Kim," said the deputy chief. "Would you like your mother?"

I shook my head. "I don't need her to call him on his lies."

"I'd be happy to take a lie-detector test," Garrett Tabor concluded. "I want this all cleared up."

They made a date.

I ran back out to the waiting room and hugged my mother.

Later I heard he passed with honors. Sociopaths recognize when people like them. They *believe* that people like them. And people really do like them. That sole truth turns every other twisted lie into a truth that sociopaths can live with, and that they believe, too. Everything else is just smoke from a distant fire.

WHEN WE GOT home, at exactly midnight, Rob called and breathlessly told us to turn on the evening news. Mom and I sat in horror with Mrs. Staples, who'd babysat sleeping Angie. The three of us found ourselves watching shaky footage of what at first looked like a snuffed-out campfire. I squinted at burned remnants of some dark clothing and the soles of barefoot track shoes. Then the reporter spoke. "Empty of cash or credit cards was a wallet with a driver's license issued the previous year to Juliet Lee Sirocco. . . ."

I tuned out his voice after that, but the information seeped through. There was no trace of her. But everything in the charred pile had belonged to Juliet, including horribly, two of her eight ringlethingles.

"The Tabor family is offering a fifty thousand dollar reward to anyone who finds her," the reporter concluded.

The pieces of the puzzle slid into place. They did not fit precisely, but just enough. Juliet had known what Tabor could do, what he *would* do if he didn't get what he wanted. I knew he'd tried begging. I knew he'd tried bribery. I would bet he'd finally tried threats. That night at the bridge, all those final things she said, they made sense.

Juliet had given Garrett Tabor what he wanted most of all—herself—in exchange for something she loved dearly.

Me.

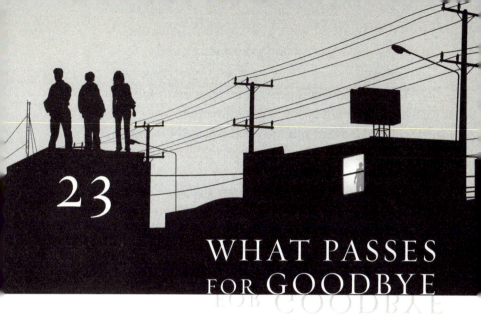

23

WHAT PASSES
FOR GOODBYE

The letter, addressed to Sherriff Thomas Sirocco, arrived four days into the search. He insisted on bringing it to me that night at 1 A.M. Not too late for a Daytimer, but right on track for the XP community. I knew he wasn't acting as a cop, but as a father. That's all he could ever be to Juliet, even now.

At our door, Tommy still looked like the dead version of himself. He hadn't even bothered to dress in his Sherriff's uniform. He wore loose-fitting jeans, a hat, and an overcoat. It was only 28 degrees out. He gave my mother and me a quick hug and then sat at our kitchen table. My eyes narrowed as he slipped on plastic gloves to remove the letter from his pocket. The envelope was postmarked Illinois. "O'Hare Airport zip code," he muttered. "International flight hub."

He flattened the paper on the table. I glanced at my mother.

"Should I touch it?" I said.

"It just means your fingerprints will be on it," he said.

"You're no longer a person of interest with Juliet, but we are. The parents always are. You know that."

I nodded and squinted at the piece of stationery.

Dearest Dad,

I want you to know that I'm okay. I realize how much this is hurting you. You know that causing you pain isn't at all what I intend. I've told you for years that this was a possibility. Now it is a reality. Don't bother to look for me. Don't send police to any of those old hotels. I won't be there.

But I am okay.

I am taking care of myself and I am staying out of dangerous situations. I'm not alone and I'm very happy to see how the other half lives, if you know what I mean.

I love you and miss you and Mom terribly. I always will. I will stay in touch with you, as long as no one tries to find me. If someone tries to find me, I will disappear.

It's important for me that I have this time on my own. It may be the only time in my life I have to really live my life normally. Live once!

So try not to worry. I'm sorry I didn't get to tell you before I left.

Please tell Alexis not to worry, either. Tell her I'm thinking about her.

Love,
Juliet

I frowned and looked up. "This isn't real."

"What makes you say that?" he demanded. I could tell

he wanted it to be real. He wanted it to be an answer. If Juliet was alive somewhere, and if he and his wife had enough patience, they would see her again. Piercing the fragile bubble of hope, the only place he could breathe, was almost more than I could bear. Parenting really is a paper doll chain. And Juliet had set it on fire a long time ago.

"You know, don't you?" I asked.

"I think some things about it are hinky."

"Which things?" I pressed. I wanted him to answer, more than I'd even known.

"You tell me, just for argument's sake," he said.

I turned back to the paper. The old familiar golf ball appeared in my throat, making it difficult to speak. "The only people who call me 'Alexis' are my mother when she's mad, and people who don't know me. You know, like school administrators. Everybody in the hospital calls me Allie. I bet even Nicola didn't know my real first name. My email address is Allie-dot-Kim."

He nodded. "Go on."

"But it's not that. The biggest thing is that she didn't mention Rob once. Rob is a part of us. If this was a real letter, she'd tell you to tell Rob everything she told me, and to tell you that she was thinking of him, too."

My mom began to cry. Tommy glanced at her, then at me. He swallowed several times, staring at the ceiling. He was fighting hard not to cry himself.

"Allie, I've never said this . . . but I'm so grateful that she has real friends like you," he managed, his voice thick. "I mean it. I thank God for you and Rob. You drive me crazy with your stunts. But you love. . . ." He paused. "We'll get to the bottom of this."

My eyes moistened. "Of course we will."

"We won't know anything until the lab looks at it," Tommy said. His voice hardened. He shoved the letter back into the envelope and stood. "I'll call you."

ROB SHOWED UP about ten minutes after Tommy left. My mother had given up any pretext of setting limits on Rob and I being together. She knew I didn't want to be alone, ever, anymore, and she didn't want me alone, either. For the first few hours, my mother allowed us some privacy. Not that we were in the mood for anything more than clinging to each other in my bed. Rob rested his head against Penguin, his arm around me. For some reason, that set me off. I cried for a good long time.

"Allie-Stair?" he finally whispered.

"Yeah?"

"I think I get now why you're going to John Jay."

I buried my head against his chest. "You do? Good. Please tell me. Because I'm not even sure I want to go anymore."

"That's not true. You do want to go. You want to go because you've always been trapped in this little room, this prison cell. You've been trapped with me, and Juliet, and XP. I mean, sometimes the room is bigger, sometimes it's the whole night, but it's still a prison cell with a door that's gonna open at a set time. And someone will come in and say, 'Time's up.' John Jay is your furlough. And that is awesome."

I chewed my lip, not wanting to cry again. That was when I saw it: the Rob I'd loved from toddlerhood, the doomed-boy-who-could-have-been-a-jock, the late-night record producer, the de-facto therapist—the countless Robs, wondrous and magical—all forced to live inside a single head their whole lives, never able to do what they wanted, but never mean or bitter about it. The United Rob.

"What?" he asked.

"Since when did you get so smart?" I said.

"It's from hanging out with you and Juliet."

"Rob. . . ."

"I know you. There are a thousand Juliets. But there's only one Allie Kim. And from now on, I hope there's only one Rob Dorn." He drew in a trembling breath. "We owe that to Juliet, no matter what happens."

I squeezed my eyes shut to block out the pain. I kissed his neck. "She never believed in the prison cell, did she?"

"Why the hell do you think she was able to convince us to do Parkour?"

I WAS JUST drifting off when the prison cell door flew open. "You have to eat more and sleep more," Mom said, apropos nothing. "Well, *eat* more. Hi, Rob."

He laughed.

"I eat all the time," I muttered groggily, extricating myself.

"You eat grapes. You were already thin. Now you look ghastly."

"Now I can be a model."

"You're angry and you're grieving, but this helps nothing," Jackie said. "No one likes to believe what she doesn't want to believe."

"Gee, Mom, did you just make that up?"

"No need to take it out on me, Allie." She folded her arms across her chest and arched her eyebrow at Rob, hoping to enlist him as an ally the same way she enlisted Angie. *Oh, God,* I thought. *Now we're like some loser married couple who lives at home. Maybe it's time to move into that cabin at Ghost Lake.*

"See?" I said. "You're mad and you're not even calling

me Alexis." I was furious at the seeming willingness of people in charge to fall for the dumbest excuse for a solution. "I know Juliet better than anyone, Mom."

"In some ways. In other ways, you don't know her at all."

I glanced at Rob. He shrugged. No wonder Mom wanted to enlist him as an ally. They both spoke the truth. I struggled to a sitting position.

"I want to know if they checked for Garrett Tabor's fingerprints," I stated. "You know, at Lost Warrior."

"Why would Garrett Tabor have fingerprints in a criminal system?" Rob asked.

"When you work with kids, you have to pass background checks." I glanced at my mom. "Right, Mom?"

"Ah," Rob said. "But he's smarter than that, Allie-Stair. He doesn't leave traces." *Kind of raised that way*, I thought, shivering.

Rob wrapped his arm around me. "Do you think there's a chance it's real?"

"There's always a chance," Mom put in. "Your father up and vanished, too, Alexis. It was convenient. Maybe this way out was convenient for her. Maybe Juliet was the one who left no traces."

The next day, the $50,000 reward offered by the Tabor Clinic was withdrawn. A new bulletin listed Juliet as a "Missing Person." Suddenly, she was nobody's little girl.

THE NEXT NIGHT, as I was heading out to meet Rob up at the cabin at Ghost Lake, I found my mom in the kitchen, crying.

My heart seized. It was the six o'clock news. I caught a glimpse of the river, under floodlights, of the newscaster, his face grim.

"They don't know," Jackie finally said. "They don't know if it's her." There were still streaks of light in the sky. My mother got up and pulled the shades. "The body they found doesn't fit Juliet's description. And it's much . . . well, let's wait and see, Allie."

"Go ahead and say it, Mom. I can take it. It's what I want to do with my life—"

"Not when it comes to your best friend."

"Please say it. I'll think worse."

My mom nodded, blinking rapidly. "You can sit with me and watch. I'm sure they'll go over it again. The state of the body isn't quite compatible with Juliet. This person would have died more recently. And while she might resemble Juliet superficially, there was damage to the face and hands from aquatic life. . . ." Fish had nibbled her. Crabs had plucked at her beautiful lips. "But also perhaps from trauma."

"From rocks and being in the water," I said.

"Maybe."

"From being hurt by someone else?" I had promised that it was okay for my mother to say these things, but now my body betrayed my rational mind and I began to over-breathe, a kaleidoscope of sparkling confetti before my eyes. "What about her clothes? The black bodysuit with the blue stars on it?"

Jack-Jack looked at me with a fierce animal protectiveness, and I knew that there had been no clothes. Involuntarily, I heard myself make the kind of sound a person would make if she were gut-punched without warning.

"Allie, Allie. I'm sorry."

"Dental records will show right away," I croaked. Juliet's teeth were perfect, and one was a perfect fake, an implant, a permanent tooth placed when one could not be surgically re-rooted after she literally knocked it out with a ski pole.

My mother said, "There was damage there, too. That won't be definitive." Quickly, she added that the girl who had been pulled from the river had short dark hair, which was dyed, and was much thinner and less well developed in terms of musculature than Juliet. "So it really may not be her at all, Allie. People drown all the time. No one knows if this girl has water in her lungs. No one knows how she died."

"What about her tattoo?"

Mom shook her head.

"You got all this from the news?" I finally yelled. My throat clogged.

"I called Tommy. . . . " She turned back to the television.

Because I'd already lost Juliet, I almost prayed that it was her. I almost willed her long lonely voyage to be over. If someone had starved her and beaten her, there must have come a moment when she'd won before she succumbed to defeated agony by letting life go. I almost prayed that she thought of herself as a hero, having saved me, having taken the devil's bargain. I almost prayed for all that. But I couldn't. Because even if there were a chance that Juliet was still out there, running from Tabor, it meant some other father and mother's child had died. It meant the paper doll chain had been set ablaze once more. *Juliet, come back,* I pleaded. *Come back. Help me fight him.*

"I want a second opinion," I told my mother.

"What?"

"I want Dr. Stephen to have someone else do the autopsy."

"Allie, you're beyond the point of rational. I understand—"

"Is there a way to request that legally?" I interrupted. "Can her parents request that legally? To replace Dr. Stephen just this one time?"

"Only if they have some reason to believe he's incompetent," my mother said. She choked over the words. "And his brother has cared for Juliet all her life. He has samples of Juliet's blood and tissue, and her fingerprints as part of the research study."

"Exactly! The research study. That's why. I think he may be too . . . close to it. And he's coming all the way back from South America. He'll be exhausted."

"It's because Garrett gives you the creeps. That's why. But Stephen is the nicest guy in the world. He's crushed over this. They all are, baby."

"Mom, please, just ask someone, okay?"

In the end, it was Dr. Stephen who asked for assistance, from an FBI pathologist. Juliet was still a minor when she died, and foul play or kidnapping was a possibility.

ROB ENDED UP coming over. Angela woke up around two o'clock and got into bed with Rob and me, curling into my body like an oversized shrimp. My mother had told her that a girl had died, but that we were hoping it wasn't Juliet, and that we would have to wait for the doctors to tell us. Angie knew about Nicola's death, although she hadn't known Nicola other than to say hi. What we both knew as the daughters of a nurse was that in the medical world, good news travels fast. The morning lasted forever.

The phone rang at six. The three of us sat upright in bed.

Mom said softly, with an almost religious hush, "Thank you. I will tell her."

But she didn't have to.

24

ASHES

A t Ghost Lake, a cordon of Iron Harbor cops blocked the road so that no one could intrude on what was a private family ceremony, with only a few close friends included. Reporters were still on the prowl. Citizens of the town placed cards and wreaths for the Siroccos in their mailbox, as they'd done at Nicola's grave.

No one's funeral is ever held at ten o'clock at night, so this was my first. It was Rob's first, too. The Siroccos insisted on including us. Juliet wasn't even going to be buried at Torch Mountain Cemetery. Her ashes were going to be scattered over the water at one of the places she loved the most, *by* those she loved the most.

Only as I took a step out on the old pier did the reality of the past two days sink in. It had been a flurry of anger and disbelief and sleeplessness. But there was no argument to be made anymore.

DNA tests had proved that the body found in the river was Juliet's. And Dr. Stephen's report was supported by the

FBI medical examiner. Even a Tabor couldn't have bribed the
federal government. The report pointed out the coldness of the
water as a factor in how well-preserved the body still was, and
the loss of teeth possibly accidental, as a result of gum damage
due to rapid weight loss. She had died by accident shortly after
cutting her hair in a punk crop and dyeing it. No one could
explain any of the physical anomalies, other than to suggest
that starving herself for a week was a reliable way to dramati-
cally change her appearance quickly, as part of some kind of
plan to escape.

The FBI physician was also a criminalogist. She suggested that undetected neurological damage might have
prompted Juliet's abrupt mood swings. The blaze that had
consumed Juliet's belongings could have been phony, a delib-
erate diorama meant to suggest that someone was shedding
her past. But if true, then why up on the back side of Torch
Mountain, among old mine shafts that pitted the slopes?
The likelihood of that doused fire being lost forever was far
greater than the slim chance someone would stumble upon
it. . . .

I tried to shut off the squirming thoughts as I awaited
my turn to speak. The uncles went first. Then her grandma,
Rosa. Then the cousins. Then Rob. . . .

I tried to remember Juliet, to conjure her up. Instead,
my normal brain went on strike. It was Occupy Allie Kim
for my normal brain. (Was there ever even a normal brain?)
I thought of my outfit: a brand new short black dress Gina
had bought for me as a gift and as condolence, as she knew
I couldn't go shopping. (Juliet would have dug its style.) I
thought of how the whole thing seemed like a long prank,
and that Juliet herself would leap out at any moment and
yell, "Psych!"

I blinked at Rob. I hadn't even heard what he'd said. He held and released a fistful of the stony mix, like ash and shell. He turned to me, tears staining his cheeks.

This was no prank, no hoax.

Without thinking, I wet a finger and poked the gray matter, then dotted my tongue. Like the night sky above us. I hadn't planned it, but Rob did the same. As long as we lived, Juliet would be part of us.

It was my turn. I cleared my throat. I tried to remember what I'd prepared.

"Juliet . . . there's nothing to say except that I loved her. Part of what I loved most is that I never knew everything about her. People like us want a little privacy. A little mystery. It's all we have. But I know this much. Juliet wanted everyone she loved to soar and be daring. So I'll sleep well tomorrow . . . seriously. I will, knowing she is out there taking flight. Forever."

I blinked again. I found myself staring at the shadows of people who were here for my best friend. I thought about the kids who'd glimpsed us in the playground, years ago, who had no mechanism to deal with what we were.

"I wanted to read a poem." My throat caught. "These lines were written four hundred years ago, about a skylark:

"Hail to thee, blithe spirit!
Bird thou never wert—
We look before and after,
And pine for what is not:
Our sincerest laughter
With some pain is fraught;
Our sweetest songs are those that tell of saddest thought."

Rob took my arm. We turned and walked away then, from Ghost Lake, where we had laughed and fished and skinny-dipped and drank wine, where, I think, Juliet had spent some of the happiest nights of her life. We left her there.

Neither Rob nor I ever went back.

AROUND MIDNIGHT, AFTER Juliet's funeral, I went home to cold-pack my head like a fresh fish. Rob had gone home. My mother had gone to the Sirocco house to be with the family. My sister had gone home with Gina. Maybe they all knew that I had to be alone. All I wanted was to hide from the grief and the hot, close pounding of the pain.

Bonnie had graciously left me with a packet of a few knockout pills, not enough to put me in any danger.

I took all five. They might as well have been M&M's.

When I finally slept, it was only for a few hours. I kept dreaming of her, asleep with her open palms next to her head. *Hail to thee, blithe spirit....*

It was silent when I awoke.

I glanced at the phone at my bedside table. I had three new messages.

My mouth was pasted thick with the debris of dreams, already fading. There are biological reasons that you have a sensation of spinning in the extremes of anxiety. You over-breathe or breathe too shallowly; your heart rate builds and your glands release the hormone flood that will let you run and scream or stand and fight. If you do neither, you can black out. I'm guessing I did. I've never fainted again and I'd never fainted before.

But the last thing I recall was pressing the button to listen to the message, and then staring up at the blank ceiling Juliet and I had filled with hopes and dreams over a lifetime of lying next to each other.

"ALLIE," MY MOTHER was saying. "Alexis. Are you hurt? Don't move, sweetie. Everything feels okay pulse-wise. Did you fall?"

"I'm fine," I said.

"Don't speak," she said. "It's just too much of too much. You're sweating and it must be seventy in here."

My mother didn't think it was so very strange. I hadn't been eating or sleeping much; the pills might have made me groggy. I was not bruised, just sort of slumped in a gangly but not untidy heap near my bed.

"Mom, I need some time alone," I told her.

"Alexis, you need a hot meal. That's not a request. It's almost four."

"Four in the morning?"

She sighed. "Of course in the morning."

My heart began to thump, remembering I'd heard Juliet's voice.

First: *"Allie. Call now. Hurry."*

Then, weepy: *"Bear! Call me. Call back right now!"*

Finally: *"Allie-Bear. Don't call. Don't call until I tell you. Wait."*

I began to blink rapidly. *Juliet. Juliet. . . .* Maybe she'd called long before she'd died, and her phone had been damaged so the calls hadn't been received until now. The first call was time-stamped during her funeral. I'd called for her and she'd called back. But that was insane. It was sickening. I knew her phone hadn't been found. But did that mean. . . ?

Madness, I know, is anesthetic: Garrett Tabor could have

gotten the phone and forced her to prerecord a series of messages, just to torment me. First, she cries out, stubbornly, releasing a wail of pain only at the last blunt moment. Then she's like a child, crying hard—not for me, for anyone. Then she's collected. How could that be faked? It was her. It was Juliet. It was part of a plan, not coincidence. But a plan for what?

My mother shook me. "Allie! Look at me!"

"Just give me two seconds, Mom," I said.

She stood and marched to the door. "I want you downstairs, dressed, and at the kitchen table by 4:15 at the latest."

Hustling, I backed up my phone on my computer. I got dressed: sensible jeans, sensible sweatshirt. I didn't want to freak out my mom any more than she already was. For the first time since Juliet had disappeared, I felt in the moment, invigorated, *focused*. I had to act now. If I had no proof that she was alive, at least I had proof that she had been alive long after even the autopsy suggested she was. These recordings and Garrett Tabor were connected in some way. She'd foiled *his* plan for her. It wasn't evidence, but it was suspicious enough to mount an investigation. It could be put together in a chain that would be enough to indict him for something.

I quickly tidied up in the mirror over my bureau.

But then another thought occurred to me. If she *was* dead, then Garrett Tabor was pulling the strings. He'd somehow orchestrated this. He wanted to scare me so badly that I'd know: if I said a word, it would be the word that would pull the trigger on something even worse than the worst possible thing. That something-even-worse would really happen then—an apocalypse, and it would be my fault. Juliet would never be redeemed, and my own life would be nothing but ash. Still, if there was an off chance, literally a ghost of a chance. . . .

I clung to this knowledge like an overfilled glass of water. It could tip and spill. I could tip it by telling Rob or my mother or Tommy. I could run to them now and say, take this glass from me. But they wouldn't be able to take it. If I did not lose my mind then, I never would.

I CAME DOWNSTAIRS to find my mom arguing with Deputy Sherriff Sonny Larsen.

"No," Mom was saying. "You can't come in until I make sure that Alexis is properly dressed and has eaten."

"You'll need to keep the door open then. This is a serious charge."

Thank you, universe! I thought, bounding down the stairs. *Thank you, thank you!* I hadn't had to say a thing. He'd been caught and charged! Here were the Marines! The balance had been restored. The glass would not spill. They'd got him. Somehow, they'd put the pieces together themselves.

"Allie," my mother said, stepping aside. "Deputy Chief Larsen. . . ."

"Miss Kim," said Officer Larsen. Her sour smile almost looked like a sticker, pasted on her blocky face. "I have here a complaint against you for assault and battery."

I blinked at her. "I'm sorry?"

"You and your mother need to come with me now."

"Is this a joke?" I asked, my heart hammering against my ribcage. I felt guilty, even though I knew I'd done nothing wrong. "What's happening?"

"Yes, please tell me what the hell is going on," Mom demanded.

"Garrett Tabor filed a complaint this morning after he was treated for serious burns to his neck at Divine Savior Hospital emergency room. He is still in the hospital, under care."

"What does that have to do with me?" I asked, even though I felt a flood of relief. Somebody *had* gotten to him.

"We need you to come down to the station," Officer Larsen said.

"I'll drive my daughter," Mom said.

"She'll need to come in the squad car," Officer Larsen said.

"The hell with that!" Mom barked. "Call Tommy Sirocco!"

"He's been notified," Officer Larsen said.

I clung to my mom's arm, feeling as if I were trapped in some waking nightmare. Would I wake up?

"She's not under arrest," Jackie protested, pulling me close. "You arrest her, or I will drive my daughter. Now, I am going to call my friend Gina Ricci to take my daughter Angela to her house. Allie, sit down, and—"

"I'll let you make your arrangements," Officer Larsen interrupted. "But I'll follow you all the way. Running lights."

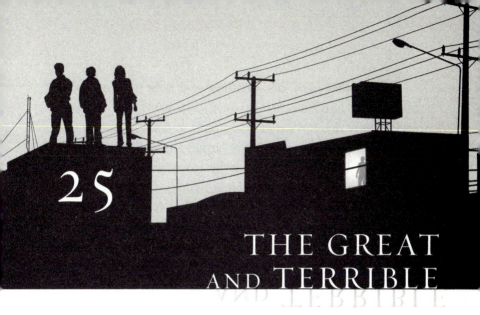

25

THE GREAT
AND TERRIBLE

The ski mask.

Even when Sonny Larsen placed it on the interrogation table in front of my mother and me, I wanted not to believe it.

Panic turned to horror. It came to me in a flash, in my mind's eye, like the police reports I'd studied for John Jay. The facts were cold and sequential. Juliet had tossed her brand new ski mask to me at Watching Rock, insisting that she wear mine instead. I'd given the ski mask back to her in the hospital room. And she'd never worn it.

"Recognize this?" Officer Larsen asked.

I shook my head, almost hyperventilating. "Yeah, but—"

"Alexis, what's going on?" my mother murmured.

I couldn't speak. Officer Larsen flipped open a laptop and pressed the pause button. I found myself in the very surreal position of watching Garrett Tabor, his face and neck blotchy with burns and blisters, accuse me of attacking him.

His story was as follows:

I'd broken into his penthouse. I'd been scoping for months; he had video to prove it. He also knew I babysat for a family there, though he'd prefer to leave them out of it, so he wasn't mentioning their name. Upon breaking in the balcony, I'd lit the burner on the stove and doused him in his bed with scalding water. He'd managed to rip off my ski mask during the attack, but it was definitely me. He'd caught a glimpse of my face.

I could feel the blood draining from my cheeks, from my chest, pooling at my feet. Garrett Tabor was beyond mad. He'd disfigured himself to frame me? He'd ingratiated himself with Sonny Larsen, which would only discredit Tommy Sirocco, his victim's father? There truly was nothing he couldn't do. And his claim would be impossible to refute.

My mind whirled down a series of dead ends. Garrett Tabor had no doubt caught the three of us on surveillance cameras when we'd traced at Tabor Oaks. Plus, his tissue would be all over the outside of that ski mask; mine alone would be all over the inside. A DNA test would prove that beyond any shred of a doubt. He knew it, didn't he? He knew that even if I protested, I'd be proved a liar.

I hated myself, but my only thought was: *Juliet, you didn't set me up . . . did you?*

No. Of course she didn't. But if she wasn't dead now, she would be soon.

"I know that Alexis's grief is overpowering," he continued on the tape, his eyes brimming with tears. "Mine is, too. I've spent my whole life working with kids. The problem is that this troubled girl doesn't understand my relationship to Juliet. I loved her like a daughter. Juliet Sirocco endured physical and emotional pain most of us can't even conceive of. I spent hours of my life trying to talk her out of committing suicide, trying to get her to go on. I also know that Alexis Kim thought I hadn't done enough. . . ."

I only caught snippets of the rest. Garrett Tabor said he had gone straight to the ER, where his friend, Dr. Lauren Wilenbrand, had treated him. *She'd* convinced him to make a formal complaint. It was she who'd pointed out that indeed, he'd been hurt, badly hurt. And if I could do so much damage to someone who was a relative stranger, what else could I do?

Would he press charges? Would he try to intervene if the county pressed charges?

He had no interest in punishing me. He just wanted to get back to Bolivia, back to the important work his family was doing. If I would agree to mandatory psychiatric treatment . . . perhaps he could see his way out of this. He knew that I was undone by grief. I had lost a great deal.

I gaped at Officer Larsen, unbelieving.

Garrett finished: "This town, Iron Harbor, where my family has devoted itself to helping others for four generations, has been through hell. It's time for that hell to end."

WHEN I FINALLY was able to collect myself, I asked to take a lie-detector test. My mother had to pay for it, because I wasn't formally charged with anything. The results showed that I was being truthful when I said that I believed that Garrett Tabor was responsible for Juliet Lee Sirocco's death. When the operator submitted his report, however, he added that I was being truthful when I said that *I* was responsible for Juliet Lee Sirocco's death. I was being truthful when I said I had nothing to do with Garrett Tabor's injuries.

A few days later, I received a letter from Iron County Social Services.

If I would agree to twenty hours of community service, to

be served over the winter holidays, there would be no formal charges. And an added bonus? The Cryer family would not be notified, either.

LYING IN ROB'S arms that night, I cried and talked and cried. And he listened, until I talked myself into the understanding that to fight back, I would risk a felony blot on my record as an adult. Goodbye, career as an investigator. That would be the equivalent of handing Garrett Tabor my sword.

But Rob insisted that he believed my version of events. Of course he did. No way would I have snuck out of my house to break into Tabor's penthouse. My mother believed me, too. Angie believed me. They knew I'd been at home that night, even though they hadn't seen me there. That was all that mattered. Now their eyes, too, were on Garrett Tabor.

But I was not finished. I made arrangements for a confidential conference call with Barry Yashida, my advisor. He was a former FBI agent. I told him everything. My acceptance into John Jay still stood; I was not a convicted criminal. If he doubted me, he never let on. He told me that he admired my forthrightness. I made a recording of the phone messages for Dr. Yashida, and set up a phone conference. Then, with Rob and my mother present, he listened as I laid out my version of the events of the past six months.

The process took three hours.

Although my mother gasped and recoiled when I explained about the girl in the empty apartment and gave Juliet's account of her relationship with Garrett Tabor, she did not speak of it or ask about it—then or later. Finally, I forwarded the videos we'd made of the Dark Stars, as they provided a sample of Juliet's voice.

Dr. Yashida called me back within the hour. The voice analyst could not be more than 75% sure that the voice on the phone messages matched the voice on the video. But 75% was hardly insignificant. Percentages far less had stood up in court. The only problem was determining the time of origin . . . and given the DNA results, the case appeared closed. I understood. I thanked him for his time.

"I'm proud of you, Allie," Mom kept telling me throughout the whole awful ordeal.

I only hoped she meant it. This wasn't over.

A FEW NIGHTS later, I went to Tessa's at Tabor Oaks for the last time, just to say goodbye. They were moving to a little lake town in Wisconsin; her mother, too, to a town where Tessa's sister lived.

NO PART OF their decisions linked to anything that had befallen me, but I rejoiced. Tessa made forlorn noises about my coming along, as a summer nanny. I was tempted. Tavish was adorable, and Tessa's belly was enormous. She would pop at any moment. The idea of running away and caring for two innocent children . . . for a fleeting instant, I almost felt like Juliet. *Break free. Soar. Live once.*

But no. I would never leave Rob, or my mother, or Angie. Not until I'd proven what had really happened. I couldn't go away to college. I would go to John Jay, but online and by Skype, even if I got the chance to leave.

"Allie, I hate to do this to you, but would you mind hanging out for a half hour while I just run to the store and grab some ice cream?" Tessa asked. Her tired eyes twinkled as she massaged her swollen tummy. "I'll pay you double."

"Please. It's on the house. Just save some ice cream for me."

"You're a lifesaver," Tessa breathed—and then was gone.

Tavish, who had been running around all day like the toddler madman he was, was already conked out. I had the place to myself. *A lifesaver*. I walked to the window. If only that were true. . . . The early winter wind in the treetops was a doleful sigh, the waves stroked the shore: *Now? Now?*

That's when I spotted it.

A dim light: bouncing, low to the ground, bobbing along the bluff. Every few moments, the light descended, disappeared and then reappeared, wobbling, side to side, closer, and then closer.

Why had I thought he would stop? Logic? People like Garrett Tabor didn't stop. They never stopped, until they were caught or eliminated everyone who stood in their way. They did not stop until they were forced. He had watched my shadow, alone in the apartment with Tavish. He had waited patiently, knowing that I would take his bait and step outside onto the balcony.

His silhouette stood in stark relief against the seam between the sky and dark water. Three floors and a hundred yards separated us, and still, when he waved the flashlight across the balcony, I had to stifle a shriek. Far off, miles down the road, a rumble and whine suggested Rob's Jeep. But the sound of possible salvation died away. I held my breath.

Then he aimed the big light directly at my face.

I winced. Naturally: a lifetime of recoiling from the light.

I could call the police. But what would that do? In the eyes of the authorities, I was the attacker, the culprit. I could only thank my lucky stars Tessa and her family didn't know. But then, he'd probably orchestrated that, too. From the corners of my vision, I tried to scope the lights throughout the building. It was late. Only nightlights, and few. I was all by myself and he knew it.

Maybe you can't stop them until after they do what they do. . . .

Perhaps as reparation, Juliet had offered her own life. But what could I offer Juliet, my best friend, my heart, in return for that? Could I avenge her? Even if I had wanted to hide and pretend, it was too late for me to die without really having lived.

The light swept playfully, an arc.

If Tabor wanted war, fine.

Kicking off my shoes, I stepped on the first rung of the metal railing. Finding my balance, I stood on the second and threw both my arms up in a raised V.

"I am Allie Kim!" I shouted, louder than I realized I could.

The light beam froze on my face.

"I am Allie Kim!" I repeated. "The Great and Terrible. And I will end you!"

His light went out.

Turn the page for a preview of the forthcoming

WHAT WE LOST
IN THE DARK

I

ALL THE
LOST PIECES

Picture yourself in a helicopter, looping slowly down from heaven.

First, it looks like a child's map of what Earth offers: green and blue and beige. The green resolves into broad hills, thick with trees: a green beard chopped off by the craggy throats of glacial bluffs, dropping away to sparkly beaches. Even from this great height, the water is so clear that you can see the bottom, and the bottom could be hundreds of feet from the surface. You think it's a sea. But no; it's a lake, massive and majestic. The greatest of all lakes, it's called Superior.

Now you descend.

You can tell the red pines from black spruce at this height. You begin to hear the restless fingers of the wind among all those branches. Closer, you spot the little town. It's named after a harbor as narrow as a creek but as deep as a river. No one pays attention to the small freighters that load and unload there. Everyone sees the big, winged yachts with their showy masts, polished deck rails, and ironic names. *Nick's Waterloo. Enter the Titan.*

Touch down gently. Your rotors spin slower and then fall silent. The helicopter disappears.

There's a town square, just a little too old and well-used to have been tacked on for tourists, although tourists flock to Iron Harbor for reasons I've never been quite able to fathom. At the center stands a monument to Amos Hayden of the Union's First Minnesota infantry regiment. The town's Civil War hero, he was a miner's son. At Gettysburg, when nothing except a doomed charge with fixed bayonets could hold back the Rebels, the general turned to the First Minnesota, the soldiers who were closest to him. Two hundred and sixty-two men charged, and two hundred and fifteen died. Not a single man deserted. It was over in fifteen minutes. They gave their lives for an idea that not all of them probably even understood.

Amos Hayden was only seventeen. His statue is here, but he still sleeps far away in the ground.

Was he brave or only young?

Did he have a moment to think of his mother? Or the lakeshore where he skipped stones, or the summer stars so close you felt you could reach up and play with them like beads? Did a girl love him and wait for him? Did he know that he might never again open the door on an icy wind that slapped him until he glowed?

Tonight, nobody is thinking of Amos Hayden dying young and alone. It's late fall, and people visiting this town are taking advantage of the warmth of an extended autumn. They stroll past the Flying Fish restaurant and Borealis Books, with its neat, scalloped wooden fringes—each painted to resemble a famous volume of prose. Even the tall, pale girl with the uncombed auburn hair, who stops in front of the statue and stares . . . the tall, pale girl who is me . . . even she isn't really thinking of Amos Hayden, although I remember looking up into his chiseled young face, which would always be young.

Only later, when I passed by the scene of the only true breakdown I would ever have in my life, would I really stop to consider Amos Hayden and wonder how the most innocent of heroes and the pond scum of sinners could rise from this one small place.

That Sunday night was only a few weeks after my best friend's body was found. It was the night that I walked into one of Iron Harbor's two clothing stores and stole a poncho.

I had never stolen so much as a pack of gum.

If all the boutiques in Beverly Hills had opened for my own personal plunder, and I could run through them and keep whatever I wanted until my arms and shopping carts were filled, I would have chosen a rhinestone cat collar sooner than a poncho. And I don't even have a cat.

The poncho I pulled down was woven in shades of green, from mint to forest—thick and subtly striped with the kind of oily, expensive feeling that seems to scoff at all weather. Ladies from Chicago bought these to wear on their sailboats. The store was the typical wannabe Native American thread-and-head shop required on the map of every tourist town.

I slipped the thing on.

Then, I walked out the door.

The owner, an old, bearded hippie guy everybody called Corona, watched me curiously. He didn't say a word.

Corona's store was one of the few places that Juliet and Rob and I had never been able to break into. (We'd tried, but Corona is in the gifted program for theft prevention.) Yes, I call it "breaking in," but we never broke a thing. We were way too good for that. We left things just as they were, or a little tidier. Juliet could be light-fingered when it came to expensive wine and trinkets, but Rob and I kept her in check. She was the first one to get a set of lock picks (which you can buy online), and we quickly followed her lead. The *tres compadres*, we roamed the night, from fancy faux-Swiss ski chalets in the hills where we sipped champagne in the owners' hot tubs, to the music store where we pounded our palms on drums or ran our fingers over the electric guitar strings in an unmelodious twang.

We owned Iron Harbor, Minnesota.

It was ours, all twenty blocks.

Really, though, Iron Harbor, and our place in it, in its night landscape, was mostly Juliet's. Juliet was always at the wheel, no matter who was really driving. Rob and I rode shotgun to her one desire—the desire to be free. Not free of us, her closest friends on earth, but of this place and her life in it.

Now she was free, of the former and the latter.

Wearing the poncho like a shroud, I reached the end of the street. Then I stopped and burst into tears. It was a warm night, sixty-eight degrees at nine o'clock. It's never this warm this late in the year, so far north . . . I was practically in Canada, minus the checkpoint.

Corona joined me at the corner. He was a tall, old guy, thin to the point of gauntness, with a face I now noticed was lined not with the wrinkles of care, but with decades of quiet amusement. His eyes brimmed with a surpassing kindness. Why had we ever even *tried* to break into his little store? As we gazed at each other, I saw that he knew that we had tried, and it was already forgiven.

"It's okay, little dude," he said.

Corona took the phone out of my hand and scrolled through my favorites list until he found *Mom*.

She was there within five minutes, jumping out of the minivan, leaving the driver's side door hanging open. I might as well have been a toddler for the way my mother held up my arms and slipped the poncho over my head. Then, she stroked my hair. "Oh, Allie . . . oh, Allie."

"I stole this from him," I confessed. My teeth started to chatter.

Corona just shrugged. "It's okay. I don't care if she keeps it, even."

Everyone knew about Juliet. Everyone knew I was crazy.

"I *stole* this!" I repeated, raising my voice.

Corona gave my mother a level look.

Mom sighed. "Allie," she said. "Honey. Time to go home."

"Why don't you call the cops?" I glared at her, and then at Corona. "Call Tommy. Call Mr. Sirocco." I bit my lip. "No, don't call him. But call someone." Even I knew that was too over the top. Tommy Sirocco, in addition the chief of the Iron County Sheriff's Department, was Juliet's father. "Doesn't anybody around here ever do anything? Doesn't anyone care when someone does something wrong?"

"You aren't a bad person. You didn't do anything wrong, tonight or ever. You couldn't have helped her, Allie," Mom said, pulling me close. I shook my head, squeezing my eyes shut and struggling against my mother, literally kicking at her shins with the toes of my ballet flats, now really acting like a toddler. *That's a lie,* I thought. *I knew, I knew, I knew.*

"Allie, no," Jackie said, pulling me closer. Both of us were sweating. "It's not your fault."

I might as well have spoken aloud. I never had to speak for Jackie Kim to know exactly what I was thinking. Maybe it was because I was chronically ill, with something that would probably kill me sooner rather than later, so she's never paid anything but ultra-close attention. Maybe it was just Jackie's ultra-vigilant nature, because despite a basic optimism, Jackie is so overprotective of her family that she makes the Secret Service look like a bunch of stoners. My mind seemed to provide my mother with near-constant printouts of my every emotion.

She handed Corona the poncho.

I let her guide me to the front seat, pulling the safety belt across me. She turned the AC on to arctic blast. I glanced in the rearview mirror. My nine-year-old sister, Angela, was curled in the backseat, bony arms wrapped around her knees, a fringe of thick black hair hiding her face, trying hard not to look at me.

I opened my mouth wide and screamed as loudly as I could.

Angela flinched. "Allie?" she croaked. "Are you . . . sick?"

"You loved her, too," I said, breathless, my throat an open wound. Angela would know that I meant Juliet, the friend who had treated her like a little sister and a little princess. I glanced back at Angie. I was tormenting her. She swallowed, rubbing her eyes.

My mother concentrated, backing the car out into Harbor Street.

"Allie, we all loved her," she said.

"But nobody knows the truth! Nobody who's alive, anyway. I *should* do community service. Not for what that freak said I did. For being a goddamn fool."

"Don't talk about it like that. It's just a job," said my mother. "Think of it as an opportunity. You would have wanted a job like this anyhow."

I glanced at Angie from the edge of my eye.

Angie's Asian features glowed pale, stretched tight. This

was not the capable, strong Allie she knew. She expected grief but she didn't expect this moaning, fragile thing her big sister had become. I hadn't expected it either.

We left poor Corona standing there on the corner, holding his green poncho. He offered a halfhearted wave.

"Remember, Allie, when we talked about this?" my mother said. "It will be intercession at school, starting next week. The mini semester. Like winter break, as far as the world is concerned. I explained to Angie how this would help you at college."

I had just started college online at John Jay, the first school in the world to grant a major in criminal justice. John Jay had never before offered an online degree. I was part of the first class.

"The experience will be invaluable. It's a good résumé item." With one hand still on my arm, my mother piloted the car into around the corner onto our street. "The days will go past so quickly. This time will always be a terrible memory. But it's over now. Allie? Do you hear me?"

"I hear you," I said.

"Do you believe me?"

"I believe you, Jack-Jack," I said, using the name I used to tease her. At least one of us should relax. I didn't believe her, at all.

"I believe you," Angie said. I had to smile.

"No one will punish you anymore. It's over," my mother added.

On both counts, she was wrong.

A week later, when I showed up for my community service, the first person I saw was Garrett Tabor, the man who murdered Juliet and who knows how many other girls. The man who would have also murdered me.

2

ONCE AGAIN, FOR THE FIRST TIME

"Good evening, Allie," said Tabor. "How are you?"
"I could be better," I told him. "If you were dead."

It astonished me that I could speak at all, much less summon up a barb.

I could see the fabric of my T-shirt rising and falling with the whomping of my heart. How could he fail to see it, too? Didn't he know this was all bravado? I glanced around to find the night supervisor. There had to be one.

Please let it not be Garrett Tabor.

"I'm sorry, Allie," Garrett Tabor said. "I've felt a great deal of sadness about what happened. I've had time to reflect on everything. I realize how impaired your judgment was. I'm sorry for that."

"Leave me alone."

"I'm not trying to bother you. I'm trying to move past this."

"You're crazy," I said. "Who else is here?"

"Just us," he said. I put my hand on the handle of the

door behind me. It was locked. Tabor explained, "It's the medical examiner's office. It has to be locked. There's a code you punch in."

A code. He would know it. The medical examiner was Garrett Tabor's father, Dr. Stephen, and Dr. Andrew Tabor ran the Tabor Clinic. Iron Harbor was the name of this place only by virtue of geography. It should be called Taborville.

I stared now at the scion of that great family of healers.

Blondie. The child's nickname I had given him the first time I saw him would always spring to my mind. It owed to a streak of platinum down the wavy dark pelt of his hair, a blanket over the twisted brain beneath.

Blondie.

Garrett Tabor: trusted coach, privileged son, genetic researcher, and serial killer.

Yes, serial killer.

Does that surprise you?

That he is one, or that he's walking around?

The great majority of them are walking around. The great majority of them look like everyone else. Some of them even look a little better, unless you catch the unguarded glance— the flat gaze of the predator, as sympathetic as a grizzly. Mostly, they present a front that's civil, lively, even charming. That's how they get people.

Garrett Tabor and I had a short, blunt, potent history.

I was here because Garrett Tabor's word was better than mine. He claimed that after my friend Juliet's death, I had scaled the balconies to his apartment at the Tabor Oaks Condominiums, broken in wearing a ski mask, and poured boiling water on him as he lay unprotected in bed. That part was pure nonsense. *I poured boiling water on him?* I took the time to put a teakettle on the stove, able to find the stove and the kettle in an apartment I'd never been in, with Tabor separated from the kitchen by one wall? If I'd gone to all the trouble to catch him alone and vulnerable, why didn't I just hit him with a hammer? Still, Tabor had the surveillance tapes of Rob, Juliet, and I climbing the outside walls "to case my place," he said. He had the second-degree burns rippling along his neck and shoulder, not to mention a ski mask I'd once owned, to prove it.

What was true was that I was a gifted climber.

Rob and Juliet and I had practiced the urban discipline called Parkour, and we were so skilled that there was almost no vertical surface that we couldn't boulder up or leap down from. We had indeed traced the Tabor Oaks, although that was before Garrett Tabor lived there.

The Tabor Oaks was the first place I remembered seeing him and his blond streak. We were doing what Parkour people call a "trace," jumping from the roof of one building to the next, then preparing to swing down. When my foot touched the first balcony, I saw him. In an empty, uncurtained apartment, he bent busily over the still, colorless, half-naked body of a young woman whose name no one would probably ever know. She laid helpless, her clothing and dignity torn away by the same immaculate hands I was now staring at.

Had I called the police? Who wouldn't?

You bet I called the police.

I called them then, and again later, when Garrett Tabor forced me to jump from the third story of a parking garage, breaking my arm so badly I had to have surgery.

I called when he threatened me, while I was babysitting a little boy, and again when he cornered me in a local cemetery.

It was always my word against his. His word always prevailed.

Except once.

After Juliet's memorial service, when I got the phone calls, I didn't risk calling the police. Dr. Barry Yashida, a former FBI evidence expert, was my college advisor, and there was no one else in the wide world I trusted except him: a man I'd never met face to face—only on Skype, and then just twice. He had done exactly what I asked him to do, in confidence, and he had *kept* my confidence, in hopes of a future time when the information he gave me could be useful.

It wasn't even the horror of Juliet's disappearance, or the confirmation that Juliet's DNA matched the badly mauled remains pulled from the river three weeks later. It was her *voice*.

I'd never heard her phone go off. I was deep in sedative-soaked sleep after the incomprehensible experience of reciting a poem and then accepting a handful of ash—all that remained of the wild and splendid beauty, Juliet—to scatter in the dark waters of Ghost Lake. When I awoke the following night, my breath stopped when I saw the screen: five calls had come from Juliet's phone, the phone that was never found.

Dead for weeks, Juliet left me five pleading, chilling phone messages.

After I cried and screamed in Rob's arms until I was too limp to do anything but stand in the shower and fall asleep, I made copies of those calls. I copied the files onto my computer, and then onto a CD. I gave Rob the CD and he burned several copies, locking one in his fireproof ceiling safe. Maybe he was only humoring me because he knew I had *Xeroderma Pigmentosum*, or XP, the deadly "allergy" to sunlight. And while I never accept pity, I accepted that he was willing to accept my version. He simply said that he had a great deal of experience with things that could not have actually happened but had.

Dr. Yashida sent a courier for the copy I made for him. An FBI analysis compared the voice on the phone calls with the audio of old videos Juliet and I made, of us skiing, or dancing, or modeling the clothes we'd bought. At least three were a near-perfect match for her voice. Of the last messages, less than two seconds long, when she was screaming for her mother, the analysts couldn't be sure.

They did believe those were also real.

While I was certain, utterly certain, that those calls had been recorded long ago, they did the job they were meant to do on my head. They were a heartless ruse from a soulless creature to convince me that there was the slimmest chance that Juliet was still alive and needed me. The subtext was clear.

If I told anyone the truth, the unthinkable would happen. If Juliet were somehow alive, then she would die, and her death would be on me.

ACKNOWLEDGMENTS

This is a work of fiction. As such, any and all errors of fact are the author's alone. I wish to thank my friend and fellow author Dr. Gay Walker for her help in understanding the hope of gene therapy for families afflicted with real diseases such as *Xeroderma Pigmentosum*, and my son Dan for dabbling in Parkour and not letting me know about it. Always, but especially through some harrowing recent times, I owe a great debt to my extraordinary friends, to my even more extraordinary children, and to my beloved agent and longtime friend, Jane Gelfman. A salute to Soho designer Janine Agro, and cover designer Michael Fusco for making this all look so grand, and my editor Daniel Ehrenhaft, for making it sound even better than it looks.